TALES FROM THE DECAMERON

Tales from the Decameron

Giovanni Boccaccio

Selected and adapted by Mark Cohen

NEL SIGNET CLASSICS
Times Mirror

★

This translation first published as a Four Square Classic in 1962
© The New English Library Ltd., 1962
Reissued in this NEL Signet Classic edition January 1969

*NEL Signet Classics are published by The New English Library Limited from Barnard's Inn,
Holborn, London E.C.1. Made and printed in Great Britain by Richard Clay (The Chaucer Press),
Ltd., Bungay, Suffolk*

45000221 7

CONTENTS

Third day: second tale

GROOM SWEEPS QUEEN

AGILULF, King of the Lombards, like his predecessors made
Pavia his capital. He married Tuedelinga, the widow of a
former King of the Lombards. She was beautiful, intelligent, and gracious, but had an unfortunate taste in lovers. In
the period of prosperity induced by the King's enlightened
rule, it happened that one of the Queen's grooms fell
deeply in love with her. Though his birth was humble, he
had a natural dignity far above it, and very much
resembled the King in looks and figure.

Despite his social position, he was not too brash to realize
the presumption of his love, but he had told no one and not
even the Queen had guessed it. Although he despaired of
ever attracting her, he secretly gloried in having set his cap
so high. Because of his love he was far more attentive to
the Queen's wants than any of his fellows. So it happened
that whenever the Queen went riding she tended to take
the horse that he had groomed. He considered this a great
honour and never left her stirrup, thinking himself lucky to
be allowed to touch just her clothes. It's proverbial that
love waxes as hope wanes. Certainly in the case of the
groom, so serious and hopeless was his passion that it sometimes made him despondent enough to contemplate suicide.
However he courted it, he was determined on one thing:
his death must disclose his undying love for the Queen. It
must provide him with one last chance to gain at least some
satisfaction for his passion. He didn't dream of either
speaking or writing to the Queen, because he knew this
would be useless. Instead, he decided to try and manage
sleeping with her. This he could only do by getting into her
room, and that could only be achieved by pretending to be
the King. He knew his master did not sleep with her every
night, and so for several nights he kept watch in the palace

hall that lay between their two rooms, to see what the
King wore and how he behaved. On one of these nights he
saw the King leave his room, wrapped in a great cloak, with
a burning torch in one hand and a stick in the other. He
saw him cross the hall and knock quietly on the Queen's
door once or twice with his stick. The door was then opened
and the torch taken from his hand. Having observed the
King's system and being set on copying it, the groom
acquired a mantle, a torch, and a stick like the King's. He
then took a bath to remove the smell of the stable—for it
might both offend the lady and sabotage his plan—he put
on his disguise and hid in the hall. Having waited for everyone else to go to sleep, he considered the time was ripe for
what might mean either success or the longed-for death his
presumption had earned him. He lit the torch with the
tinder he had brought, wrapped his cloak round him,
approached the Queen's door, and knocked twice with the
stick. The door was opened by a sleepy chambermaid who
removed the torch. Silently he took off his cloak, drew the
curtains that hid the sleeping Queen, and got in beside her.
He pretended to be grumpy, because he knew that in that
mood the King would not hear a word from anybody.
Without either of them saying a word, therefore, he took
her passionately in his arms and enjoyed her several times.
Reluctant as he was to leave, the groom feared that to pro-
long his pleasure might prove fatal, so he got up, took his
cloak and the light, left without a word, and returned to
his own bed.

Hardly had he gone, than the King got up and—to her
astonishment—went to the Queen's room. She was reassured, however, by the obvious good humour in which he
got into bed, and she said:

'Well, my lord, this is something new! You've only just
left me after more than your usual ration and now you're
back for more. Are you sure it's wise?'

From these words the King at once gathered that she
had been tricked by someone whose looks and dress had
been imitated from his own. He also realized that as neither
the Queen nor anyone else had detected the trick, it was
best not to disabuse her by mentioning it. Many would

not have been so acute, but would have stupidly blurted out:

'Oh, it wasn't me! Who can it have been? How did it happen? How did he get in?'

Such remarks would not only have given the Queen needless embarrassment, but might also have revealed what was less shameful to himself when hidden. So, not giving away his distress either by his expression or his words, the King replied:

'Does it look as though I weren't up to enjoying you once and then coming straight back for more?'

'Of course not,' answered the lady. 'I was only thinking of your health.'

The King said: 'I rather think I'll take your advice and leave you here and now.'

He put on his cloak and left the room, furious over the trick he saw had been played on him. He was determined privately to punish the offender whom he considered must be a palace-retainer. Whoever he was he must still be on the premises. The King therefore lit a lantern that threw only a small light, and went up to the dormitory over the palace stables, which was so long that almost all the male servants in the palace slept there. He reckoned that the man who had just done what the Queen had described, would still be suffering from a pounding heart and a racing pulse after so much strain. He started cautiously with one of the head-grooms, and went from bed to bed feeling every man's pulse. They were all asleep except the one who had just visited the Queen, and he was terrified when he saw the King and guessed what he was doing. Fear increased his heart-beat even more than his late exertions. He was certain that the King would detect this and kill him. He thought of several possible courses, but finally, noticing the King was unarmed, he decided to pretend to be asleep and see what the King would do. Having tested so many and found no one who was obviously guilty, the King reached the offender himself and noting the speed of his heart-beat, said to himself:

'This is the fellow.'

As he was anxious not to give his ulterior motive away,

he merely took out a pair of scissors and cut off some hair (which it was then fashionable to wear long), on one side of the man's head, so as to be able to recognize him next day. Having done this he went back to his own room. The groom was fully conscious of what the King had done, and quite shrewd enough to realize its point. So he got up at once, took one of the several pairs of scissors that were used on the horses, and went through the dormitory quietly cutting off hair just above everyone's ear. He did this without disturbing anybody and then went back to bed.

Next day, as soon as he was up, and before the palace gates were opened, the King summoned all his men-servants. When they stood bare-headed before him, he looked closely to see whether the one whose hair he had cut was there. He noticed that the majority of them were cropped in the same way, and said to himself:

'This man I am trying to catch certainly shows great cunning, for all his humble rank.'

Realizing that he could not achieve his object without making a fuss, and not wanting to risk a major show-down for such minor revenge, he contented himself with a word of warning that would remind the offender he was a marked man. He turned to them all and said:

'Don't let the man who did it, do the same thing again, and go all of you in peace.'

Any other man would have questioned, racked and tortured them, and so revealed what was much better left secret. Suppose he had discovered the man and wreaked full vengeance, his own dishonour would have been increased, not reduced, and it would have sullied his wife's reputation.

Everyone who heard the King's statement was thoroughly impressed and wondered what it all meant, except for the man to whom it referred that is, and he wisely kept the secret to himself during the King's lifetime, and did not risk his neck on an escapade like that again.

Fourth day: second tale

ANGELS FEAR TO TREAD . . .

THERE lived in Imola a man whose life was vile and
debauched. He was called Berto of Massa. His appalling
behaviour at last got him so evil a reputation among his
fellow citizens, that on principle no one ever believed him,
whether he was speaking the truth or not. When he found
there was no scope left for his crookedness in Imola, he
despaired and moved to Venice. He hoped to find a new
opening for his talents in that hell-hole. There he paraded
a shameful past and an air of deep humility. He was determined to out-Catholic the best of them, so he became a
friar minor under the name of Brother Alberto of Imola.
He assumed the austerity as well as the friar's habit and
laid great stress on penitence and abstinence. He was tee-
total and vegetarian—that is, only the best wine and meat
passed his lips. No one would have known him for an ex-
forger, pimp, and murderer turned religious leader who
still managed to practise his old professions on the quiet.
Once he became a priest he was always moved to tears by
the Passion of Our Lord—whenever he was celebrating
Mass before a large congregation. His tears were cheap
and could be turned on and off like a tap. In fact his combination of sermons and tears so took the Venetians in, that
he became the trustee and executor of practically everyone's will. He acted as banker, confessor, and advisor to a
great many men and women. The wolf had indeed become
a shepherd whose local reputation for sanctity put even
St Francis of Assisi in the shade.

It so happened that there was a lady called Lisetta—one
of the Quirinos—among those confessed by the holy friar.
She was the young and silly wife of a big merchant who
was away in Flanders with his fleet. Like the typically
stupid Venetian lady that she was, she fell at the friar's

5

feet but did not come clean with all her sins. When Alberto asked her if she had a lover, she answered in high dudgeon:

'Come, reverend friar. Haven't you got eyes in your head? Haven't you noticed that I'm made of better stuff than the rest? I could have as many lovers as I wanted. But my charm's the sort which oughtn't to be just thrown away. I'm not giving myself away. You've not seen many women in the same class as me. Why, I'd be a credit to paradise itself.'

She blew her own trumpet so hard, the friar was deafened. He summed her up as being none too bright and thought she'd prove a walk-over. He fell for her on the spot but did not make a pass at her there and then. He decided it would be more convincing if he laid into her for her pride and suchlike. She countered by calling him a fool, who didn't know quality when he saw it. He did not want to hurt her feelings, so he put an end to the confession and sent her off with the others.

A few days later, he and a close friend paid a visit to Lisetta's house. He took her on one side in a neighbouring room out of sight of prying eyes, and there threw himself at her feet crying:

'For the love of God, forgive me, dear lady, for what I said to you last Sunday, about your beauty. As a result I was given such a beating that same night that I've only just got up from my bed.'

'Who was it punished you?' asked the Lady Muck.

'I'll tell you,' said the monk. 'That night, I was praying as usual, when a sudden bright light lit up my cell. Before I could turn to see who the visitor was, a handsome young man was standing over me. He held a heavy stick, and clutching my habit, he yanked me to my feet and beat me fit to break every bone in my body. When I asked him what I had done to deserve this, he replied: "It's because you dared to disparage the sacred charms of Lady Lisabetta, whom I adore more than anyone except God Himself." So I said: "Who are you?" And he told me he was the Angel Gabriel. I said: "Lord, please forgive me!" He said: "Only on condition that you go and ask her pardon as quickly as possible. If she doesn't relent, I'll visit you again and give you a hiding you'll remember for the rest of your life." I daren't tell you what he said afterwards until you've pardoned me.'

This so tickled Lady Fat-Head's vanity, that she took the friar's story for gospel truth. She replied almost at once:

'Didn't I tell you, Brother Alberto, that my beauty was out of this world—But, God bless me, I'm sorry for you really. You'd better have my pardon before worse happens to you—as long as you tell me what else the angel said, that is.' 'I shall be only too happy,' came the answer, 'now I'm forgiven. I warn you, however, make quite certain you don't repeat a word of what I'm about to tell you. Unless you want to ruin the stroke of luck that has made you the most privileged woman alive. The Angel Gabriel asked me to say that he is so devoted to you that if he hadn't been afraid of frightening you, many's the time he'd have come and spent the night with you. I'm to tell you that he'd like to pay you a visit one night. Being an angel, he could come in angelic form, but then you couldn't touch him. So for your sake he'll come in human shape. Just you let him know which night suits you, and who you would like him to come as . . . and he'll be there. So you can count yourself the luckiest woman in the world.'

Lady Swell-Head said she was honoured to be the lady of Angel Gabriel's choice. She had always been very partial to him herself and she'd make a point of burning a fourpenny candle before his shrine, whenever she was passing. He was more than welcome to visit her as often as he liked, and she'd take care to be alone in her room. It was on the strict understanding however, that he was not to be unfaithful with the Virgin Mary. He was supposed to be very fond of her, and it certainly always looked like it. Wherever you went, he was down on his knees in front of her. As to what he looked like, that was up to him, but she didn't want to be frightened out of her wits.

Alberto agreed: 'Well said, dear lady. I'll arrange it just as you say. But you could do me an enormous favour, without putting yourself out. If only you'd allow him to come as me. He'd then free my soul by borrowing my body while he's with you. Then my soul would be in paradise.'

'Agreed,' answered Madame Smug, 'I'd be only too pleased for you to have some consolation for the bruises you received on my account.'

'Good,' said the friar. 'Then he'll come tonight, so leave your outer door unlocked, then he can get in. Since he's coming in human shape he'll need a door.'

'Of course,' she replied.

Off went the friar, leaving the lady so excited that her vest parted company with her behind. It seemed centuries to have to wait.

Meanwhile Brother Alberto, realizing that he had to show the human and the angelic stuff he was made of that night, primed himself with sweets and energy-giving foods, to insure staying in the saddle. Having got leave of absence, he and one colleague set off that evening to a woman friend. Alberto had used her house before as a base for sporting excursions. He disguised himself and when the time came, went to the lady's home. With the help of the stage properties he had brought with him, he became an angel and went upstairs to her bedroom. On seeing the dazzling vision, she fell at her angel's feet. He blessed her, raised her to her feet and pointed to the bed. She obeyed only too willingly, and he took his place beside his acolyte. Alberto was a fine figure of a man and in good form. Lisetta, who was sexy and pretty enough herself, found him better company than her husband. That night he rode the course several times, and she was thoroughly satisfied. He described the Kingdom of Heaven to her in the process. Just before dawn, he gathered up his equipment and went off to rejoin his colleague, whom their faithful friend had kept company in case he was afraid of sleeping alone.

As for Lisabetta, when she had breakfasted she went off with a friend to visit Brother Alberto and tell him of the Angel Gabriel's visit. She reported his statements on the glories of eternity and his behaviour. Alberto replied:

'I've no idea how well you did with him, but he came to see me last night, and as a reward for my services as a messenger he bore off my soul to a land of flowers and roses—more beautiful than any in this world. I didn't know what my body was up to, but my soul enjoyed itself in that delightful place until this morning.'

'Haven't I been telling you?' said the lady. 'Your body was with the Angel Gabriel in my arms. If you don't believe me, just look at your left pap. I kissed the angel so passionately there, the mark will last for days.'

'Really!' said the friar. 'Then I'll do what I haven't done for a long time—undress, and see if you're right.'

This farce continued for some time before the lady went off home. After that Alberto paid her regular visits in his angel kit, and no one stopped him. But one day Lisetta was having a gossip about sex appeal, when she took it into her silly little head to brag about her own conquest.

'If you only knew who my admirer was,' she bragged, 'you'd be left standing.'

The other gas-bag was all ears. Knowing her companion's weak spot, she answered:

'That's as may be, but as I don't know who you're talking about, I'm not convinced.'

'My dear,' gushed the poor fool. 'Strictly between you and me, I'm referring to the Angel Gabriel. He loves me better than himself, for he says I'm the most beautiful woman in the world, not to mention the Island of Elba.'

The other woman burst out laughing at this, but controlled herself in the hope of hearing more.

'Well I never!' she said. 'If it *is* the Angel Gabriel—and of course it must be if you've got his word for it . . . but I didn't know angels were that way inclined.'

'That's just where you're wrong, you poor fool,' came the reply. 'Why, he's much better at it than my husband. He says it goes on upstairs too, but he thinks I'm better looking than any of that lot, so he's very keen on me and he drops in fairly often. Now do you understand?'

As soon as the other chatter-box had got the story, off she went, bursting to pass it on to someone else. When she met a group of other ladies at a party, she told the story in full detail. It soon got round to the husbands, then to another circle of ladies, and then to yet another lot. In under two days it was right round Venice. Among others, Lisabetta's relations got to hear of it. They privately decided to hunt this angel and see if they could put him to flight. For this purpose they kept watch for several nights. As luck would have it, Alberto was still ignorant of the current rumour, so one night when he'd come to enjoy the lady yet again, her relations caught him with his trousers down. They had seen him arrive, had approached the door, and were just about to open it, when Brother Alberto heard the noise and guessed the danger. He jumped up, and there was nothing for it but to throw open a window overlooking the Grand Canal and dive into the water. It was very deep, but he was a good swimmer. He reached the other side safely, and managed to get into a house he found open. Alberto threw himself on the mercy of the owner, begged him for God's sake to save his life, and invented a story to explain his visit in the nude and at that time of night. The man felt sorry for poor Alberto, but since he had an engagement he lent him his bed, ordered him to stay there till his return, locked him in and went about his business.

When the lady's relatives broke into her room they found the angelic bird had flown, abandoning its wings. They made up for their frustration by hurling abuse at Lisabetta and having reduced her to a heap, they went off home with the angel's effects.

Early next morning the merchant who had given Alberto asylum was on the Rialto. He heard the story of the Angel Gabriel's nocturnal visit to Lady Lisabetta, of the intruders, and of the angel's terrified plunge into the Canal, from which no one had seen him emerge. He at once identified the man he was harbouring at home. When he got back he confirmed his suspicion and after much haggling with the friar extracted fifty ducats from him as hush-money. When the bargain was made Brother Alberto tried to get away, but his host warned him:

'There's only one solution. We hold a fête today and people are led about in various disguises—bears, savages, and suchlike. This ends with a hunt in the Piazza San Marco, and rounds off the fête. Everybody goes his way, leading whoever he brought in tow. If you are prepared to let me take you in one of the disguises, I can get you away safely, before anyone cottons on to who you are. I can't

see any other way of getting you away unrecognized. The
lady's relatives must have suspected you're hiding somewhere in the area, because they've got guards posted.'

Brother Alberto didn't like the idea of this disguise at
all, but he agreed, because he was terrified of the relations.
He told his benefactor where he wanted to get to, and left
the choice of disguise to him. His companion smeared him
from top to toe with honey, stuck feathers in it, and put a
chain round his neck and a mask on his face. Himself he
armed with a stout stick and two big dogs (reprieved from
the slaughterhouse). Then he sent a herald to the Rialto to
announce that anyone who wanted to see the Angel
Gabriel had only to go to the Piazza San Marco. He had a
true Venetian sense of honour! So away he went with
Alberto at the end of the chain, and pushed his captive
through a mob howling: 'What on earth is it? What on
earth is it?' When he got to the square, what with those
who had followed him and those who had heard about him
on the Rialto, there was a large crowd. He fastened his
wild man-animal to a column in a very prominent place,
as if waiting for the hunt to start. The victim was pestered
by bluebottles and horse-flies, who were attracted by his
coating of honey. His master had only waited for the square
to fill before pretending to release his wild animal but in
fact only tearing the mask off Brother Alberto's face.

'Gentlemen,' he shouted, 'as no boar has appeared and
so the hunt is off, I'm going to compensate you with a sight
of the Angel Gabriel himself. He comes down from heaven
nightly to bring joy to the ladies of Venice.'

As soon as the mask was off, everyone recognized Alberto.
A great shout went up against him, he was abused in
language so obscene it would have made the most hardened
crook alive wince. They pelted him with whatever refuse
came to hand. They had baited him for a long time before
his fellow friars got to hear of it. Half a dozen of them
dashed to the square, shoved a habit on him, loosened the
chain and led him back to the friary in an uproar. There,
after a short spell in prison, he is believed to have died.

Fifth day: ninth tale

A BIRD IN THE HAND

There lived in Florence a young man called Federigo, son of Filippo Alberighi. He was the finest knight and the noblest courtier in Tuscany. Like most other gentlemen, he fell in love with a lady. Lady Giovanna was considered one of the most beautiful and gayest women in Florence. In order to win her love, Federigo fought at tournaments, threw parties, gave presents, and spent his inheritance recklessly. But she was a good woman as well as a beautiful one and was unconscious of what was being done for her, and of who was doing it. Federigo spent far more than he owned, and all to no end. His money could obviously not last for ever and the time came when he was almost destitute. Only a little farm which could barely support him, and one of the finest falcons in the world, remained to him. He was more deeply in love than ever, but seeing it was impossible to live on in town in the manner to which he had been accustomed, he retired to his farm in Campi. He lived there alone, hawking and learning to accept his poverty.

At about the time of Federigo's bankruptcy, Giovanna's husband, who was very rich, fell ill. He realized he had not long to live, and drew up a will leaving all his property to his son who was then a minor. Since he was devoted to his wife, however, he made a provision that if his son died without lawful issue, the fortune passed to Giavanna. Having made these arrangements, he died.

Giovanna was now a widow, and she retired that summer, as so many ladies do, to a country estate that lay near Federigo's. Her boy chanced to get friendly with Federigo, and became keen on hawks and hounds. Having seen Federigo's falcon fly many times, he passionately wished it were his. He did not dare to ask Federigo for it, because he knew what it meant to him.

It was at this stage that the boy fell ill. His mother was terribly upset, as he was her only child. She was devoted to him and watched at his bedside throughout the day, to keep him cheerful. She asked him if there were anything he wanted. He had only to say the word, and if it were at all possible she'd move heaven and earth to get anything for him. After much coaxing the boy said:

'If you could only get me Federigo's falcon, mother dear, I'm sure I'd soon get better.'

This brought his mother up sharply and gave her food for thought. She knew that Federigo had loved her for a long time, without so much as a friendly glance from her. 'How can I send him a message or go and ask him for his falcon,' she asked herself, 'which by all accounts is a superb one and his last remaining joy? I wouldn't be so cruel as to deprive him of the one crumb of comfort left to him.'

So, although she knew the bird was hers for the asking, she was in a quandary. Not knowing what to say, she did not reply to her son. Finally, however, maternal love conquered, and she decided to put his mind at rest by going herself, not sending for the falcon.

'Keep cheerful,' she urged her son. 'Don't worry, you'll soon be better. For first thing tomorrow I promise I'll go and get you the falcon.' The child was so delighted he began to improve at once.

Next day, Giovanna and another lady, as if on a social visit, rode over to Federigo's cottage and asked to see him. The weather had been unsuitable for hawking for several days, so Federigo was in the garden seeing to a few small things that needed his attention. When told that Giovanna had come and had asked to see him, he was pleasurably surprised, and hurried to meet her. As soon as she saw him, Giovanna came forward radiating feminine charm. She said as he greeted her :

'Good morning, Federigo. I've come to make amends to you for all you went through in your excessive love for me. In recompense, my companion and I have unceremoniously asked ourselves to lunch with you this morning.'

Federigo replied with great humility:

'Madam, I can't think of anything I lost through loving

you. In fact you did a great deal for me. If I was ever worth anything, it was thanks to your influence and my love for you. Indeed if I had all my fortune over again, I'd gladly trade it for this charming visit to a man who can offer you only the meagrest hospitality.'

He then apologetically welcomed her to his home. He led her into the garden and having no one else suitable to keep her company, introduced her to the wife of his workman: 'Here is the only person I have to entertain you while I superintend the meal.'

Though he was desperately poor, this was the first time the ill-effects of his extravagance had irked him. This morning his straits were all too apparent, as he couldn't find anything to offer the lady, for whose sake he had been so widely hospitable in the past. This distressed him deeply. He cursed his bad luck, and dashed to and fro frantically, but couldn't find a brass farthing or even anything pawnable. The time was getting on, and he had set his heart on giving Giovanna some taste of hospitality. His pride was such that he couldn't bring himself to ask his own workman for help. In his dilemma, he happened to catch sight of his fine falcon, on its perch in the little living-room. In desperation he took it in his hand, felt that it was plump, and decided it would make a dish fit for a lady. Without more ado he wrung its neck, and ordered the maid to pluck, spit, and roast it. He laid the table with a spotlessly clean cloth and hurried gaily back to the garden. He told Giovanna that such lunch as he could offer was nearly ready. The lady and her friend rose and came in to eat the meal Federigo had so painstakingly provided. They had no idea they were eating the splendid falcon.

When the meal was over, and they were sitting over it, chatting pleasantly, Giovanna thought the moment had come for her to explain her motive in coming. So she put her cards frankly on the table and told Federigo:

'In the light of the past and my virtuous behaviour to you (you probably considered it callous obstinacy), you will be flabbergasted by my cheek, when I tell you my main reason for this visit. But if you had a son of your own, and knew how one feels about them, I am sure you'd at least partly forgive me. You have no son. I've got one and I can't claim to be any less maternal than the rest. It's this power that drives me—I can't help it—to ask for something from you. I know it's inexcusable to ask you for what you rightly value above everything else, especially when you've been so battered by bad luck that it's the only thing left that gives you pleasure and recreation. I'm referring to your precious falcon. My boy has so set his heart on it, I'm terribly afraid that if I don't take it back to him, he'll get worse and I may lose him. So I implore you—not for the sake of your love for me, since that shouldn't bind you—but because of your own noble nature. You've already shown it in your generous welcome to us. I'm appealing to this, in asking for your bird as a present: then I may say I've saved my son's life, and I'll never forget that I owe it to you.'

On hearing Giovanna's request, Federigo was so miserable at being unable to offer the falcon which had already been served up to her, that he broke down and couldn't utter a word. At first she thought this owing to his unwillingness to part with the beloved bird and his determination to refuse her; but she waited patiently for him to answer:

'Since the day God ordained I should fall in love with you, I have more than once miserably cursed my misfortunes. But that was nothing compared to the trick destiny has played me this time. I can't forgive that bad luck when I think that you never deigned to come and see me in my palmy days, and now you visit me in this poor little house and ask a small favour, and I just can't oblige you. I'll explain why.

'When I heard you would do me the honour of staying to lunch, remembering your breeding and your noble character, I thought it only right and proper to entertain you as royally as was in my power. I thought of the falcon you have just asked me for, and since it was an exceptional one, I decided it would do for you. So I had him served up to you on a plate this very morning. I thought I'd done you well, but now I see you would rather have had him for something else. I'm so cut up at not being able to help you, I'll never be the same again.' Then he showed her the evidence of the bird's feathers, beak, and claws. On hearing Federigo's story and seeing the bird's remains, Giovanna's first reaction was to blame him for sacrificing such a magnificent bird to a lady's lunch. But deep down she was most impressed that her host's generosity had been unaffected by his poverty. Having been thwarted in her attempt to get the bird, and still anxious for her son's health, she left in deep depression, and went back to her boy.

Either because of his disappointment at not getting the falcon, or because the disease itself was fatal, the boy died a few days later. His mother was inconsolable. For some time she did nothing but cry and reproach herself. But, as she was still young, and now very rich, her brothers were continually imploring her to remarry. She would rather have remained a widow, but under this pressure she thought of Federigo's sterling character, and his great nobility in killing the falcon in her honour, so she told her brothers :

'If only you'd let me, I'd rather stay a widow. But if you insist on my remarrying, the only husband I'd think of is Federigo degli Alberighi.'

Her brothers laughed at her and said:

'You silly woman, what are you talking about? You can't possibly want Federigo. He's penniless.'

'I know you're right about that,' she replied, 'but I'd rather have a somebody with no money than a rich nobody.'

Her brothers saw she was adamant and as they knew Federigo to be a thoroughly good man despite his poverty, they gave him their wealthy sister. So Federigo was married to the woman he had adored so long. Possessing happiness and wealth (which was spent more sensibly than before) Federigo flourished to the end of his days.

Sixth day : tenth tale

TALE OF THE MIRACULOUS FEATHER

You may know Certaldo: it's a town in the Val d'Elsa. It's
small now but it used to have many wealthy and aristocratic inhabitants. For a long time it was the happy hunting ground of a friar of St Antony. He came once a year
to sponge off anybody fool enough to give him charity.
Brother Onion (that really was his name!) always got a
warm welcome, as much for his name as for anything else,
because that area is known throught Tuscany for its onions.
He was slight, red-haired and jolly—a thorough character.
Though he was totally ignorant, he spoke so glibly that anyone who didn't know better would have called him a great
orator—up to Cicero or Quintilian perhaps. For miles
around he was almost universally known, in some capacity
or other—either as a gossip, friend, or lover.

One August the friar was paying his regular visit to
Certaldo. It was Sunday morning and all the locals from
outlying farms came to mass in the parish church. The
friar took this opportunity to address them:

'Ladies and gentlemen, you will know that it's your
annual practice to grant the poor humble servants of our
lord and master St Antony a tithe of your harvest. Some
give a lot, some a little—it depends how rich you are and
how religious. In return St Antony watches over your farm
animals. In addition some of you, especially those who are
entered as honorary members of our brotherhood, pay a
modest yearly subscription. I've been sent here to collect
these offerings by my superior, the abbot himself. So in
God's name, be outside the church this afternoon when you
hear the bells ringing, and as usual I shall preach my
sermon, and you may kiss the cross. Since I know how devoted you all are to my lord and master St Antony, I'm
then going to show you as a special favour a genuine and

17

holy relic which I brought back myself from the Holy Land. It's none other than one of the feathers the Angel Gabriel dropped in the Virgin Mary's room in Nazareth after the Annunciation.'

He said no more and the service was continued.

Among the large congregation which heard this speech were two young scallywags, called Giovanni del Bragoniera and Biagio Pizzini. Though they were good friends of Brother Onion and went about with him a lot, the idea of the relic so tickled them that they made up their minds to play a trick on him and his feather. They learnt that Brother Onion was to lunch in town that morning with one of his friends. As soon as they knew he'd be safely at his meal, they were out of the house like a shot and on their way to the friar's lodging. Their plan was that while Biagio distracted the servant's attention, Giovanni was to ransack the friar's baggage in search of the feather (or whatever it was). Then they'd remove it and see how he got himself out of the situation, when he tumbled to it.

The friar's servant, Guccio, sometimes known as 'the Whale' or 'Scum-face' or 'Porker', was even more of a crook than those painted by Lipo Toppo (whose name is of course a household word!). His master used to say to his friends:

'My servant has nine characteristics, any *one* of which would have been the ruin of all the goodness and wisdom possessed by Solomon, Aristotle, and Seneca. Just imagine what it must be like to have all nine characteristics without a scrap of goodness and wisdom.'

Whenever he was asked to enumerate these nine qualities, he would chant:

'They are as follows:
He's careless, disobedient and obscene.
Rash and rude, if not insane.
He lies, is lazy and unclean.

He's got other lesser vices hardly worth mentoining. His most amusing foible is wanting a wife and a house in every port. With his big black greasy beard he's convinced he's irresistibly attractive and that every woman he meets is in love with him. Given half a chance, his woman-chasing would become a full-time job. But he's certainly very useful to me. If someone comes for a very private interview, he has to put his spoke in. If I'm asked a question, he's so afraid I'll be at a loss for an answer, that he chips in with "yes" or "no" as he thinks fit.'

When Friar Onion left this crook at his lodgings, it was with strict instructions not to allow anyone near his property, especially the bag that held the sacred object. But Scum-face took to the kitchen like greased lightning, especially if he saw a maid there. In this kitchen there was a slut, short and tubby, grotesquely malformed, with breasts like dung-heaps, a hideous face, all sweat, smoke, and grease. Guccio abandoned his master's property, was out of the room, down to the kitchen and had fastened on his prey before you could say Jack Robinson. Though it was August, he sat by the fire and gossiped on to the girl Nuta. He told her he was a 'self-paid man' with a fabulous fortune in two-shilling pieces, quite apart from those he more or less gave away. He could say and do even more miraculous things than his master. Unabashed by a hood that dripped with enough grease to float a battleship; doublet that was torn and patched, inlaid with dirt around the neck and under the arms, and discoloured with every shade in the rainbow; shoes that were falling apart; and socks that were in ribbons, he spoke to her in the most lordly terms. He said he was tempted to give her a new set of clothes, tidy her up, and raise her from her humble position to better things. Though she'd not have much of her own, there was always a chance . . . He went on in this vein, with a succession of promises that sounded fair enough but as usual were just pure wind. The two young men found the Porker so pre-occupied with Nuta, that they saw their job was already half-done. With no interference they went to the friar's room, which was not locked, and found the bag and the feather. It was in the bag, wrapped round with taffeta, sitting in a little box. They thought this precious object that their town had been promised a sight of, must be a parrot's tail-feather. That might well have passed muster with Certaldo, for at that time such Oriental luxuries were practically unknown in Tuscany, though since then they have been imported throughout Italy on a ruinous scale. Though they were not totally unfamiliar, they wouldn't have meant a thing to anybody in that part of the world. The locals lived the simple unspoilt life of their ancestors, and would never have heard of, let alone seen a parrot.

The young men were delighted at having found the feather. Wondering what to put in its place, they picked up some charcoal that was in a corner, and filled the box with that. They closed it, made sure that the room looked exactly as it had before, and left unnoticed, crowing over the feather. They waited impatiently to hear what Brother Onion would say on seeing the charcoal.

After mass the gullible townsfolk went home from church, and soon the news spread that the Angel Gabriel's feather would be on show that afternoon. A man told his next-door neighbour, a woman chatted to a friend, and as the morning wore on the town filled to bursting with crowds of people all agog to see the feather.

The friar ate a hearty lunch, took forty winks and was up early in the afternoon. Noticing the huge crowd that was gathering to see the feather, he sent and asked Scum-face to bring him the bag, and go and ring the bells. Guccio reluctantly tore himself away from the kitchen and its maid and fetched the things required. He arrived at the church porch very bloated from drinking too much water, and in obedience to his master started clanging the bells.

When the crowd had gathered round the door, the friar began his sermon—quite unaware that the box had been tampered with. He started with some self-congratulation. Next the general confession was solemnly chanted, and two candles were lit. Then the friar bared his head, carefully unwrapped the taffeta and took out the box. With a few introductory words in praise of the Angel Gabriel and the relic, he proceeded to open it. When he saw that it contained nothing but charcoal, his suspicions did not fall on the Whale, for he knew him to be too stupid for a practical joke like that. He didn't even blame his servant's negligence in letting someone else tamper with the box. But he inwardly cursed himself for entrusting the box to someone he knew to be careless, disobedient, slovenly, and thick-headed. However, the friar didn't turn a hair; he merely raised his face and hands to heaven, and said loudly:

'O Father, eternally blessed be Thy power!'

Then he closed the box, and turned to the crowd.

'Ladies and gentlemen,' he said, 'I should tell you that when I was young my abbot sent me to the east, with instructions to find the Porcelain Privileges. As you know,' he added mysteriously, 'these could have been sent by registered post, but the other side values them far more highly than we. On this mission I set off from Venice, crossed Greek Street, rode through Portugal Place, past the Roof-Gardens. Then from Pimlico, I fought my way to the Isle of Dogs. But what's the point of mentioning everywhere I passed? Once through the Straits of St George, I was soon at Truffles, and then Buffles—both densely populated and full of people. I moved on to Flim-Flam, where I came across many fellow friars and other clerics, all of them busily cultivating their comfort for the love of God. Nothing was too much trouble for other people, as long as they weren't put out themselves. Up and down the land they paid for everything in cardboard cash. I eventually reached the Abruzzi, where the men and women cross the mountains in clogs, and pigs' insides make sausages' outsides. A little further on I met people who ate stick-bread and drank their wine from bags. Next came the Grubby Mountains, where all the water runs downhill. Indeed I went on as far as the Double-Dutch East Indies, which really is a whale of a place. I swear by my habit I saw wing collars fly, incredible though it may sound. If you want a witness ask that great merchant Fleshpots. (And do you know I found him cracking nuts there and then selling the shells retail!). Since I could not find the object of my search, and from there the journey is by water, I turned back. In the end I got to the Holy Land. (In summer there a loaf of bread costs a penny cold and nothing hot; would you believe it?). I met Holy Father Please-Don't-Blame-Me, the Patriarch of Jerusalem. He respects my order and our lord and master St Antony so much, that he was good enough to show me all the holy relics he had handy. It would take me years to describe them all, but I'll tell you about a few of them:

'First : the Holy Ghost's finger, in mint condition. A curl from the Seraph who appeared to St Francis. A nail from one of the Cherubim, a rib from the Sacred Word of Don't-Look-Now. A garment belonging to the Holy Catholic Church herself. A ray or two from the Star of the East seen by the Magi. A tube of St Michael's sweat from his battle with Satan. The jaws of death St Lazarus actually went into, and many other relics. As I was only too happy to copy him out a portion of Box Hill in the Vernacular, and a chapter or two of Capricians which he had hankered after for a long time, he was generous enough to give me a share in his holy relics. I got a tooth from the Holy Cross; a fraction of the sound from the temple-bells of Solomon; the feather of St Gabriel I mentioned to you; a clog belonging to St Gherardo of Villamagna, which I gave quite recently to Gherardo Bonsi in Florence, because he's very keen on him. I was also given some of the charcoal used in roasting the blessed martyr, St Lawrence.

'I brought all these back with me and have them still. It is true that my superior won't allow me to show them publicly until he's convinced that they're genuine. Now, however, this *has* been established, because the Patriarch wrote describing the miracles they had performed. I am therefore at liberty to show them. But, in my anxiety for their safety, I always keep them with me.

'To be honest, I keep the Archangel Gabriel's feather in a little box so it doesn't get damaged. The charcoal which roasted St Lawrence is kept in a box so similar, that I often muddle them up. I'm afraid this has happened today: I meant to produce for you the box which holds the feather, but I've brought the charcoal one instead. I won't say by mistake, because I think it's God's will. He Himself gave me the charcoal, for, as I recall, the feast of St Lawrence is the day after tomorrow. God realized that if I showed you the charcoal used in the roasting, I'd rekindle the devotion you should be feeling in your hearts. My hand was directed not to the feather I intended to bring, but to the blessed charcoal saved from burning by the sweat from that sacred body. So, my children, come forward humbly with bared heads. But first let me promise you that whoever has the sign of the cross made over him with this charcoal, will be completely insured against fire for a whole year. No flame will have power to touch him.'

After this speech the friar chanted a hymn in praise of St Lawrence, opened the box and revealed the charcoal. The silly crowd gazed in awe, then pressed forward and thronged around Brother Onion. They offered up even more money than usual, and all clamoured for him to touch them with the charcoal. The friar took it in his hand and started drawing large crosses on veils, white blouses, and jerkins. He had frequently proved, he claimed, that whatever the charcoal lost in this way, it regained on being put back in its box.

So it was that the friar set his mark on the people of Certaldo, and did very nicely out of it. Thanks to his quick reactions, he turned the tables on the thieves who had hoped to show him up as as fool. As part of the audience, they were most impressed by his improvisation, his rhetoric, and his elaboration of the story. They almost died laughing. When the crowd dispersed, they went up to him, gaily owned up and gave back the feather. The year after it proved to have just as much sales appeal as the charcoal.

First day: fourth tale

THE POSITION WITH WOMEN

IN a not very distant part of Lunigiana there was a flourishing community of monks, more numerous than any found there today. In their number was a young brother who was so hale and hearty that even vigils and fasts could not keep him subdued. One afternoon, when his fellows were asleep, the young man went for a walk round the church, and happened to meet a young and very pretty girl. She must have been a local peasant's daughter, because she was gathering herbs in the fields. At the sight of her he was so overcome with lust that he quickly went up to her. As she had a sympathetic nature, they soon came to an understanding and, unnoticed by anyone, went into his cell. As luck would have it, they enjoyed themselves rather noisily, since he was over-enthusiastic. This woke up the Abbot, who walked slowly past the monk's cell and heard the noise inside. To make out the voices more plainly, he stalked up to the door of the cell, and didn't take long to find out there was a woman inside. First he considered breaking open the door, but changed his mind and returned to his room to wait for the monk to finish.

Much as the monk was enjoying his intercourse with the girl, he was still a little anxious. He thought he had heard footsteps in the dormitory, and through a peephole had had a good view of the Abbot spying at the door. He realized that the Abbot might well have detected the presence of the woman, and he was very frightened at the thought of the punishment he would incur. He hid his distress from the girl, however, and racked his brains for some way out of his predicament. Then he hit on a brilliant scheme to solve his problem. Pretending he was sick of the girl, he told her:

'Now I am going out for a moment to arrange getting

you out of here without being seen. Stay here quietly till I get back.'

He locked the door, and bore off the key with him. He went straight to the Abbot's room and handed it to him, as a monk who was going out was supposed to do, saying nonchantly:

'I wasn't able to bring in all the firewood I cut this morning, so, with your permission, sir, I'll fetch the rest now.'

The Abbot, who wanted to investigate the monk's crime further and who did not realize that his spying had been spied on, was pleased with the turn of events. He took the key willingly and gave his permission. After the monk had left, the Abbot wondered what to do next. Should he summon the whole monastery and throw open the cell door, so that they would be witnesses to the crime, or should he collect the girl's statement first? It struck him that she might be related to someone who would take exception to her public exposure, so he decided to find out who she was before taking further action.

He approached the cell softly, slipped in and closed the door behind him.

The girl, recognizing the Abbot, panicked and cried bitterly in shame. He looked her up and down, fully appreciating her attractions. Despite his age, he felt as violent a desire for her as the young monk had. So he said to himself:

'Poor me! Why don't I get my bit of fun, when I get the chance? Life's depressing enough, without letting an opportunity like this slip. Here's a pretty girl, and no one will be any the wiser. Why shouldn't I, if she'll oblige? Who's to know? No one's ever likely to—and a sin that's hidden is half-forgiven. I shan't get a chance like this again, and it would be ungrateful not to take God's gift.'

Having persuaded himself from his original intention, he approached the girl, tried to console her, and gradually made his intentions clear. The girl was only flesh and blood, and was easily persuaded to accommodate the Abbot. When he had fondled her, he lay down on the monk's bed. Perhaps he felt his weighty presence might overpower one so young. Anyway he didn't lie on her, but made her lie on him instead, and enjoyed her for some time.

The monk had only pretended to go to the wood and was hidden in the dormitory, and on seeing the Abbot enter his cell he was overjoyed at the success of his plan. He was further reassured by hearing the Abbot lock the door. He crept from his corner and found a little hole through which he could see and hear everything that the Abbot did. When the Abbot was satisfied, he locked the girl in the cell and returned to his own room. When he met the monk a little later, supposedly back from the wood, he decided to give him a terrific dressing down and then lock him up, so that he'd have the girl to himself. He therefore summoned him, laid into him fiercely, and with a stern expression sentenced him to imprisonment. The monk promptly countered :

'I have not belonged to the Order of St Benedict long enough, sir, to know every one of our rules intimately. You described the position with fasts and vigils but not with women. But now that I have seen your demonstration, I promise you, if you'll pardon my offence, I will never repeat it, but always follow your example, and do it your way.'

The Abbot was shrewd enough to see that the monk had not only outwitted him, but had even outspied him. Nor, in his shame, could he punish the monk for a crime he had himself committed. He pardoned him on condition that he kept the secret, and they smuggled the girl out of the monastery. But let us not jump to the conclusion that they never invited her back.

Seventh day: ninth tale

THE RIGHT HAND MAN

ARGOS is an ancient city of Achaia, whose fame derives
from its line of kings, rather than its size. Among its inhabitants was Nicostratus, an aristocrat who late in life was
fatally lured into marrying a great lady. His wife Lydia was
a lively and charming woman. Nicostratus kept the considerable household of servants, dogs, and hawks that was
incumbent on a man with his wealth and position, who was
also an enthusiast for hunting. One of his servants, a very
talented and handsome fellow called Pyrrhus, was Nicostratus' right hand man. Lydia fell so deeply in love with
him that she couldn't keep her mind off him for a moment.
Either because he was blind to it or superior, Pyrrhus
gave no sign. This increased her suffering so unbearably
that she made up her mind to admit her love to him openly.
She called her maid Lusca, in whom she had great faith.

'My presents to you should have been enough to command your unquestioning loyalty. So please make sure that
what I'm just going to tell you only reaches the ears it is
meant for. You can see for yourself, Lusca, that I'm healthy
and in the prime of life. I have everything that anyone
could wish for; my only complaint is that my husband's so
much older than I am. When it comes to you-know-what, I
don't do so well. Since I've got the same appetites as anyone else of my age, and fate's saddled me with a decrepit
husband, I've got no one to blame but myself if I'm not
happy and flourishing. So as to round off my happiness,
I've decided on Pyrrhus as the most suitable man for my
lover. In fact I'm so in love with him, that I'm miserable if
I'm not with him, at least in spirit. I think I'll die if I
don't get him soon. If my happiness means anything to you
tell him in any way you like, and beg him to come whenever you go and fetch him.'

27

'Indeed I will,' the maid reassured her.

And at an opportune time and place, she took Pyrrhus on one side and delivered her mistress' message as best she could. Pyrrhus listened with amazement, for it came as a shock to him, and he suspected the lady was just testing him.

'You can hardly expect me to believe that message came from our mistress, Lusca,' he said tartly. 'Be careful, because if she did say that, she can't mean it. And if she is serious, I'm so indebted to my master, who's far too good to me, that I wouldn't dream of doing a thing like that to him. So, Lusca, please don't ever mention it again.'

Lusca wasn't the least put out by his snub and replied:

'Pyrrhus, I'll mention this and anything else I'm told to by my mistress, whether you like it or not. You're a plain fool.'

Lusca was annoyed by his attitude and repeated the conversation to her mistress. It almost killed poor Lydia. But a few days later she brought the matter up again.

'You know, Lusca,' she said, 'we couldn't expect the first attack to succeed. I think you'll have to try again. This sense of duty of his *is* a pain in the neck. Choose your moment and then tell him of my passion, and do your damnedest this time. This suspense will be the death of me. Besides he will begin to think I was making fun of him, and he's more likely to loathe than love me.'

Lusca comforted her and then went to look for Pyrrhus. Luckily she found him in a good mood.

'Pyrrhus,' she said, 'only a few days ago I told you how passionately our mistress loves you. Now I've come to repeat it, and to warn you that if you remain callous, she'll not live much longer. I appeal to you to give in to her. I've always thought you had sense, but you're behaving like a pig-headed idiot. You should be flattered with an aristocratic, beautiful woman like her doting on you. You should thank your lucky stars, having a thing like that drop into your lap. A fellow couldn't wish for anything better. You'll have no more financial worries. None of the other servants would be in such a privileged position. None of them would be so well off for arms, clothes, horses and money—all you need do is give our lady your love.

'Just think about what I've said. Take a grip of yourself.
Remember, you don't get offered a chance like that twice
in a life-time. If you don't take it, you'll only have yourself to blame when you're down and out. A servant doesn't
owe his master anything like the loyalty he owes friends
and relatives. He just has to give his master the treatment
he gets from him, if possible. Do you really think that if
you had a daughter, a mother, a sister, or a wife who attracted Nicostratus, he'd think twice about it, like you with his
wife. You'd be a fool if you credited that. Take it from me,
if he didn't get what he wanted by asking nicely, he'd certainly use force without so much as a by-your-leave. So let's
pay them in their own coin. Take a chance when you're
offered it. Don't look a gift horse in the mouth, go and
meet her halfway. If you don't, quite apart from it being
the death of her, you'll go on kicking yourself for the rest
of your life and wish you were dead.'

Since his first interview with Lusca, Pyrrhus had been
brooding on what she had said. He'd decided that if she
came back, he'd change his tack and agree to everything
the lady asked, as long as he could be sure it wasn't just a
trial. So this time he replied :

'Lusca, now I'm prepared to admit you're right. But
Nicostratus is no fool. As he has given me a great deal of
business responsibility, I bet it's all his idea, and he suggested Lydia should test me this way. So, just to set my mind
at rest, I'm going to ask three things of her. If she does
them, I'll do anything she wants without another word. I
demand these three things: killing Nicostratus' favourite
falcon before his own eyes; cutting off a lock of his hair for
me; and getting me one of his best teeth.'

This seemed a pretty tall order to Lusca, and worse still
to her mistress. However, love is very optimistic, and an old
hand at stratagem, so she was determined to have a try. She
sent Pyrrhus word by Lusca that his command would at
once be obeyed to the letter. She added that, since he was
so convinced of Nicostratus' cleverness, she'd actually
arrange for them to enjoy each other in his presence, without him taking it seriously.

Pyrrhus waited anxiously to see what she'd do. Some

days later Nicostratus gave his usual grand dinner to a group of gentlemen. When the tables were moved back, Lydia came into the hall from her room in a dress of green silk covered with jewellery. In front of Pyrrhus and everyone else, she went up to the perch where Nicostratus' favourite sparrow-hawk stood. She untied the bird, and as though about to lift it on to her hand, took it by the jesses and battered it to death against the wall.

'Oh! What have you done?' cried Nicostratus. As answer she turned to the men sitting at the table, and said:

'My lords, I would hardly be up to revenging myself on a king who had done me wrong, if I wasn't brave enough to get my own back on a sparrow-hawk. Let me tell you this bird has deprived me of the time a gentleman owes his wife. At crack of dawn Nicostratus is up, has mounted his horse, and has gone off to fly his hawk in the country, leaving poor me alone and miserable in bed. For a long time I've been wanting to do what I've just done. The only thing that stopped me was my desire to do it in the presence of men who would understand and sympathize, as I hope you will.'

These words convinced the guests that she was as devoted to Nicostratus as her actions implied. They all started laughing, and turning to Nicostratus, who was still livid, they said:

'You can't help admiring a lady who'll get her own back on a sparrow-hawk!' So when the lady returned to her own room they laughed off the affair and turned Nicostratus' anger to amusement.

Pyrrhus, having witnessed the proceedings, said to himself: 'The lady's made a fine beginning. It's a good sign for our future happiness, if she can keep it up.'

Lydia certainly did. Not long after killing the sparrow-hawk, when she and Nicostratus were in her room, their kissing turned to horse-play. He pulled her hair in fun, and this gave her a chance of fulfilling Pyrrhus' second order. She grabbed at a little tuft of her husband's beard, and laughingly pulled it out. When he grumbled, she said:

'You've got no reason to look so miserable. I only pulled half a dozen hairs out of your beard. You can't have felt it more than I did when you were pulling my hair.'

So they continued the game and the laughter, but she kept the hairs very carefully, and sent them to her beloved that same day.

The third labour presented some problem. But she was quick-witted and love had given her the incentive, so she soon hit on a plan. Nicostratus employed two pages from good families, sent by their relatives to be taught etiquette. One of them carved at meal-times, and the other poured out drink. Lydia summoned them both and asked them to keep their heads averted when serving Nicostratus, because their breath smelt. She told them this was to go no further, and they believed her and did as they were bid. She said to Nicostratus one day :

'Have you noticed what those boys do when they're serving you?'

'Indeed I have,' he replied, 'and I've been on the point of asking for an explanation, more than once.'

'Well you needn't bother,' answered his wife. 'I can tell you the reason, but I didn't like to say, in case it hurt your feelings. As other people have been noticing it too, I may as well break it to you. They turn their heads away because your breath smells so bad. It used not to be like that, so I can't think how it happened. But it's very unpleasant when you mix with gentlemen. We must cure it somehow.'

'I wonder what the trouble is,' said Nicostratus. 'Do you think I've got a rotten tooth?'

'It might well be that,' she answered, and leading him to the window, made him open his mouth. After examining it closely, she gasped: 'Oh, Nicostratus, how can you stand it? One of your teeth is not just decayed, it's rotten to the core. I'm sure if it's left there much longer it'll infect all the others. If I were you, I'd have it out at once.'

'I agree with you completely,' he said. 'So get me a dentist at once.'

'Good Lord, you don't need a dentist for a thing like that,' answered Lydia. 'I'm sure we can get on perfectly well without him. I'll take it out myself. These dentists do the job so brutally. I couldn't bear seeing you, or thinking of you, at their mercy. I'm determined to do it myself, so if the pain's unbearable, I can stop at once, which is more than a dentist would do.'

So Lydia ordered the necessary instruments, sent everybody away except Lusca, locked the door, popped the pincers in his mouth and clamped on to a tooth. Lusca held the patient down, so that he might scream with pain, but couldn't move. Lydia wrenched a tooth out by brute force, and swapped it with a horribly decayed one Lusca had with her. She thrust this at Nicostratus who was half-dead with pain, and said :

'Look what you had there. Wasn't it far gone?'

Her husband believed her, and was glad that now the tooth had come out, his breath would cease to smell. He grumbled about the agonizing pain he had suffered, but it had eased a little. Having been coaxed and made a fuss of in various ways, off he went. Lydia sent the tooth to her lover at once. He was now fully satisfied and placed himself completely at her disposal. She, however, despite her gnawing impatience to be with Pyrrhus, wanted to make assurance doubly sure. To carry out her final promise, she decided to pretend illness. One day, after dinner, Nicostratus came to see her, bringing only Pyrrhus. She asked to be taken down to the garden for the good of her health. Nicostratus took one side and Pyrrhus the other, and they carried her downstairs and set her on the lawn underneath a magnificent pear tree. Lydia had already briefed Pyrrhus on what to do, so after a while she said to him:

'Pyrrhus, I should dearly love some of those pears. Do climb up and shake some down.'

Pyrrhus was up the tree in a flash and had begun to shake down the pears when he cried out suddenly:

'Shame on you, sir! What are you doing? And, my lady, you should be ashamed to let him, in my presence. Do you think I'm blind? A moment ago you were supposed to be very ill. You must have got better pretty quickly, to behave like that. Besides you've got quite enough bedrooms for the purpose. If you must play about like that, go and do it in one of them. It would certainly be more decent than doing it in my presence.'

At that, the lady turned to her husband and said:

'What *is* Pyrrhus talking about? Is he out of his mind?'

'No, madam. I'm far from mad,' he cried. 'Don't think I can't see.' Nicostratus was flabbergasted.

'Pyrrhus,' he said, 'I think you're suffering from hallucinations.'

'No, my lord,' he answered. 'I'm certainly not dreaming —nor are you. You're tossing about so violently, that if this tree rocked like that, it'd lose every pear.'

'What can he mean?' asked Lydia. 'Does it really look the way he says? If only I were well enough, God knows I'd get up there myself and see if what he claims is true.'

Meanwhile up in the pear tree Pyrrhus kept on in the same strain. Nicostratus ordered him to come down.

'Now,' he said, 'what do you say you saw up there?'

'I suppose you'll think I'm suffering from hallucinations,' replied Pyrrhus, "but I honestly saw you covering your wife. On my way down, I saw you get up and sit where you are now.'

'Then it certainly was an hallucination,' said Nicostratus, 'because while you were up the pear tree we haven't budged an inch, except to where we are now.'

'Don't let's beat about the bush,' said Pyrrhus, 'I saw you all right, and you were certainly covering your wife.'

Nicostratus was so amazed by this time that he said:

'I've got a good mind to see if everyone up in this tree sees miracles.' So he climbed up.

Meanwhile his wife and Pyrrhus were enjoying each other. Nicostratus saw what was going on and shouted: 'Oh, you foul woman! What are you doing? And you Pyrrhus, who've always been so reliable.' And he started climbing down. But both Lydia and Pyrrhus said : 'We're sitting quite still.'

As he descended they moved to where they had been before. Nicostratus at once began to abuse them.

'Well, now I'm prepared to admit what you said about that pear tree's true,' said Pyrrhus. 'I just didn't realize it produced delusions, till I saw it happen to you too. If you don't believe me, just think a moment. Is it likely that an exceptionally virtuous and clever woman like your wife would do a thing like that before your very eyes, even if she did want to make a fool of you? Not to mention me, though I'd rather be torn to pieces than think of doing such a thing, especially in your presence. It's obvious that that pear tree produces some optical illusion. Nothing would have convinced me that I didn't really see you copulating with your wife, except your saying you saw me do the same. I'd never even dream of it, let alone do it.'

Lydia then got up and burst out furiously:

'God forgive you, you can't know me very well. Can you imagine that if I wanted to put you to shame, I'd be capable of doing a thing like that; and under your nose too? If I ever did have a mind to it, I'd do it in one of our bedrooms, don't you worry. And you wouldn't catch me arranging it so that you'd be likely to find out.'

Then Nicostratus believed them both, and was convinced that neither of them would have dreamed of doing such a thing in front of him. He stopped blaming them and drew attention to the fact that this extraordinary vision should occur to everybody who climbed the tree. But Lydia pretended to be still distressed by his having imagined such a thing of her.

'One thing's certain,' she insisted, 'neither I nor any other woman is going to be insulted again because of that pear tree. Go and fetch an axe, Pyrrhus. Clear both our reputations by cutting it down. Though it'd be better to use it on Nicostratus' head, if he lets himself be taken in as easily as that. Even if your eyes really did see that vision, your mind oughtn't for one moment to have accepted it as real.'

Off went Pyrrhus to fetch the axe; he brought it back and cut down the pear tree. Then Lydia turned to Nicostratus and said :

'Now my honour is cleared, my anger has evaporated.'

Nicostratus humbly begged her pardon, and was generously forgiven, as long as he never again allowed himself to think such a thing of the wife who loved him more than herself. The poor tricked husband went back to the house with her and her lover. And Pyrrhus and Lydia often enjoyed each other again—though with less discomfort. If only we could all say the same . . .

Fifth day: fourth tale

THE NIGHTINGALE

Not long ago there lived in Romagna a noble aristocrat called Lizio of Valbona. He was on the verge of old age when his wife Giacomina gave birth to a daughter. She grew up as beautiful and charming as any girl in the district. As she was the only child still at home, she was the apple of her parents' eye. They guarded her fiercely and hoped to arrange a distinguished marriage.

A certain Ricciardo, one of the Manardis from Berettinoro, a handsome and lively young man, was such a frequent visitor at their house, and got on so well with the Lizios that he became almost one of the family. He was so often in the company of this beautiful, vivacious, and well-behaved young lady, that he was soon desperately in love with her. He was very careful, however, to keep his passion secret. This did not prevent the girl soon finding out, and far from minding she fell equally in love with him. Ricciardo was delighted, and was often on the point of speaking out, but felt too shy. He did finally pluck up courage, took his chance and said:

'Caterina, I implore you, don't make me die of love.'

To which she replied:

'I could say the same to you.'

This reply was so cheerful and encouraging, that Ricciardo continued:

'If you come to any conceivable harm, it'll be over my dead body. But you could save both our lives.'

'You can see how closely I'm watched, Ricciardo,' she said. 'I really can't see how you can get to me. If you can think of anything I can do respectably, you've only to say the word.'

After a little thought, he hit on an idea:

'My dear Caterina, the only thing I can suggest is that

35

you somehow manage to sleep out on the balcony overlooking your father's garden. If I knew you were sleeping out there, I'd move heaven and earth to climb up to you, however high you are!'

'If you're brave enough to come,' said Caterina, 'I'll somehow manage to be there.'

He promised he would, so they kissed furtively and parted.

As it was near the end of May, the next day the girl started grumbling to her mother about not being able to sleep the night before, because it was terribly hot.

'What are you talking about?' said that good lady. 'It wasn't at all.'

'Mother dear,' answered Caterina, 'you mean you don't find it hot. Probably you didn't, but remember girls are warmer blooded than middle-aged women.'

'That's true, my dear,' answered her mother, 'but you really can't expect me to regulate the temperature to suit you. We must put up with it, and take what weather's given us. Perhaps it'll be cooler tonight, and you'll sleep better.'

'I only hope so,' said Caterina with feeling, 'but it's not normal for it to get cooler as summer comes on.'

'But what *do* you expect me to do about it?' asked her mother.

"If you and Father didn't mind,' came the answer, 'I'd like to make up a small bed out on the balcony, next to his room and over the garden. If I slept out there, I'd be cooler, sleep much better than in my room, and be able to hear the nightingale.'

'Don't worry, dear,' said her mother, 'I'll ask father, and if he says yes, we'll do that.'

Lizio, however, was no longer young, and was inclined to be prickly. When he heard all this he shouted:

'What's this nonsense about a nightingale to sing her to sleep? If I had my way she'd have crickets chirping her a lullaby as well.'

When this was reported to her, Caterina, more from spite than from the heat, not only had a sleepless night herself, but kept her mother awake with her grumbles.

So next morning the lady went to her husband and pleaded:

'You've not got a scrap of feeling for the girl. What harm would it do for her to sleep on the balcony? She didn't get a wink all night for the heat. Besides, you can't blame her for wanting to hear the nightingale; she's only young. Children love things romantic like themselves.'

At this, Lizio gave in:

'All right, make up any bed there you can. Hang a bit of curtain round it, and let her listen to the nightingale to her heart's content.'

As soon as she heard this, the girl had her bed made up, so that she could sleep out that night. She watched out for Ricciardo and gave the signal agreed on; so he knew his next move.

When Lizio heard his daughter get into bed, he locked the door from his own room onto the balcony and went to bed himself. When everything was quiet, Ricciardo climbed the wall, with the help of a ladder, and holding on to some projections on another wall. With enormous effort and risking a dangerous drop, he got up to the balcony. The girl welcomed him silently but joyfully. They kissed long and passionately, went to bed together, and enjoyed each other for almost the whole of the night. They raised a song from the nightingale a good many times. Since the night was short and their appetite large, it was nearly day before they fell asleep. Thanks to the hot weather and hot work, they had thrown back the bed-clothes and fallen fast asleep. Caterina's right arm was around Ricciardo's neck and her left hand held him by what, ladies, shall be nameless.

They were still asleep in this position, when Lizio got up at crack of dawn. He remembered his daughter was sleeping on the balcony, so he opened the door quietly, saying to himself:

'Let's see whether the nightingale sang Caterina to sleep last night.'

He went quietly up to the bed and drew the curtain aside. There lay Ricciardo and his daughter, asleep and naked, as I have just described. Lizio recognized Ricciardo, crept to his wife's room, and called out:

'Get up at once and come and look. Our girl was so keen on the nightingale, that she's gone and caught it and has trapped it in her hand.'

'Is that possible?' she asked.

'You'll see, if you hurry up,' he replied.

So she dressed hurriedly, and quietly followed her husband to the bed. Drawing the curtain, Giacomina could plainly see her daughter holding the nightingale she'd been so keen to hear. As a mother she saw how misplaced her trust in Ricciardo had been, and wanted to beat the daylights out of him. But Lizio said:

'My dear, for my sake don't say a word. Since she's caught him, she can have him. He's young, rich, and a gentleman. We couldn't wish for a better son-in-law. But if he wants to stay in my good books he must agree to marry her on the spot. Then he'll realize he's put the nightingale in his own cage, and not in anyone else's.'

The lady was relieved to find her husband was not furious, and satisfied that her daughter had slept well and managed to catch the nightingale, she said no more.

Ricciardo awoke not long after this conversation. Seeing it was broad daylight, he gave himself up for lost and woke Caterina:

'Oh, my darling, we're done for! Daylight's caught us napping.'

At these words Lizio stepped forward, drew back the curtain, and answered: 'We'll survive.'

When Ricciardo saw him, his heart went into his boots. He sat up in bed and said:

'Sir, for God's sake have mercy on me! I know I'm a foul swine, and hanging's too good for me. You can do what you like with me. But please, in God's name, spare my life and don't kill me.'

'Ricciardo,' said Lizio, 'my affectionate trust in you deserved something better. But as it's turned out this way, and you've been carried away by your youth, you can save your own life and my shame by marrying Caterina. Then you can do what you did last night for the rest of your lives, as is only right. That's the way you'll satisfy me and save yourself. But if you reject this offer, say goodbye to the world.'

During this speech Caterina had let go of the nightingale, covered herself up, and started crying bitterly. First she begged her father to forgive Ricciardo. Then she implored Ricciardo to accept her father's offer, so that they could sleep peacefully together for the rest of their lives. But he didn't need much persuasion. What with a shame-faced desire to make amends, a frightened reluctance to die, and a lover's desire to possess his mistress, Ricciardo willingly agreed to Lizio's terms. So the father borrowed one of his wife's rings and on the spot Ricciardo was married off to Caterina.

Then Lizio and his wife made themselves scarce, saying: 'Now relax! That's much more important than getting up.'

When they had gone the couple embraced and since they had only done six laps during the night, did another two rounds and so ended their first training bout.

When they got up, Ricciardo and Lizio discussed the matter more formally. Some weeks later, as was only proper, Ricciardo married the girl again, publicly. He took her ceremonially to his own home and gave a splendid wedding reception. For many years to come they lived happily, catching the nightingale together day and night, to their hearts' content.

Fifth day : tenth tale

THERE ARE GAMES TWO CAN PLAY AT

NOT long ago there lived in Perugia a wealthy man called
Pietro di Vinciolo. He was there to live down his wide-
spread reputation; and as a blind, rather than from any
personal desires, he got married. Fate was obliging enough
to send him a plump young red-head who was so highly-
sexed that what she needed was two husbands, not one who
really preferred women of his own sex.

She soon summed up the situation and knowing herself to
be attractive and feeling entitled to some fun, she was not
unnaturally piqued. She had frequent feuds with her husband and their life was not a bed of roses. She saw that
this was only making her more miserable and having no
effect on her husband, so she said to herself:

'This man neglects me miserably, and goes tripping after
queers, whereas I'm all for doing it the normal way. I
accepted him as my husband, brought him a large dowry on
the assumption that he was a man, and expected him to
want what's only natural. If I'd thought he was anything
else, I'd never have taken him on. He knew I was a woman,
why did he marry me if women weren't his cup of tea?
It's unbearable. If I'd wanted to give up the things of this
world, I could have done it in a convent. I plumped for
life but I'm not likely to get any fun from him. I might
wait till I was grey, moaning over all the chances I'd
missed, but I wouldn't get any change out of him. Anyway
he's a walking example himself of how to console yourself with a bit of fun on the side. It'd be all above board
for me to have a fling, but it's criminal with him. I should
only be flouting convention, but he's illegal and unnatural.'

She had this debate with herself several times, before she
secretly set about putting her theory into practice.

She got friendly with an old harridan who took after

Saint Verdiana, the patron saint of vipers. She was always at church when the indulgences were being given, telling her rosary, droning on about the lives of the Holy Fathers and Saint Francis' stigmata. Pietro's wife opened her heart to this so-called saint.

'My child,' said the old woman, 'God, who knows everything, knows you would be absolutely right to do this. Apart from anything else it's right, because a girl of your age oughtn't to throw away the best years of her life. There's nothing worse than kicking yourself because of the chances you've missed. What are we women good for when we're old, except watching the stove? I can tell you this from experience, if nobody else can. Don't think I don't blame myself when I think of the time I wasted. Not that it was entirely thrown away—I wouldn't have you take me for a complete fool—but I didn't get the best out of it. When I look at myself now, an old hag who couldn't raise a flicker in anyone, believe me, it hurts.

'Now with men it's different. They're equipped from birth for lots of other things, not just sex. Anyway they're usually better old than young. But that, and having children, are the only things women are any good at, or respected for. If you can't prove it in any other way, just take a look at how we're always ready for sex. Men aren't. And a woman can tire out a lot of men, without showing the strain. Since this is our sole function in life, you're only doing what's right if you give your husband a taste of his own medicine. Then, when you're old you'll have no cause for complaint. In this world if you want something, you've got to take it. Especially women—*we've* just got to seize our opportunities as they come. For you don't need me to tell you that when we're old neither our husbands nor anyone else will spare us a glance. No, we're sent away to the kitchen, to console ourselves by talking to the cat and washing up. They go so far as to make doggerel of us:

> "Always give young girls the pickings,
> The old ones can make do with kickings."

—that sort of nonsense.

'But let's get down to brass tacks. You couldn't have

chosen a better person than me to come and tell your troubles to. I'm not afraid to give the most high-class men a piece of my mind. And I can get the toughest customers to eat out of my hand. Just tell me who you fancy and leave the rest to me. Remember, my dear, I'm not rich, but I'd like you to have a place in all my paternosters and indulgences, and I will dedicate candles and pray to God for your loved ones who have passed away.'

On that note the old crone ended, and she arranged with the young woman to way-lay a certain young local and send him to her. The young wife described the man in full detail, so there could be no mistake, presented the old crone with a piece of salted meat, and sent her packing.

It wasn't long before the old woman brought the young man to the wife's room. A little later she brought another one who had caught the lady's fancy. For though she was still afraid of her husband, she didn't believe in letting a good chance slip.

One evening her Pietro was asked out to dinner with a friend called Ercolano, so his loving wife ordered her old go-between to procure the nicest and most handsome lad in Perugia. He was duly delivered, and the two of them were just sitting down to supper, when they heard Pietro at the door, asking to be let in. At that, the woman gave herself up for lost. She wanted desperately to hide the young man, but the only place handy was the hen-house in a shed near the room where they were eating. She shoved him under that and covered him with a decrepit mattress-cover, only that day emptied of its straw. Then she hastily opened the door to her husband, saying as he came in:

'You *have* swallowed your meal fast.'

'We didn't even get a mouthful,' said Pietro.

'Why on earth not?' asked his wife.

'Ercolano, his wife and I were just sitting down when someone sneezed close to us. It happened twice, and we pretended not to notice. But when there was a third and a fourth and so on, it wasn't easy to ignore them. Ercolano was annoyed with his wife anyway, for having kept us waiting at the door so long before letting us in. He flamed up:

' "What's going on? Who is it sneezing?" He got up and

went to the bottom of the stairs, where there is a little
wooden cupboard. It's the sort that everybody has for
storing oddments in. He thought the sneezes came from
there, so he threw open the door. He was greeted by a
suffocating stench of sulphur. We'd had a whiff of it before,
but when Ercolano grumbled to his wife, she'd explained :
"I've only just finished bleaching my veils in sulphur, and
you have to sprinkle it on a plate and expose them to the
fumes. I put the plate under the stairs, but there are still
traces of the smell !"

'Once the door was open and the smoke had cleared a
little, Ercolano looked in and saw the sneezer. In fact
thanks to the sulphur the man was still at it. Despite all
those sneezes the poor man was practically suffocated by
the sulphur, and looked as if he'd soon be past sneezing or
anything else. On seeing him Ercolano bellowed:

' "Now I see why when we came in just now, we were
kept waiting at the door so long. But damn me, I'll pay you
back, if it's the last thing I do !" His wife saw she'd been
caught red-handed and didn't try any blarney. She just ran
for it—I don't know where. Ercolano ignored her departure,
and just went on asking the sneezer to come out. But the
fellow was so flattened that he didn't budge an inch, for all
the threats. So Ercolano caught hold of one of his legs,
dragged him out, and then ran off for a knife to kill him.
But I wasn't keen to have the police after me, so I got up
and stopped him killing the fellow, or even laying a finger
on him. By defending him I raised the alarm, and some
neighbours appeared, removed the lad—more dead than
alive—and took him off somewhere or other. So our supper
got so messed up by all this that I didn't finish it, in fact
I didn't even get a mouthful.'

Pietro's story showed his wife that others had the same
good ideas, though not such luck. She longed to spring to
the other woman's defence, but she thought it would put a
better face on her own if she laid into someone else's vices.
So she started on this tack:

'Well, what goings on ! That woman's a proper saint, a
pillar of virtue. Why I'd have trusted her with any secret;
she seemed really religious. A woman like her who's old

c

enough to know better. The worst of it is that it's a shock-
ing example to young people. Such things shouldn't be
allowed. A low-down hypocritical woman like that. She's
a disgrace to the city's good name, and an insult to her sex.
Throwing away her principles, her marriage vows, and her
reputation. Fancy bringing that down on herself and her
husband—there's a good man for you, honest as the day,
and treated her wonderfully. Good God, I've got no sympathy for women like that. Hanging's too good for them,
they should be burnt at the stake.'

Then she suddenly remembered her lover was still on the
premises, under the hen-house, and she tried to hustle
Pietro off to bed, for it was getting late. But he was
more interested in food than bed, and wanted something
to eat.

'Supper, indeed!' snorted his wife. 'Of course supper's
our big meal, the nights you're out. Do you take me for
Ercolano's wife? There's nothing to stay up for. Go on off
to bed. That's the best thing for you.'

Now it so happened that just that evening Pietro's
workers had brought him up some stuff from his farm in
the country. They stabled their donkeys next door to the
hen-house, but forgot to water them. One of the donkeys
got so thirsty he slipped his head from his halter, broke
loose, and started sniffing round in search of water. He got
to the hen-house. The boy underneath had to crouch on
all fours and the fingers of one hand protruded. As bad
luck would have it, the donkey trod on the hand. The poor
boy screamed with pain. Pietro was astonished to hear there
was somebody else in the house. He ran out of the room, for
the boy's moans continued, and the donkey did not shift
his hoof from the fingers.

Pietro called : 'Who's there?' and ran to the hen-house;
he lifted it and there was the lad. Quite apart from the
pain caused by the hoof, he was terrified of what might
happen to him. Pietro recognized him as a very promis-
cuous young man he'd been after himself for some time.

'What are you doing here?' he asked.

The only reply was an appeal for mercy, in God's name,
so Pietro went on:

'Get up! Don't be afraid, I shan't hurt you. But tell me, how did you get here, and what are you doing?'

The young man then confessed the whole story. Pietro was as delighted to have found the boy as his wife was distressed. He took his hand and led him to the room where his wife was waiting in agony. He sat down in front of her and said:

'Only a moment ago you were abusing Ercolano's wife, saying she ought to be burned alive, and calling her a disgrace to her sex—but you didn't say the same of yourself. Even if you didn't dare own up, you'd got a cheek to call her names, when you knew you were just the same. All you women are alike, always trying to cover up your own lapses by picking on somebody else's. May you all be struck by lightning, you wicked crew.'

His wife remembered that hard words broke no bones, and noting her husband's obvious pleasure at holding a handsome young man's hand, took courage and said:

'I'm not surprised you damn all women black and blue, since you've always hated our guts. But, by God, you'll not get your way. Besides, what have you got to complain of, I'd like to know! A fine thing it's come to when you start comparing me to Ercolano's wife. She's a bloody little hypocrite. She gets a fair deal from him, he treats her properly, and that's more than I can say for you. You see to it I don't go naked: I'll give you that. But I don't fare so well otherwise. God knows how long it is since you last slept with me. I'd rather do without clothes and shoes, and get a little bit of fun in bed, than get all those belongings and your present treatment. Look here, be reasonable, Pietro. I'm a woman like the rest, and I've got the natural appetite. If you won't give me it, you can't blame me for looking elsewhere. At least I do you the honour of keeping off stable-hands and servants.'

Pietro saw she'd be at it all night. As she meant nothing to him, he said:

'Now, let's have no more of this, woman. I'll give you satisfaction the way you want. But would you be kind enough to give us some supper. I don't think this lad has had a bite to eat, any more than I have.'

'That's true,' replied the wife. 'He hasn't had a thing. We were just sitting down to supper when, bless me if you didn't blow in.'

'Off you go then,' said Pietro, 'and get us some supper. Then I'll settle this little problem, and you'll have nothing to complain of.'

The lady saw her husband had calmed down, so she got up and soon had the supper she'd prepared back on the table. And a very pleasant meal they had, the swine of a husband, the wife, and the lad. I can't call to mind just how Pietro arranged things satisfactorily for them all, afterwards. But I do remember that when the young man found himself in the square next morning, he was a little hazy about whether he had spent the better part of the night with the husband or the wife.

But I would like to add just this piece of advice: 'Tables can be turned'. Even if you can't act on it just now, remember for future reference—there are games that two can play at.

THE HOLE IN THE WALL

THERE lived in Rimini a merchant rolling in money, land, and property. He had married an extremely beautiful woman. He was terribly jealous of her, on the grounds that he adored her, thought her ravishing, and found her behaviour to himself wonderfully accommodating. He therefore concluded that everyone else must adore her, find her ravishing, and hence that she must be equally obliging to everybody. So you see what a silly, misguided fool he was. Being so bitterly jealous, he kept her rigidly under lock and key. A strait-jacket in a death cell is nothing to it. It was not that the poor woman couldn't go to a wedding or a party or to church, she wasn't allowed out of the house at all. She didn't dare look out or be visible at a window for any reason at all. She led a depressing life which was all the more unbearable for her knowing herself to be blameless. Her husband's unwarrantable suspicions seemed so unfair that she decided to give him justification and herself consolation. As she was not allowed near the window, she couldn't lure any attractive passer-by, but she knew there was a gay and handsome young man living next door. It struck her that if only there was a hole in the dividing wall, she could keep watch for him. As soon as she caught sight of the gentleman, and could speak to him, she would offer him her love. If he were interested and it could be managed, she'd try and meet him occasionally. This would make it easier for her to bear her miserable life until her husband came to his senses. She carried out a thorough search when her husband was out, and finally found a chink in the wall in a remote corner. Squinting through it she could just make out the room which lay on the other side.

'If only that were Filippo's bedroom,' she said to herself,

for that was the name of the man next door—'Half the battle would be won.'

She made tentative researches through her maid who was very sympathetic, and found out that it was the young man's room, and that only he slept there.

So she went to the crack in the wall often, and whenever she reckoned he was there she dropped something like a pebble through. In the end she managed to get him to come to the other end of the crack to see what was wrong. She called him in a whisper, and he recognized her voice and answered. She leapt at her chance and told him the whole story as briefly as possible. He was delighted and worked away at the crack until it was much larger though no more conspicuous. They had many conversations there together, and held hands, but that was as far as they dared go, with the jealous husband on the prowl.

Towards the end of December, the lady announced that if allowed she'd like to go to church on Christmas morning, to confess and take communion like other Christians.

'And what sins have you committed,' he asked, 'that need confessing to?'

'Well,' she replied, 'I'm no saint. You do keep me locked up tightly enough, but I'm still mortal, you know . . . anyway, I don't intend to confess to you. You're no priest.'

This made her husband highly suspicious, so he started thinking of a way to find out about all these sins of hers. With a plan in mind, he gave his permission. But she was only to go to their own local chapel; she must go early in the morning, and must only confess to their own chaplain or some other priest appointed by him—to no one else, and she was to come straight home. His wife had an inkling of the motive behind this order and complied without a murmur.

On Christmas morning the lady was up with the lark, dressed, and off to the church selected by her husband. He too was up early and reached the same church, just before her. Everything had been arranged with the priest in charge. He put on the vestments and one of those hoods tilted forward to hide the face, as worn by many clergymen. In this disguise he sat himself in the chair.

The wife asked for the vicar. He came, but on hearing that she wanted to confess, he declined to officiate himself, but offered one of his colleagues, instead. So off he went and sent her poor jealous husband. Though he looked solemn enough, the light was bad, and he'd pulled the hood well over his eyes, it didn't get him anywhere. She recognized him at once, and said to herself.

'Thank God! The jealous devil's taken orders! But I'll give him what he's asking for, don't you worry.'

So she pretended to be taken in, and sat herself at his feet. (I ought to mention that he'd popped some pebbles in his mouth to disguise his voice. So he was sure that he was totally unrecognizable.) When she came to confess, the lady told him she was married, and, among other things, that she was in love with a priest who slept with her every night. This was a blow right between his eyes. If he hadn't been desperately anxious to know more, he'd have put a stop to the confession and escaped. He stood his ground, however, and said:

'What? Doesn't your husband sleep with you?'

'Oh yes!'

'How on earth can the priest sleep with you as well, then?'

'I don't know how he does it, Father,' came the reply. 'But doors don't keep him out. However firmly they're locked, they open at his touch. He says that when he gets to my bedroom door he speaks certain words, which send my husband to sleep. Then he opens the door, in he comes, and sleeps with me. It always works like that. Every time.'

'Well, it's immoral,' said her husband, 'and you must stop it at once.'

'I doubt if I'll ever be able to do that, Father,' she replied. 'I'm too much in love with him.'

'In that case, I can't give you absolution.'

'Poor me!' she moaned. 'I came here to make a clean breast of it. I'd give it up if I could.'

'I am indeed sorry for you, my dear,' came the answer. 'You seem to be well on the way to losing your soul—but I'll promise you this: I'll pray to God especially for you.

Perhaps that will help. I'll also send you one of my curates from time to time, to find out if my prayers have had any effect. If they have, I'll know what to do next.'

'No, don't do that, Father,' she implored. 'Don't send anyone to my home. If my husband found out, he's so jealous, he'd be bound to think they'd come for something immoral. I wouldn't hear the last of it for a year.'

'Don't worry, my dear. I'll arrange it that he'll never mention the matter to you.'

'If you can do that, I've nothing against it then.'

So ended her confession, and when she had received her penance, the lady got up and went off to mass. Meanwhile her poor frantic husband took off his priest's vestments hurriedly, and dashed home, racking his brains for a way to bring the priest and his wife together, and then take his revenge on them both.

The wife came home from church and saw from her husband's face that she had ruined his Christmas, though he tried to hide from her what he'd done and what (he thought) he'd laid bare. He was determined to lie in wait by the front door for the priest that very night. He announced to his wife:

'I'm dining out and I shan't be in till morning. See to it the front door, the one on the stairs, and the bedroom door are properly locked. Otherwise, go to bed at whatever time you like.'

'All right,' she answered, and soon as she got a chance she went to the crack and gave the usual signal. As soon as Filippo heard it he was there. She then told him what she'd done that morning and what her husband had said after the meal.

'I'm sure he won't leave the house,' she added, 'but will keep watch by the door. So if you can come in tonight over the roof, we can be together.'

'Lady,' replied the young man, 'trust me.'

That night, the husband armed himself and hid silently in a room on the ground floor. His wife locked all the doors, being especially careful with the one on the stairs, so as to prevent her husband coming up. When the time came, her lover climbed over the roof. They went to bed together, and a very enjoyable time they both had. At daybreak he went home.

Meanwhile the poor benighted husband, supperless, comfortless, and blue with cold, kept guard by the door, expecting the priest every moment. Towards daybreak he collapsed, and lay down and slept on the floor. It was nine o'clock by the time he woke up, and the front door was open. So, pretending he'd just come home, he went upstairs to breakfast. Not much later, he sent to his wife a lad disguised as a priest's server to ask if 'a certain person' had visited her during the night. The lady understood exactly what he was getting at, so she replied that he hadn't come that night and that if he had given her up, she might be able to forget him, however delightful the memory was.

To cut a long story short, the husband spent many nights in the same way, in the constant hope of catching the priest. Meanwhile his wife enjoyed herself with the lover. Finally the husband could bear it no longer, and cross-questioned his wife to make her reveal exactly what she had told the priest when she confessed that morning. She said she had no intention of telling him, and he had no right to ask. Then he pounced on her:

'You wicked woman! I know what you said, for all that, and I insist on knowing who this priest is that you're in love with. This man who practises black magic to sleep with you. Otherwise I'll make mincemeat of you.'

'It's untrue that I'm in love with a priest,' she replied.

'What! But didn't you say as much to the priest who took the confession?'

'He can't have told you that,' she answered. 'Were you there in person then? I certainly never told him any such thing.'

'Then tell me who this priest is, and don't beat about the bush.'

'Well what a lark!' she said with a grin. 'Fancy a clever man falling for that one, like a lamb to the slaughter. Not that you're a clever man—not since that fatal moment you took it into your head, for some reason that's beyond me, to be so bitterly jealous. You've behaved so ridiculously that I can hardly claim any credit. Maybe you're incapable of

seeing the nose in front of your face, but I'm not that
blind. That I'm not. I saw at a glance that priest was you.
But you were asking for it, so I decided to let you have it.
If you were as clever as you took yourself for, though, you'd
not have picked on such a fatheaded way of spying on
your wife. And you wouldn't have indulged in such preposterous suspicions. You'd have realized I was telling the
truth, but was absolutely innocent for all that. I told you
I was in love with a priest. I meant I loved you, though
you don't deserve it, and hadn't you turned priest? I told
you that no door got in his way when he felt like sleeping
with me. When you want to come to me is there anything
stopping you? I told you the priest slept with me every night
—and don't you? Then you sent the curate along. You
know as well as I do that the nights you didn't visit me, I
told him the priest hadn't come. Anybody but you, who
were blinded by jealousy, would have had sense enough to
see the point. But you had to stand guard at night by the
door, and expect me to believe you'd gone out to supper and
for the night. Have some sense and pull yourself together.
You haven't always been like this. You look an awful fool to
someone who knows you as well as I do. And let's have no
more of this keeping me locked up. God knows, if I felt
like being unfaithful, I could have as much fun as I liked
without you ever finding out—even if you had a hundred
eyes in your head instead of two.'

After this lecture, the jealous fool who thought he'd been
so clever in spying on his wife, felt crestfallen. He could
only congratulate her on her sharpness and virtue. Before,
he'd been jealous with no justification, now he was justified
but not jealous. So the shrewd woman now had practically
a free hand. She didn't have to scheme to get her lover
over the roof any longer. She let him in by the door, and
by using a certain amount of tact, had a very enjoyable
time with him and found life much pleasanter.

Ninth day: second tale

THE NUN'S STORY

In Lombardy there is a convent with a high reputation for
leading the holy life. Among the nuns there was one young
lady of good birth and exceptional beauty. Isabetta—that
was the girl's name—while talking to a visiting relative at
the gate one day, fell for the handsome young gentleman
who had come along too. He saw how beautiful she was
and how attracted to himself, and fell in love with her as
well. They suffered long and painfully from their mutual
and hopeless passion. In the end they longed for one another so intensely that the young man evolved a way of
secretly visiting his nun. She was nothing loath, and he
started paying her frequent visits, and highly enjoyable
they both found them. During their affair, however, one of
the other nuns happened to see him leaving Isabetta's room,
though neither of the lovers realized they had been caught.
The sister spread the news to several others. First they
thought they'd inform against her to the Mother Superior,
for that lady—a certain Usimbulda—was considered by her
nuns and by everybody else, to be deeply religious. On
second thoughts it seemed a surer means of convincing their
abbess, if they could arrange for her to catch the nun and
the young man in the act.

Isabetta knew nothing of this plan and was not on her
guard. So one night when her lover was visiting her, her
watchful colleagues soon knew of it. At what they reckoned
was the crucial moment, half their number kept watch outside Isabetta's cell, while the other half of them hurried off
to the abbess' bedroom. They knocked at the door, woke her
up, and when they heard her voice, shouted:

'Holy Mother, get up at once. We've discovered Isabetta's got a young man in her cell.'

Now that night the abbess happened to be sleeping with

a priest. He visited her quite frequently by being carried in in a chest. So urgent was the sisters' summons that she was afraid they'd push her door open in their hurry. She leaped out of bed and flung on her clothes as well as she could 'n the dark. Reaching for the veil they call a psalter, she picked up the priest's trousers by mistake, shoved them on her head and hurried out, locking the door behind her.

'Where is this female?' she cried.

Guided by the sisters, who were so jubilant at the thought of catching Isabetta red-handed that they didn't notice their abbess' unconventional headgear, she reached the cell. With their help she broke down the door. There were the lovers in bed and in each other's arms. Paralyzed at the unexpectedness of the attack, they lay there helplessly. The sisters dragged the nun away to the chapter-house where the abbess had commanded her to appear. The young man was left behind in the cell to put on his clothes and await developments. He threatened to wreak vengeance on all the nuns. If they laid a finger on his mistress, he'd fly to her help.

The abbess took her seat in the chapter-house, surrounded by all her nuns. Everyone's eyes were on the offender. She was given the dressing down of her life. People had only to get wind of her disgraceful and filthy behaviour, she was reminded, for the convent's reputation to be ruined. Many other hideous threats were made by the abbess. The sinner was far too ashamed to attempt any excuses. She stood silent and pathetic. But as the abbess became more and more eloquent, Isabetta looked up and saw the strange head-dress, with its bits hanging down on both sides. Its significance was not lost on her. So she plucked up courage and interrupted:

'Holy Mother, in God's name tie up your head-dress, and then say what you like.'

The abbess didn't understand.

'What head-dress, you vile creature? Have you the cheek to joke? Do you think what you've been caught doing isn't serious?'

'Please tie up your head-dress before you go any further,' repeated Isabetta.

By this time several of the nuns had noticed the abbess' head. When the good lady raised her hands to it, they all of them saw what Isabetta was getting at. The abbess saw herself hoist with her own petard, with no possibility of evasion. So she changed her tack, and her lecture concluded on a quite different note. The main point was that the desires of the flesh were irresistible, but that if secrecy were observed, as it had been in the past, everyone could enjoy themselves when they got a chance.

Isabetta was dismissed to rejoin her lover in her cell and the abbess returned to her priest. Often after that Isabetta had her lover in, to the envy of everyone else. The nuns who hadn't got a lover, secretly started to spread their nets for one.

Ninth day : third tale

WHEN WOMEN GET ON TOP

I MUST tell you the story of how Calandrino's aunt died and left him two hundred pounds in cash. Calandrino announced his intention of buying an estate with it. He started haggling with every estate agent in Florence, as though he were investing two thousand. But the negotiations were always broken off when it came to coughing up.

Bruno and Buffalmacco saw his game, and insisted that it would be much better for him to have a fling with them than spend the legacy on a tuppenny-halfpenny piece of land. But they got nowhere, and couldn't even get a free meal out of him. One day they were having a good grumble over this when they were joined by a fellow painter called Nello. They put their heads together to find some way of stuffing themselves at Calandrino's expense. They concocted a plan and next morning Nello met Calandrino just as he was leaving the house.

'Good morning, Calandrino.'

'The same to you, and many of them.'

Nello then backed away a little and stared at him.

'What are you staring at?' inquired Calandrino.

'Did you have a nasty night?' asked Nello. 'You don't look yourself.' This remark had Calandrino worried.

'Oh dear! What do you mean? What do you think is wrong with me?' he cried.

'Why, I wouldn't like to say. But you do look rather odd. Maybe I'm quite wrong . . .' Nello replied, turning on his heel. Calandrino was left feeling odd, but not knowing quite why. Further on he met Buffalmacco, who having seen Nello departing, approached in his turn, greeted Calandrino and asked if he were in pain.

'I really don't know,' replied Calandrino. 'Only a minute

ago Nello told me I was looking odd. Do you think there's something wrong with me?'

'Anything wrong?' exclaimed Buffalmacco. 'It must be more than just anything. You look half-dead.'

By this time Calandrino was beginning to feel feverish.

Then Bruno appeared. The first thing he said was :

'Calandrino, you must be ill. You look like death. How do you feel?' Getting the same reaction from all three was enough to convince Calandrino that he was ill.

'What shall I do?' he cried in terror.

'If I were you, I'd go home and get straight to bed, and cover yourself up well. Send a specimen of your urine to our friend Doctor Simon. He'll tell you what to do, at once. He'll come and see you and do anything necessary.'

Nello then rejoined them and all three took Calandrino home. He was reduced to a pulp and flopped into bed, gasping out to his wife:

'Come and tuck me in properly, I feel dreadfully ill.'

There he lay and at once sent a maid with a specimen of his urine to Dr Simon at Nincompoop House in the Old Market. At this point, Bruno briefed his friend:

'You stay here. I'll go and hear the doctor's diagnosis and bring him back if it's necessary.'

'Please do, old fellow,' begged Calandrino, 'and come and tell me what's up with me, because I feel very queer inside.'

Off went Bruno to the doctor, and getting there before the girl and her bottle, told him what was going on. So when the girl arrived the doctor knew his cue, and after examining the urine, told her:

'Go and tell Calandrino to keep very warm, and I'll come at once to tell him what's wrong and give him a prescription.'

The girl had only just had time to deliver her message when Bruno arrived with the doctor. The physician sat at Calandrino's bedside, felt his pulse, and soon announced— in the presence of the wife:

'Look here, Calandrino. Frankly speaking the only thing wrong with you is that you're pregnant.'

Calandrino screeched: 'Horrors. It's all your fault, Tessa,

you will insist on being on top. I warned you what would happen.'

The lady was horribly embarrassed, blushed to the roots of her hair, and silently left the room, with her eyes firmly fixed on the floor. Calandrino maundered on miserably :

'Oh dear, oh dear, oh dear! What shall I do? How can I give birth to this baby? There's nothing else for it. It's obvious now, that sexy wife of mine will be the death of me. God rot her, for spoiling my happiness! If only I was well enough I'd get up and beat her till I'd broken every bone in her body. Even if it does serve me right for letting her get on top of me. If I survive, she'll never have it that way again, even if she's dying for it.'

These words made Bruno, Buffalmacco, and Nello almost burst with holding back their laughter. Simon guffawed till his jaws ached. In the end, however, he took pity on Calandrino's frantic appeal for helpful advice.

'Don't worry, Calandrino,' he said consolingly. 'Thank God we realized your condition early enough to be able to put you right quite quickly and easily. But it will cost a bit.'

'Oh dear! But for God's sake do it, Doctor. I've got two hundred pounds which I meant to spend on an estate. Take it all, if need be, so long as you spare me childbirth. Seeing what a song and dance women make about having babies, even though it comes naturally to them, I don't know what I'd do if I had to go through with it. I think it would kill me.'

'Don't take on so,' said the doctor. 'I'll get a medicine made up for you. It's very potent and quite palatable. It'll get rid of everything and leave you feeling fit as a fiddle. But you'll have to be more careful in future and not get into that position again. For this medicine we'll need six good-sized chickens. As for the other ingredients, give one of your friends five pounds in cash, and get all the stuff sent to my dispensary, and God willing, I'll get the medi-cine concocted tomorrow morning. One glassful to be taken morning and evening.'

'Just as you say, Doctor dear,' answered Calandrino, handing Bruno five pounds and the money for the chickens.

He begged his friend as a special favour to buy the things for him.

So off went the doctor, brewed him a little something and sent it round. Bruno bought the birds, and all the other ingredients of the feast, which he, his friends, and the doctor demolished.

Calandrino drank the mixture for three mornings, and was then visited by his friends. The doctor felt his pulse and diagnosed:

'Calandrino, you're absolutely cured. You needn't stay indoors any more, and can do anything you feel like quite safely.'

Calandrino was immensely relieved. He got up and resumed his normal way of life. Whenever he got a chance he sang Doctor Simon's praises. It had been magnificent, the way he had been cured of pregnancy in only three days without any pain at all. Bruno, Buffalmacco, and Nello were also very pleased with themselves at having outwitted the stingy Calandrino. Only Tessa, who had not fallen for the story, was dissatisfied, and she had a good grumble at her husband.

THERE WERE TWO IN THE BED

IN the Mugnone Valley there lived a man who provided refreshments for travellers. As he was poor and his house was small, he couldn't put people up as a general rule, only one of his regulars at a pinch. He had a fine looking wife and two children: an attractive girl of about fifteen or sixteen who was still unmarried, and a boy of under one who was still being breast-fed.

A very gay young man from our city, who was frequently in those parts, fell passionately in love with the girl. She was highly flattered at attracting such a dashing gentleman. While busily practising all her arts to keep him in attendance, she fell for him just as deeply. They had several opportunities of consummating their love for each other, but Pinuccio (that was the young man's name) was reluctant to ruin her reputation or his own. His desire to sleep with her grew continually stronger, however, and he thought he must somehow manage to spend a night in their house. He knew that the lack of space would enable him to get at her without anyone being any the wiser. No sooner said than done.

Late one night he and a close friend called Adriano (who was in on the secret) hired two horses, stuffed a couple of saddle-bags with straw, and set off from Florence. They went a roundabout way to the Mugnone Valley, and got there after dark. They made a detour so that it looked as if they were coming from Romagna, rode up to the house, and knocked at the door. As the landlord knew them both very well, he opened the door at once.

'You'll have to give us a bed for the night,' exclaimed Pinuccio. 'We were trying to make Florence, but this is as far as we could possibly get in the time.'

'Well, Pinuccio,' he replied, 'you know how ill-equipped

I am to put up gentlemen like yourselves. But since you've only got to here and it's too late to go on, you're welcome to what I can offer.'

The two young men dismounted, watered their horses, and then went indoors. They produced the food they had brought with them, and ate with their host.

Now he had only been able to make up three beds in the one bedroom. Two against one wall, and the third opposite them, leaving only a narrow gangway in between. The least uncomfortable bed was allocated to the young visitors. As soon as he had seen them into bed, taken in by their pretence of being asleep, he gave his daughter the second bed, while he and his wife took the third. The baby's cradle was put beside the parents' bed.

Pinuccio made careful note of these sleeping arrangements. He waited until he thought he was the only one still awake, got up quietly, crept to his mistress' bed, and got in beside her. She welcomed him shyly but with great joy. He stayed and they enjoyed each other as they had been longing to for so long.

While they were in bed together a stray cat knocked something over with a clatter. This woke the wife, and thinking something serious was wrong, she groped her way in the dark to where the sound came from. At just about the same time Adriano was disturbed, not by the noise but by a call of nature. On his way outside, he found the cradle in the way. He had to move it from beside the mother's bed to his own. When he had relieved himself, he got back into bed without giving a thought to the cot.

Meanwhile the wife had discovered that nothing important had been broken. She didn't bother to light a candle and investigate more closely, but told the cat off and went back to the bedroom. She groped her way back to her own bed, but found no cradle there.

'What a mutt I am,' she said to herself. 'What on earth am I doing! Good Lord, I was going straight to the visitors' bed.'

She soon brushed against the cradle and got into the bed beside it, taking Adriano for her husband. Adriano was still awake and was very pleased to see her. He put her through her paces without a word, and a delightful time they both had.

Pinuccio had satisfied his desire, and was afraid that if he stayed he'd be caught asleep in bed with the girl. So he got up to go back to his own bed. But when he found the cradle beside it, he took it for the landlord's. So he groped his way to the next bed and climbed in. Its occupant woke up. Pinuccio, thinking he was confiding to his friend, whispered to the landlord:

'That Niccolosa certainly is a terrific bit of stuff. God! I'll bet no one's ever had such a time with a girl as I've just had with her. Do you know I was in there six times!'

The landlord was not over-pleased at this news and said to himself:

'What the devil is this chap doing here?'

Then, since he was too furious to control himself:

'You've played me a dirty trick, Pinuccio. I don't know what I've done to deserve it, but by God, I'll get my own back.'

Pinuccio was not a conspicuously discreet young man, and even though he realized his mistake, he did nothing to put it right.

'How are you going to get your own back?' he retorted. 'You can't do a thing.'

The wife then said to the man beside her:

'Listen, dear, the visitors are having a quarrel.'

'Leave them to it!' said Adriano with a laugh. 'They drank too much last night, God rot them.'

The woman had already suspected it was her husband's angry voice she could hear raised. Now she heard Adriano and realized the position at once. Being a clever woman, she got up, silently picked up the cradle, and in the pitch dark groped her way blindly to her daughter's bed with it. Then she called out to her husband as if she'd been woken up by the noise, and asked the meaning of all the fuss which he and Pinuccio were making.

'Didn't you hear what he said he'd done to Niccolosa during the night?' cried the landlord.

'Bah!' she replied. 'He's a dirty liar. He hasn't slept with her. The only time he could have done I was lying beside her myself, and I've been wide awake the whole time. Fancy believing him! You men get so tight before you go to bed, that you suffer from sleep walking and hallucinations. It's too bad you don't break your necks while you're at it. What's Pinuccio doing there? Why doesn't he stick to his own bed?'

Adriano had cottoned on to the woman's brilliant way of covering up her daughter's and her own lapse.

'Pinuccio,' he said, 'how many times have I told you not to walk in your sleep? This bad habit of wandering about fast asleep, and describing your dreams as though they'd really happened, will get you into hot water one of these days. Come back to bed for God's sake!'

Hearing Adriano backing his wife up, the landlord began to think Pinuccio must really be dreaming. He grasped his shoulder, shook him, and called to him :

'Pinuccio, wake up, and go back to your own bed.'

Pinuccio knew his cue, and started pretending to babble in his sleep. This made the landlord roar with laughter. Then Pinuccio stirred as though the shaking had woken him, and mumbled:

'Adriano, is it morning already? Have I got to get up?'

'Yes, it is !' said Adriano. 'Come on.'

In a daze Pinuccio got up from the bed and went back to Adriano. Next morning when they were getting up, the landlord started chipping Pinuccio about his dream. Everyone took up the joke, while the young men's horses were being groomed, saddled, and loaded. Then they had a drink with their host, mounted, and rode away to Florence, delighted at what had happened during the night, and the way it had happened.

After that Pinuccio found other ways of meeting Niccolosa. And since the girl strenuously maintained that the young man *had* been dreaming, her mother was left with the memory of Adriano's embraces, and the firm conviction that only *she* had really been awake that night.

THE TALE OF THE TAIL

About a year ago Barletta had a priest called Gianni of Barola. He eked out his meagre salary by saddling his mare with a pack and going the rounds of the fairs in Apulia, buying and selling goods. In this way he got very friendly with a man called Pietro of Tresanti, who did the same job, only with a donkey instead of a mare. Don Gianno in a spirit of friendliness always referred to the other, as Apulians do, as Old Pietro. He had a standing invitation to stay with the priest whenever he was in Barletta. As for Old Pietro, he was poor, and lived in a tiny cottage which barely held himself, his pretty young wife, and the donkey. But this didn't stop him doing the honours by Don Gianni when he came to Tresanti, in recompense for the hospitality he himself received at Barletta. As Old Pietro had only one bed which he shared with his pretty wife, he couldn't make Gianni as comfortable as he would have liked. The priest's mare was stalled beside the donkey in the little stable, and her master had to bed down beside her in the straw. Whenever the priest's visit was due, Gemmata was reminded guiltily of how well he entertained at Barletta. She would offer to go and sleep with a neighbour called Zita Carapressa di Giudice Lea, so that the guest could share the bed with her husband. She had suggested this to the priest several times, but he wouldn't hear of it.

'Madame Gemmata,' he once said, 'don't worry about me. I'm fine! When I feel like it, I turn the mare into a beautiful girl and enjoy her. When I've had enough, I turn her back into a mare. I wouldn't like to be parted from her.'

Gemmata was amazed by this story, but she believed it and reported it back to her husband.

'If he's a real friend,' she added, 'why don't you get him to teach you the spell. Then you can turn me into a mare,

64

and have a donkey and a horse for business. We'll double our profits and then you can turn me back into a woman when we get back at night.'

Old Pietro was not particularly bright, so he believed what she said. He took her advice and begged Gianni, as tactfully as possible to teach him the spell. The priest did what he could to make him drop the idea, but it was no good.

'Well then,' he said, 'if you're both set on it. Be up at your usual time, before sunrise tomorrow morning, and I'll show you how to do it. To be frank, putting on the tail is the most tricky part, as you'll see for yourself.'

Pietro and Gemmata were so worried, they hardly got a wink of sleep all night. They were up with the lark and called Don Gianni. He got up and came into their tiny bedroom in his shirt.

'I don't think I'd do this for anyone else at all, but you,' he said. 'As you insist on it though, I'll do it. But you'll have to do exactly what I tell you, if you want the spell to work.'

They promised to obey him to the letter, so Gianni took a candle and handing it to Pietro, said:

'Pay close attention to everything I say and do. But no matter what you see or hear, unless you want to wreck the whole operation, don't say a word. We can only hope to God that the tail will be fixed on firmly.'

Old Pietro took the candle and again promised not to say a word. Then Don Gianni ordered Gemmata to strip to the skin, and go down on all fours like a horse. She too was ordered to say nothing under any circumstances.

First he laid his hand on her face, saying:

'May this become a fine mare's head.' He touched her hair: 'May this become a fine mare's mane.' Then her arms: 'May these become a fine mare's legs and hooves.' When he touched the firm curve of her breast, a part of him stirred and stood up without being summoned: 'May this become a fine mare's chest.' He continued the catalogue to her back, belly, buttocks, haunches, and shanks. Finally there was nothing left but the tail, so he lifted his shirt, held the tool which he used for planting men, and pushed it straight down the furrow where it belonged, saying: 'May this become a fine mare's tail.'

Old Pietro had followed every move carefully up till then, but he thoroughly disapproved of the last item, and cried:

'Oh, Don Gianni, I don't want a tail. I don't want one!'

The basic sap on which all plant life depends was exhausted by this time, so Gianni drew his tool out and said:

'Oh, Pietro, old fellow, what have you done? I was just putting the finishing touch to the mare, and you've spoilt everything by speaking. I shan't be able to repeat the spell.'

'Never mind,' he said. 'I don't want that sort of tail. Why didn't you ask me to put it on myself? Besides you were placing it too low down.'

'As it was the first time,' replied Gianni, 'you wouldn't have done it as well as me.'

Then the young wife stood up and said to her husband quite innocently:

'You silly ass. You've ruined what would have been a godsend for us both. Have you ever seen a mare without a tail? God help me, if you're poor, it's certainly no more than you deserve.'

After Old Pietro had spoken so out of turn, there was no prospect of turning the young woman into a mare. Disappointed and depressed, she got into her clothes again. Pietro went back to his old profession with a donkey as before, and accompanied Gianni to Bitonto Fair. But he never asked that favour of him again.

Third day : fourth tale

TAKE CARE OF THE PENANCE

THE story goes there lived near San Pancrazio a worthy and
rich man called Puccio de Rinieri. Late in life he was
strongly drawn to religion, became a lay brother of the
Franciscan Order, and was known as Brother Puccio. The
fact that he only kept a wife and one maid, and did not
need to earn his living, meant that he could concentrate on
his spiritual development and spend much of his time in
church. Being a simple soul, not to say simple-minded, he
said his prayers, listened to sermons, went to mass, never
missed lauds (when it was the laity's turn to sing), fasted,
and mortified his flesh. Rumour even had it he was a
genuine flagellant.

His wife Isabetta was between twenty-eight and thirty,
young-looking for her age, healthy, and as plump and
pretty as an apple. With a husband who was rather old and
rather devout, she had more than a sufficient dose of
abstinence. When she only wanted to make love or go to
sleep, he recited the life of Our Lord to her, or a sermon
from Brother Nastagio, or the lamentation of Mary Magda-
len, or something of that sort.

Such was her life when a young monk called Felice returned to the friary of San Pancrazio from Paris. Puccio
became a close friend of this lively and very brilliant man.
Any question he put to him was answered with every air of
holiness, because Felice soon summed up his friend's mentality. Brother Puccio made a habit of asking him home to
lunch or supper. Like a loving wife Isabetta also became
friendly with Felice and was always welcoming.

As a frequent visitor to the house the monk noted the
healthy plumpness of the wife. He realized what she must
be having too little of, and decided to fill the gap if possible
and do both husband and wife a service. He gave her the

glad eye from time to time and she responded very favourably. Having noticed his success he took the first opportunity to announce his passion for her. He found her only too ready to accommodate him, but there seemed no means of achieving this. She would not risk herself anywhere away from her own home with him—only infuriatingly her husband was never out. The monk gave the problem a good deal of thought, and at last hit on a plan for enjoying the lady in her own house and with her husband at home but unsuspecting. So one day when he was with Puccio, he said:

'I know well enough, Brother Puccio, that your one desire in life is to become a saint. It seems to me you're going a roundabout way to it, whereas there's a short-cut known to the Pope and his immediate circle, and used secretly by them. It has to be kept dark because it would soon ruin the clergy's business. The large number who rely on alms wouldn't be able to get another farthing out of their flocks. But since you're my friend and have been very kind to me, I'll show you this way, if only I could be sure you wouldn't breathe a word to anyone else at all.'

Puccio was on tenterhooks to hear more, and he started begging Felice to show him the way. He swore to tell no one without his permission, only to follow it himself if he were up to it.

'That's enough for me,' said the monk. 'And I'll show you how to do it. Let me tell you that the holy fathers consider the aspirant to sanctity should carry out the following penance. Mark my words carefully! I can't promise that after the penance you'll be any less a sinner than you are now. But you will *certainly* be totally absolved of all the sins you've committed up to the present, and those to come will not do you any serious harm, for they'll be trivial enough to need only a sprinkle of holy water. The penitent must right at the very beginning confess all his sins in detail. Next, fasting and strict abstinence for forty days, and he mustn't go near a woman, not even his wife. You must find somewhere in the house from which the night sky is visible, and go there every evening after prayers. Have a broad shelf, placed so that you can rest your behind on it, keeping your feet off the ground. Then stretch out your arms so as to make a crucifix—you're allowed something to support them by. You keep this position, motionless and eyes fixed on the sky, until matins. If you could read you could be shown the particular prayers to recite during the night. But as you can't, you'd better say three hundred *pater nosters,* and the same number of *ave marias* in honour of the Trinity. While contemplating the sky, keep your mind on God the maker of heaven and earth, and while you're in this crucified position, remember the Passion of Our Lord. When the bells ring for matins, you can go to bed and sleep, but don't take your clothes off. In the morning you have to go to church, hear at least three masses, say fifty *pater nosters* and as many *ave marias.* Then you can do anything you like with a clear conscience and have a meal. But in the evening you must go to church again and repeat certain prayers—I'll give you them in writing because they're vital. At nine o'clock you must start the operation once again. I'm pretty confident, from my own experience of this penance, that if you do this and approach it in the right spirit, you will get a foretaste of eternal bliss—even before it's completed.'

'This penance doesn't seem terribly severe or very long,' said Brother Puccio, 'and I think it'll be easy. God willing, I'll start next Sunday.'

Then off home he went to tell his wife (with Don Felice's permission) all the details. She understood exactly what the monk meant by ordering her husband to stay at his post till matins. She considered it a first-class plan, and said she was only too happy for him to take on this or anything else which would be for the good of his soul. To receive God's blessing on the attempt, she'd join in the fast herself if in nothing else.

So everyone was agreed; and when Sunday came Puccio embarked on his penance. The monk, by arrangement, came most evenings as sòon as he knew the coast was clear. He brought great quantities of food and drink with him, and after dinner he went to bed with the wife until matins. Then he got up and left, and Puccio retired to bed. Puccio had chosen a position next door to his wife's bedroom for the penance, and there was only a thin partition between.

While the monk and the lady enjoyed themselves with energetic enthusiasm, Puccio thought he felt the floor shake a little. He paused in his hundredth *pater noster* and, without leaving his post, called out and asked his wife what she was doing. She had a sense of humour, and as she was riding the course full pelt, she could not refrain from answering:

'Oh, I'm tossing about terribly, my dear!'

'Tossing?' called Puccio. 'Why are you so restless?'

The good woman laughed aloud, with good reason, no doubt, and replied:

'Why? Fancy you asking that! However many times have I heard you say: "Foodless to bed is sleepless to bed."'

Brother Puccio took it that her tossing and turning were the result of hunger and said innocently:

'I told you not to fast, my dear. But as you insist on it, try and keep your mind off it and relax. Why, you're tossing about so much, I can feel it here.'

'Don't you worry,' replied the wife. 'I know what I'm doing. You do your job. I'd do the same myself, if only I could.'

Puccio said no more and went back to his *pater nosters*. From then on, every night during the penance, Isabetta and Felice had a bed made up in another part of the house, and had a good fling there. He went home, and she went back to her own bed just before the nightly vigil ended. Puccio was as persistent in his penance, as his wife was in her enjoyment of the monk. She said to her lover once or twice in joke:

'Puccio does the penance, we get the bliss.'

In fact she got such satisfaction out of what the monk had to offer, especially as it was such a change from the malnutrition she had grown used to under her husband, that even when Puccio's penance was over she managed to continue her diet. She arranged it all so discreetly that she had many tasty titbits for a long time afterwards.

So you see Puccio tried to earn himself a place in heaven through penance, and accidentally succeeded in putting there the monk who had been the guiding force and the wife who had been half-starved until a generous spirit had brought her what she needed.

Fourth day : tenth tale

ANAESTHETIC ADVENTURE

THE story goes that not long ago there lived in Salerno a
very distinguished surgeon called Sir Mazzeo della Mon-
tagna. At a ripe old age he married a pretty girl from the
city. He swamped her with splendid dresses, lavish jewellery, and other ladylike luxuries, so she was quite the most
pampered woman in Salerno. But this didn't stop her being
cold most of the time, because the doctor didn't offer her
much protection in bed. He spun his wife the old yarn that
every time a man sleeps with a woman he takes God knows
how long to recoup. So she was terribly frustrated. Being
sensible and spirited she decided not to put up with her present assets, but to go out and find a better investment. She
considered several young men, before she finally found one
to suit her, and staked all her future happiness on him. The
young gentleman was flattered, and returned her love.
Ruggieri de Jeroli—that was his name—was an aristocrat,
but so vile in every way, that no one could think of a good
word to say for him. He was notorious in Salerno as the
worst of thieves and crooks. He hadn't any friends left and
none of his relatives kept up with him.

The lady didn't much mind that, however, for he had
his charms. With her maid's help she managed to meet him.
However, after they had had some fun together, she began
to reproach him for his past, and begged him, if he loved
her, to reform. As an inducement, she even lent him money
occasionally.

It was in the course of their most diplomatically
managed affair that a man with an infected leg came under
the doctor's care. Doctor Mazzeo saw what the trouble was
and told the relatives that the patient would die or at least
have to have his leg amputated if the gangrened bone
weren't removed; otherwise he wouldn't like to answer for

71

his life. The relatives agreed that the bone must be re-moved, and left the patient in the surgeon's hands. It was clear that the operation would be unendurable, unless the patient were drugged. So that morning the doctor had a special medicine of his own made up which would act as an anaesthetic. He intended to operate that evening, but at the crucial moment he got a message from some of his best friends in Amalfi. There had been rioting in the town and many people had been wounded, so he was asked to go there at once. Doctor Mazzeo put the operation off till the morn-ing and set sail for Amalfi. His wife realized he wouldn't be back that night, and as usual smuggled Ruggieri in. She locked him in her room until the other members of the household were asleep. As he sat waiting in her bedroom, he worked up a terrible thirst. I don't know whether it was over-exertion, or having eaten something salty, or just habitual with him. Anyway he noticed the drug destined for the operation, took it for drinking water, drained the bottle, and was soon dead to the world.

As soon as she could, the wife returned to her bedroom to find Ruggieri fast asleep. She jogged him and tried waking him gently. But nothing happened, he didn't answer or move a muscle. She was irritated and shook him:

'Get up, dozy! If you only want to sleep, you can do it in your own home, not here.'

The shove she gave him knocked Ruggieri off the chest where he was lying, but still he didn't show any signs of life. She was rather frightened by this time and in an attempt to lift him up, shook him roughly, and tugged at his nose and beard. But with no result, he was absolutely out. She began to be afraid he was dead, but she did try pinching and singeing him with a candle flame—with no effect. She was a doctor's wife, but no doctor, and by now she was certain he was dead. As she loved him better than anything else in the world, it goes without saying that she was in despair. She dared not do more than mourn noise-lessly, but she shed many tears over him and cursed her bad luck. It wasn't long before she thought her dishonour would be added to, unless she could get rid of the body at once. In need of advice, she quietly woke her maid, showed her the terrible thing that had happened, and begged for help. The maid was astonished, and also had a go at pinching and tugging Ruggieri. As there were no signs of life she could only agree that he really was dead and should be removed.

'Where can we put him?' her mistress cried. 'So that when they find him tomorrow no one would think of him coming from here?'

'Madam, late last night I noticed a good-sized chest outside the carpenter's shop next door. If he hasn't moved it indoors, it would just suit us. We can put the body inside, slash him a few times with a knife and leave him. When he's found, no one will think of this house any more than any other. As he was a crook it will be taken for granted that an enemy killed him on a job and then put him in the chest.'

Apart from the fact that she couldn't bear the thought of wounding Ruggieri, her mistress accepted the maid's suggestion, and sent to make sure the chest was still there. The girl reported that it was, and as she was young and strapping she managed with some help to shoulder the corpse. The lady went ahead to see the coast was clear, and the maid followed, laid Ruggieri in the chest, closed it, and left him there.

Now it happened that a few days earlier two young men who were money-lenders had moved into a house not far off. They had noticed the chest the day before and thought that here was a cheap way of adding considerably to their scanty stock of furniture. They decided to requisition it, if it was still there that night. Out they sallied at midnight, found the chest, and without bothering to examine it, although it seemed rather heavy, bore it home. They put it down in their wives' room, without troubling to arrange it properly. They just left it there and went to bed.

Towards daybreak, the effects of the potion wore off and Ruggieri woke up. Though he had come round and was no longer asleep, his brain was left numb for several days. He opened his eyes and couldn't see a thing, groped about with his hands, and grasped the fact that he was in a chest.

'What's happened?' he said to himself. 'Where am I? Am I awake or asleep? I remember entering the lady's bedroom tonight. But now I seem to be in a chest. What does that mean? Did the doctor come back, or something like that, and did she hide me in here while I was asleep? I suppose that's it. That's what must have happened.'

Having come to this conclusion he lay flat and listened. As he was slumped on one side in the cramped chest, he wasn't very comfortable and he felt he must turn over. He did this so gracefully that his behind hit one of the sides. The chest wasn't standing evenly, so it was knocked off balance and fell. The row awoke the sleeping women, but they were too afraid to shout out. The crash startled Ruggieri, but since it opened the chest, he realized that he would be better off outside than inside, whatever the consequences. He had no idea where he was and began fumbling about blindly for a staircase or a door, to escape by. The women were terrified at the sound of his groping and cried out: 'Who's there?' Ruggieri didn't recognize the voice so he didn't answer. The ladies started shouting for their husbands who were dead to the world after their heavy day. The women panicked even more, got up, and dashed to the window yelling: 'Help! Thief!'

Several neighbours came running in at this summons and got into the house by the roof or somehow. The young men were disturbed by the din. Ruggieri was terrified out of his wits, not knowing where to turn, or how to escape. He was caught and handed over to the police who had hurried to the scene of the crime. The magistrate he appeared before knew his reputation as a confirmed crook. Under torture, Ruggieri admitted to entering the money-lenders' house with intent to rob, and the magistrate decided to get the matter over with, and hang him.

Next morning the news that Ruggieri had been caught rifling the money-lenders' house was all over Salerno. The lady and her maid were so flabbergasted to hear this that they really thought the goings-on of the night before must have been a dream. The additional anxiety of Ruggieri's danger reduced his poor mistress almost to a frenzy.

About half-past seven Doctor Mazzeo got back from Amalfi and asked where the drug for the operation was. He was furious when he found the bottle open and grumbled that nothing was safe in that house. His wife was preoccupied enough with other worries, and lost her temper.

'Aren't there enough serious things wrong, without your making so much fuss about a bottle of water that gets spilt?' she cried.

'If you think that was only water, you're wrong,' answered the doctor. 'It was a sleeping potion.'

And he told her what it was for. As soon as she heard this, she guessed that Ruggieri had drunk it and given the impression of being dead.

'I'm afraid I didn't know that,' she said. 'Can't you make some more?'

Doctor Mazzeo saw there was nothing for it, he'd have to reorder the drug. It was soon after that the maid came home. Her mistress had sent her to find out the news about Ruggieri.

'Nobody had a good word to say for him, madam,' she reported. 'As far as I can make out, he hasn't a friend or relative to speak up for him. It's almost certain now that the chief of police will hang him tomorrow. I did hear something else that will come as a surprise to you. I think I know how he ended up in the money-lenders' house. It was like this: you know the carpenter's shop where we found the chest for Ruggieri? He was having a terrible quarrel today with the man who owns the chest. The fellow was asking for compensation. And the carpenter swore that he hadn't sold it, it had been stolen during the night. "That's not true," said the other man. "You sold it to those two young money-lenders. They told me so themselves last night, because I saw it there when Ruggieri was caught." "That's a lie," replied the carpenter, "I never sold it to them. They must have pinched it last night. Let's go and see them." So away they went to the money-lenders' house, and I came back here. Anyway, I reckon that's how Ruggieri got to the place where they found him. But it beats me how he came to life again.'

The lady now realized exactly what had occurred, and gave her maid the doctor's information, imploring help in her task of reprieving Ruggieri without damaging her own reputation.

'Just tell me what to do, madam,' said her maid, 'and

D

I'm at your service.' They always say that necessity is the mother of invention, and the lady had soon hatched a plan, and given her maid the details. As a first step the girl was sent to Doctor Mazzeo crying.

'I must implore your forgiveness, sir,' she whispered. 'I have done you an injury.'

'How?' asked he.

'Sir,' she said, still sobbing bitterly. 'You know what type of man Ruggieri da Jeroli is? Well he fell for me. It was partly love and partly fear that made me give in and become his mistress earlier this year. I knew you were going to be away last night, and he made me let him come to sleep in my bedroom. He got thirsty and I was so afraid of being caught by the mistress in the parlour, I didn't know where to lay hands on wine or water. Then I remembered seeing a bottle of water in your room, so I ran and fetched it for him, and put it back afterwards where I'd found it. But you made a terrific fuss about it. I admit it was wrong of me, but we're all human. I'm truly sorry for what I did, but it doesn't seem right that Ruggieri should have to die just for that and the consequences. I implore you—let me go and try to save him.'

Though this confession annoyed him, the doctor replied flippantly:

'It served you right, didn't it? You hoped your young man would prove nippy between the sheets last night, but he can't have been very lively. Away you go and try getting him off, but don't you bring him into this house again, or I'll get you for last time and the next.'

The maid considered stage one had gone well. Off she went to Ruggieri's prison, and by buttering up the warders, managed to get a word with him. She briefed him about what he should say to the chief of police to save his skin. She even got an interview with the chief himself. Seeing what a fine healthy piece of goods she was, he felt like knocking her off himself. She wasn't saying no, for she realized it would put their relationship on the right footing from the start.

'You've got Ruggieri da Jeroli locked up here, sir, for robbery. He's innocent.'

Then she told him the whole story: how she was Ruggieri's mistress, had let him into the doctor's house, had given him the drug in ignorance, taken him for dead, and shut him in the chest. She described the scene she had witnessed between the carpenter and the chest's owner, and showed how Ruggieri must have got into the money-lenders' house.

The police-chief saw how easy it was to check the story. First he cross-examined the doctor about the drug, and her facts were corroborated. Then he summoned the carpenter, the owner of the chest and the money-lenders. With a good deal of palaver, he proved that the money-lenders had stolen the chest during the night and taken it home. In the end he sent for Ruggieri and asked him where he had spent that night. The prisoner replied that he didn't know, but he recalled going to sleep with the doctor's maid, and drinking some water because he was so thirsty. He couldn't remember anything after that, except waking up in a chest in the money-lenders' house. The chief of police took in all this, and got the girl, the prisoner, the carpenter, and the money-lenders to repeat their story several times. Finally he was convinced of Ruggieri's innocence and released him, but fined the money-lenders for stealing the chest. I need hardly say how relieved Ruggieri and his mistress were. Many was the time the two of them laughed with the invaluable maid over this incident (though she had suggested the knife wounds). They remained faithful to each other, and their love-affair continued more happily than before. I wouldn't ask for anything better myself—but I could do without the chest.

Second day: fifth tale

THE LONG LOST SISTER

THE story goes that a young Perugian horse-dealer called
Andreuccio di Pietro set off for Naples with some colleagues
and fifty pounds in gold in his pocket. He had never been
away from home before, but he'd heard that horses could be
bought cheap in the city. He got there one Sunday early in
the evening, and was told by his landlord there would be a
market next morning. Off he went and found a good many
horses he liked. He haggled over their price but didn't
actually clinch any bargains. To show he meant business
(and what a country bumpkin he was) he kept whipping
his purse out in full view of everybody. While he was
haggling and flaunting his money, a Sicilian girl happened
to pass. She was a real beauty—and the type who sold her
favours to any bidder. He didn't notice her, but she took
one look at him and the purse, and said to herself:

'I wouldn't say no to all that money.'

And she walked on. There was an old woman with the
girl, also from Sicily, and she turned back, ran up to
Andreuccio and embraced him. The girl stopped and
quietly watched the scene from a little way off, waiting for
her companion to rejoin her. Andreuccio turned, recognized
the old woman and seemed very glad to see her. But it was
neither the time nor the place for a proper conversation, so
before they parted, she arranged to pay him a visit at his
lodging.

The girl had noticed how well Andreuccio knew the old
woman, just as she had noticed how well-crammed his purse
was. Intending to find a way of lifting some if not all of his
money, she started guardedly asking the old woman questions: Who was he? Where did he come from? How did
she come to know him? She extracted almost as much de-
tailed information as Andreuccio could have provided him-

self, for the old woman had spent a long time in his father's household, in Sicily and then in Perugia. The girl also found out why he had come to Naples and where he was staying. Fully informed of the names and details of Andreuccio's relatives, the girl thought she was equipped to get the money she had set her heart on. Having made an ingenious plan, she went home and gave the old woman enough work to keep her busy all day and stop her visiting Andreuccio. That evening she sent to Andreuccio's lodgings a maid she had trained for such jobs. As luck would have it, the girl met the man himself at the door and asked him for Andreuccio. When he said who he was, she led him on one side and said:

'Please, sir, a lady from this town would like a word with you.' He was completely taken in because he had a very high opinion of himself and was sure that some lady had fallen for him—the handsomest young man in Naples. He replied he would be only too pleased to call on the lady, and she had only to name the place.

'She'd like you to visit her at home, if you would, sir.'

'Off we go then. I'm with you,' said Andreuccio at once, without telling anyone at his hotel where he was going.

So she led him to her mistress' house, in a slum aptly called Foul-Hole. But this he was not to know. To him it was a visit to an attractive lady in a reputable neighbourhood. He followed the girl nonchalantly to her mistress' house. When the lady heard that Andreuccio had arrived, she came to the head of the stairs to meet him. She was tall and beautiful, with a well-preserved complexion, richly dressed, and most striking. As Andreuccio approached she came down three steps and met him with open arms. She embraced him warmly but silently, as if overcome by emotion. Then she burst into tears, kissed him on the forehead, and said falteringly:

'Welcome, welcome! Oh, dear Andreuccio.'

Flabbergasted at this warm welcome, he could only reply:

'Pleased to meet you, madam."

She took his hand and led him through her boudoir to her bedroom, which was redolent with roses, orange-blossom, and other scents. There was a fine four-poster, a great many dresses hanging on pegs, and other signs of luxury and elegance. They were all so strange to Andreuccio that he was convinced his hostess must be a great lady. They sat together on a chest at the foot of the bed, and she started:

'Andreuccio, you must have been very taken aback at my embracing you and crying, since you don't know me and probably haven't even heard my name. What I'm about to tell you will come as a still greater shock. I'm your sister. I can't tell you how much it means to me that God has permitted me to set eyes on one of my brothers before I die, even if I never see the others. But probably all this is gibberish to you. I ought to explain: you may know that your father and mine spent a good deal of his life in Palermo. Thanks to his kindness and charm, he was—indeed still is—very popular there. No one could have loved him better than the lady who was to be my mother. She was a widow then, but she defied her father and brothers and became his mistress. A child was born—the sister you see before you. Not long after my birth, Pietro had to leave Palermo and return to Perugia. His little daughter was left behind with her mother. As far as I can make out, he never gave us another thought. I suppose, if he weren't my father, I'd blame him for his shabby treatment of a woman who loved him so deeply that she blindly trusted herself and her fortune to a stranger . . . not to mention his responsibilities as a father, for I wasn't low-born or anything to be ashamed of. But what'd be the point in abusing him. It's easy enough to criticize, but too late to do anything about it. That's how it was. He abandoned me as a child and I grew up much as you see me now. My mother had money and married me off to a worthy nobleman of the Girgenti family. His fondness for my mother and me made him settle in Palermo. As a keen Guelf, he was soon corresponding with the King of Naples. Frederic of Sicily found this out before the plot was fully hatched and we had to escape from Sicily when I was on the point of becoming the first lady of the island. We were forced to leave practically everything behind, and took as little away with us as we could. Hardly anything in comparison to the enormous wealth, the estates and palaces we had to abandon. We found asylum here, and thanks to King Charles, who compensated us for what we had lost in his service, my husband, your brother-in-law, has a generous pension, and an estate and a mansion, as you can see for yourself. So that's how I come to be here, where thank God (for it's none of your doing) fate has reunited me with a dear, long-lost brother.'

The she embraced him with more tears, and kissed his forehead. She made this story convincingly accurate and told it most glibly. Andreuccio remembered that his father really had lived in Palermo. He knew from personal experience how easily young people fall in love. He had the evidence of her tears, endearments, and sisterly kisses. He swallowed the story hook, line, and sinker. When she had finished, he answered:

'You can't blame me for being surprised, since Father, for some reason, never mentioned you or your mother. Or if he did, I'd forgotten. So that as far as I was concerned, you didn't exist. I'm especially delighted to have found a sister here, because I was lonely and it's so unexpected. I think anybody, whatever their rank, would be overjoyed at acquiring such a sister; especially a mere tradesman like me. But tell me one thing: how did you know I was here?'

To this she replied:

'I was told this morning by an old woman who often comes round here. She claims to have worked for Father a long time, in Palermo and Perugia. If it hadn't seemed better for you to come here than for me to visit your lodgings, I'd have found you before.'

Then she started asking after all his relatives by name. Andreuccio answered everything and became more and more convinced by this dangerous imposter. They talked on and on, and it became very warm. Sweets and Greek wine were offered Andreuccio. As suppertime approached he got up to leave, but his sister wouldn't think of it. She pretended to be very hurt, kissed him, and said:

'Oh dear, that's how you feel about me. Fancy meeting

your own sister in her own house for the first time, and wanting to go away and dine in lodgings. You must eat here. I'm only sorry my husband's away, but you'll see a lady can be hospitable.'

Andreuccio was at a loss and could only mumble:

'Devoted to you as I am, it would be very rude to stay, because they'll wait supper for me all evening.'

'Good God,' she exclaimed, 'can't I send them a message not to wait for you? Though surely the politest thing to do would be to invite all your friends to dinner here. Then if you insist on going, you'd have company.'

Andreuccio replied that he could do without his friends for one evening. If she wanted him to stay, he'd be only too pleased. So she went through the motions of sending a message to his lodgings not to expect him for dinner.

They went on talking until supper. During the meal itself, she deftly managed to draw out the large number of magnificently served courses till it was dark. Andreuccio tried to leave after the meal, but she wouldn't hear of it. Naples was not a place to wander in after dark, especially for a stranger. She had told his lodgings he wouldn't be back for dinner, or for the night either. He believed her and in his innocence was happy to stay the night. For the rest of the evening they found plenty to keep them talking late. Finally, well into the night, she vacated her own room for Andreuccio, and left a page to administer to his wants. She and the maids went off to another room.

The night was boiling. As soon as Andreuccio was alone, he peeled off his jacket and laid his socks at the head of the bed. He felt a call of nature and asked the boy where to go. He pointed to a door in one corner of the room: 'In there.'

Unsuspectingly, Andreuccio went in, but unfortunately trod on a board, whose end was unattached to the joist. It fell, and he with it. Thank God, he wasn't hurt, though it was a considerable drop. But he was covered in muck from head to foot. I'd better explain, in case you're in the dark, that he'd fallen into a narow closed alley. It was the sort you often get between houses. There were two planks over this gap, resting on joists on either side. On them stood a stool. It was one of the planks that gave way under

Andreuccio. When he landed in the gap, he shouted for the boy, who had heard the fall and dashed off to tell his mistress what had happened. She came back to her room at once, and found Andreuccio's clothes and money easily, for he was silly enough to carry his purse on him for safety. Having snaffled the prize she had played so skilfully for, by posing as the sister of a Perugian though really she came from Palermo, she didn't bother further about Andreuccio. She barely stopped to close the door he had dropped through.

When the lad didn't answer, Andreuccio shouted out. But with no result. Then he began to suspect a trick had been played on him. He scaled the low wall that separated the alley from the road, and easily recognized the door of the house. He ran to it, shouted, and battered at it till its hinges shook. But again it got him nowhere. He now saw his predicament only too clearly, and he broke down :

'Oh, what a fate ! Losing fifty pounds and a sister, at one stroke . . .' and a lot more in the same vein.

Then he started thumping at the door and bellowing again, until he woke a good many of the neighbours. They got up—livid at the din. One of the maids of the house came sleepily to the window, crying petulantly :

'Who's knocking down there?'

'Oh, don't you recognize me?' asked Andreuccio, 'I'm Andreuccio, Madame Fiordaliso's brother.'

'If you've had too much to drink, lad,' she snapped, 'go away and sleep it off and come back tomorrow. I don't know Andreuccio, and haven't an idea what you're babbling about. Go away and let us get some sleep !'

'But don't you understand?' said Andreuccio. 'You must see. Well, if that's how you Sicilians treat your blood relatives, forgetting them as quickly as that, at least you can give me back the clothes I left and I'll be off fast enough.'

She replied with a giggle :

'You must be touched in the head, man.'

And with that she disappeared, closing the window behind her. His position now stared Andreuccio in the face. He was hopping mad, quite prepared to use violence where appeals had failed. He picked up a large stone, and started beating even more fiercely on the door again. As a result, many neighbours who had been woken up, took him for some thorough tough who had invented a story just to infuriate the woman. At this racket, they all came to their windows, and like an army of local dogs yapping at an intruder, they bellowed in chorus:

'It's disgusting, coming and talking such boloney to a respectable woman at this hour. For heaven's sake get out and leave us in peace. If you want to quarrel with her, do it tomorrow and cut it out now.'

The woman's bodyguard hadn't put in an appearance yet, but just sat silently indoors. Perhaps this stirred him, for he appeared at a window, and bellowed in a gruff, threatening voice:

'Who's down there?'

Andreuccio looked up at him standing in the window, yawning and rubbing his eyes as though he had just woken up. He had an unkempt black beard, and looked to Andreuccio like a pretty tough customer. He answered with a tremor:

'The lady inside is my sister, and . . .'

The bodyguard interrupted, bawling out even more viciously:

'I've a good mind to come down there and beat the day-light out of you, you bloody fool. Drunken swine. Can't you let us sleep in peace?'

At that he withdrew and slammed the window. Some of the neighbours knew what the man was capable of, and whispered to Andreuccio:

'For God's sake, get out, man. You'll get massacred if you stay.' This advice seemed friendly, and what with the look and sound of the man as well, Andreuccio despaired of ever getting his money back. He set off miserably, back towards his lodgings, the way he had so misguidedly come with the maid the day before. But he smelt so abominably that he decided to stop off for a bathe in the sea. He turned left up a road called Catalan Street, that led to the higher part of the city. Happening to see two men approaching with a lantern, he was afraid they might be watchmen or some-body equally dangerous, so he scuttled off to hide in a ruined house. The next moment they came in after him, as if deliberately following. One of them dropped some crowbars he had over his shoulder, and they both started examining and discussing them. Then one of them suddenly stopped and said:

'What on earth is it? I've never smelt anything so foul in all my life.'

He raised his lantern a little and caught sight of poor Andreuccio.

'Who's this?' the man asked in amazement.

Andreuccio was tongue-tied, but when they flashed the light over him and asked how he had managed to get so filthy, he told them the whole story. Trying to pinpoint the place of the crime, they agreed that it must have been at Scarabone Buttafucco's house. One of them turned to Andreuccio and said:

'Well, you may have lost money, but you can thank your lucky stars you had that fall. If you hadn't, you can bet that as soon as you were asleep you'd have been killed and lost your money and your life. What's the use of crying over spilt milk? You'll never get a farthing back. And if he ever gets to hear that you've mentioned what happened, you're done for.'

The two men had a short discussion on the side and then said:

'Look here! We're sorry for you and we're going to make you an offer. If you come in with us on a little scheme, we promise your cut in the share-out will be much more than what you've lost.'

Andreuccio was so desperate he was quite ready to agree.

It seemed that Lord Filippo Minutolo, Archbishop of Naples, had just been buried with a ruby on him worth over five hundred in gold, as well as some other valuable stuff. The two men planned to strip the Archbishop of his jewellery. Andreuccio approved of the scheme at once, for his greed had got the better of his sense. So off they all went to the cathedral, but Andreuccio's smell was so appalling, that one of the others said:

'Can't we find some way of cleaning him up a bit, and getting rid of that ghastly stench?'

'Yes,' said the other, 'we're just near one of those wells that always has a large bucket and chain. It's quite close and we can wash him down properly.'

Finding a rope there but no bucket, they decided to lower him into the well, to wash himself. When clean he was to tug at the rope and they'd haul him up. So down he went, but just as he had finished cleaning himself and tugged on the rope, a party of night watchmen came past. It was a hot night and they'd just had a long chase after some crook, so they wanted a drink of water. The two men made a surreptitious getaway on seeing them, and the parched watchmen approached the well, undid their belts and stripped off their weapons and tunics. They pulled at what they thought was a bucket full of water. Imagine their terror when Andreuccio appeared over the edge, let go the rope and firmly gripped the well head. The watchmen dropped the rope as if they'd been stung, and were off as fast as they could go. Andreuccio was so taken aback that if he hadn't had a tight hold on the well's edge, he would have fallen down it again, which would undoubtedly have resulted in serious injury, if not death. He was even more bewildered when he alighted on dry land and found an assortment of weapons lying about which he knew didn't belong to his companions. He felt vaguely uneasy, but couldn't put a name to his fears. He cursed his vile luck, and without daring to touch the weapons, he wandered aimlessly away from the well. He hadn't gone very far before he was rejoined by his two cronies, who were on the way back to haul him up. They were astonished to see him and asked who had pulled him out. Andreuccio said he didn't know, but he carefully described what had happened, and what he'd found by the well. They laughed at realizing what had occurred, and told him what made them run for it and who must have pulled him out. Then without more ado—for it was midnight by this time—they went on to the Cathedral. It was easy enough to break in and locate the splendid marble tomb. Despite its enormous weight, they managed to lift the lid with their iron crowbars high enough for a man to worm in. Then they propped it up. A debate followed:

'Who's going in?'

'I'm not.'

'Nor am I. Let Andreuccio.'

'Not me.'

Then they both turned on him saying:

'What, you won't go in? By God, if you don't, we'll batter you to death with one of these bars.'

The terrified Andreuccio climbed into the tomb, saying to himself:

'These fellows are making me go' in so as to cheat me. When I've handed everything out to them, and I'm sweating blood to climb out, they'll shove off and leave me empty-handed.'

So he made up his mind to look after number one. He remembered them mentioning a valuable ring, so as soon as he was inside the tomb, he transferred it from the Archbishop's finger to his own. He passed out to the others the crosier, the mitre, the gloves, and the other accoutrements. When he'd stripped the Archbishop to the shirt he shouted to his accomplices that that was the lot. They insisted there was a ring and ordered him to search everywhere. He pretended to, and shouted from time to time that he couldn't find it. This kept them in suspense for a bit, but they were as clever as he was in their own way, and kept egging him on to look more carefully. Then they seized their chance, took out the bar that propped up the lid, and disappeared, leaving him shut in. He set his shoulder and head repeatedly against the lid, and strained every muscle to budge it. But he couldn't shift it an inch. In the end the hopelessness of his position overcame him and he collapsed on top of the Archbishop. Anyone looking at them would have been incapable of deciding which was the deader body.

On regaining consciousness he broke down. His situation seemed desperate. If he didn't die of starvation first, and escaped being poisoned by the evil smell from the worm-infested body, he would be hanged as a grave-breaker as soon as the tomb was opened. Such mournful meditation was cut short by the sound of a considerable number of voices and footsteps in the church. Andreuccio guessed the intruders might be on the same mission as he and his colleagues. He was more terrified than ever. Soon the party broke open the tomb, propped up the lid and started arguing about who was going in. Nobody was keen, and the debate continued until at long last one of them—a priest—scoffed:

'What are you all so afraid of? Do you expect to be eaten alive? I'll go in myself.'

Then, resting on the tomb's edge, he started to lower himself in, feet first. Andreuccio jumped up at once, grabbed one of the priest's legs and started tugging him in. The poor fellow yelled his head off, and wriggled back out. All the others retreated in panic, as though all hell had been let loose on them. Andreuccio jumped out of the open tomb, with the ring still on his finger. He left the church the way he had come and wandered about, until early next morning he got to the sea. He branched off and luckily reached his lodging, where his landlord and friends had been worrying the whole night about him. He told them his adventures and the landlord advised him to leave Naples on the spot. So home he went to Perugia, having invested his money in a ring instead of the horses he had meant to buy.

Third day : first tale

ONE INTO NINE WON'T GO

JUST near here there was (and still is) a convent with a very
holy reputation—which for its own sake shall remain
nameless. At the time I'm describing, there were nine young
nuns, including the abbess. Their very beautiful garden was
looked after by a real fool, who became fed up with the
money he was getting, squared the convent steward, and
moved back to his home town, Lamporecchio. Among the
neighbours who welcomed him home was a healthy young
labourer called Masetto, quite good-looking for a peasant.
Masetto asked the returning native where he had been
working all this time. Our friend Nuto told him. Masetto
also asked what his job was at the convent.

'Oh,' answered Nuto, 'I kept their fine, big garden tidy.
Occasionally I used to cut firewood nearby, draw water,
and do other odd jobs. But the ladies hardly paid enough to
keep me in shoe leather. They were all so young and they
were the very devil. There was no making them happy. If
I was busy in the kitchen garden, one of them would say:
"Do this." Someone else would say: "Do that." A third
would snatch the hoe from my hands and say: "No, not that
way." They'd go on bothering me until I had to leave off
work and go away. So, what with one thing and another, I
couldn't stand it any longer, and I came home. The steward
asked me to send a suitable substitute when I got home, and
I promised to. Good luck to him, but I shan't put myself
out to find him someone.'

Nuto's rambling story made Masetto feel quite faint with
longing to serve these nuns. He gathered too that he might
he able to satisfy this ambition. But he saw it would be fatal
to give anything away to Nuto, so he replied:

'I think you were quite right to come away. One man
and all those women—it'd be real hell. More often than
not, they don't even know their own minds.'

So ended the conversation, and Masetto was left to think out some way of arranging to live in the convent. He knew he was quite up to Nuto's job, so he had no worries on that score, but he was afraid he would be turned down as too young and good-looking. After a good deal of thought he came to the conclusion that:

'The place is a long way away, and nobody will know me. I'll probably get in if I pretend to be dumb.'

Thus decided, he shouldered an axe, and without a word to anyone about where he was going, set off to present himself at the convent, dressed as a beggar.

The first person he met when he entered the courtyard of the convent, was the steward. He signed to him in deaf and dumb language, and begged to be given something to eat. He was prepared to cut firewood in exchange. The steward fed him at once and then presented him with the logs which had been too tough for Nuto. Masetto was strong enough to make short work of them all. As the steward had to go to the wood, he took Masetto with him, made him cut firewood, and load it on the donkey and then signed to him to take it back to the convent. He managed this so well that the steward kept him on several days and gave him more odd jobs.

One day the abbess happened to see him and asked her steward who he was.

'He's a poor deaf and dumb fellow, madam, who came here begging a couple of days ago,' said the steward. 'I thought it only fair to take him in and give him a chance to prove himself useful. If he knew enough to run a kitchen-garden, and was prepared to stay, we could do far worse. We certainly need him, and he's strong and ready to turn his hand to anything. You wouldn't have to worry about him larking with your young ladies, either.'

'God bless me, that's perfectly true,' answered the abbess. 'See if he'd make a gardener, and if he would, try and persuade him to stay on. Give him some shoes, an old habit, speak to him kindly, make a fuss of him, and feed him up well.'

The steward promised to do this.

During this dialogue Masetto had stopped nearby, pretending to sweep the courtyard. When he heard the steward and the abbess, he crowed to himself:

'Just let me get inside, and I'll make that kitchen-garden look like it's never been worked before.'

The steward put him to work in the kitchen-garden, and seeing how well he did it, invited him in sign-language to stay on. He made it clear that he was ready to do just what the steward wanted. So he was taken on in dumb-show, given charge of the kitchen-garden and instructed what to do. The steward had other things to see to, so he went off and left Masetto there. As he worked there day after day, the nuns started teasing and poking fun at him. As people so often do with deaf-mutes, they used the obscenest language they knew, assuming he didn't understand. The abbess seemed unaware of this; perhaps she thought of him as a eunuch as well as a mute.

One day when he was taking a short pause after some hard work, two nuns who were strolling in the garden came up and stopped to watch him, as he lay pretending to be fast asleep. The braver of the two said:

'If I could trust you to keep a secret, I'd mention something I've often toyed with—it might appeal to you too.'

'Out with it,' said the other, 'I promise not to tell a soul.'

The frank one started:

'Has it ever occurred to you how restricted we are here, with no man allowed within miles of the premises except the old steward and this mute? I gather from ladies who come visiting that nothing in the world touches the bliss a woman gets out of having a man. More than once I've thought of experimenting with this mute, since there's nobody else handy. Why, you couldn't find anybody in the whole world so suitable; he couldn't split if he wanted to. Look what a thick oaf he is—all brawn and no brain. What do you think of the idea?'

'Oh, what a suggestion!' gasped the other. 'Remember we've dedicated our virginity to God.'

'But think what a lot of vows keep on being made to Him which no one ever sticks to. What's our vow? I'm sure *He* can get an odd substitute or two to take our places,' replied her friend.

'But what would happen if we became pregnant?' the other insisted.

'Now you're just seeing troubles before they come. It'll be time enough to think about that, when it happens. There are millions of ways of keeping it dark, as long as we don't blurt it out ourselves.'

Her friend was reassured, and became even keener than her friend to try out this animal-man.

'All right, then,' she agreed. 'How are we going to manage it?'

'Well, it's past twelve now, so all the other sisters except us are bound to be asleep. Let's search the kitchen-garden and see there's no one about. If we're safe, all we need do is to lead him over to that shed where he shelters when its raining. Then one of us stands guard while the other is with him. He's so stupid he'll do whatever he's told.'

Masetto didn't miss a word of this conversation, and was only too ready to oblige. He couldn't wait to be taken in hand by one of them. They reconnoitred to make sure the coast was clear. Then the originator of the plan approached and shook Masetto. He jumped to his feet, and when she shook his hand winningly, he grinned inanely. She led him to the shed, and he did what was required without having to be asked twice. When served, she changed places with the other, like the good friend she was. Masetto, still pretending to be an idiot, obliged. Before leaving they both felt like trying again to see how the mute kept his seat.

Afterwards, when they were having one of their frequent discussions of the event, they agreed that it was just as delightful as they had been led to believe. So, whenever they got a chance, they enjoyed themselves with the deaf-mute.

One day it so happened that another of the nuns looked out of her cell window and saw them. She told two others. The three debated reporting the culprits to the abbess, but changed their minds and instead made an arrangement to take out shares in Masetto. By a succession of flukes the other three nuns eventually joined the firm.

The abbess had not tumbled to any of this, when one scorching day she happened to come upon Masetto as she was walking in the garden. He was so continually in the saddle at night, that he had to take it very easy by day, so he was stretched out asleep in the shade of an almond tree. He lay quite exposed, for the wind had ruffled up his clothes in front. The good lady noticed this, and secretly felt the same sexual urge her nuns had given way to. She woke Masetto, bore him off to her room, and kept him there several days. Despite constant complaints from her nuns that the gardener was neglecting the kitchen-garden, she repeatedly savoured the delectable sin she had been the first to blame others for. When she did finally allow him to return to his room, she was continually sending for him, and was exorbitant in her demands. Things came to such a pass that Masetto was incapable of satisfying so many women, and realized that if he didn't drop his performance as a deaf-mute, it might end in disaster. So when he was with the abbess one night, his impediment disappeared and he blurted out:

'Madam, they say that a cock can easily serve ten hens, but I think ten men would be hard put to satisfy a single woman. I'm expected to serve nine of you and I just can't take it. What I've gone through already has reduced me to a pulp. You must either relieve me of my post or ease my load in some way.'

The abbess was dumbfounded at hearing the supposed mute speak out like this, and cried:

'What's all this? I thought you were dumb.'

'So I was, madam,' said Masetto, 'not from birth actually, but as the result of an illness which struck me dumb until just tonight. Thanks be to God, I've recovered.'

The lady believed this and asked him what he meant by having to serve nine. Masetto told her the position, and she realized that all her nuns had outployed her. Seeing how ruinous for the convent's reputation it would be to dismiss Masetto, she privately made up her mind to arrange for him to stay on. She called all the nuns together, and they all made a clean breast of their past sins. Everyone, including Masetto, agreed to the story for public consumption. Thanks to the prayers of their powerful patron saint, it ran, Masetto had been cured of his long dumbness. As the old steward had just died Masetto was appointed to succeed him. The nuns arranged among themselves for him to serve them without overdoing it. During his service he procreated many a good little religious, but it was all so highly organized that there wasn't a hint of scandal in the abbess' lifetime. This continued until Masetto was getting on in years, and expressed a desire to retire to his home with the fortune he had collected. It was no sooner said than done.

So Masetto who had left Lamporecchio with an axe over his shoulder, returned in his old age. He was wealthy and a father, but had been clever enough as a young man to avoid the bother and expense of bringing up his children. He always claimed that that was the treatment given anyone who cuckolded the Lord.

Third day: third tale

THE PERFECT GO-BETWEEN

IN our city of Florence duplicity flourishes at the expense
of love and faith. It was not many years ago that there was
an exceptionally beautiful, charming, vivacious, and intelligent lady living there. Though I know her name, she and
the other participants in this story will remain anonymous,
because there are people still alive who may find this story
offensive instead of merely amusing. She was an aristocrat
who had married a cloth-manufacturer, and she could not
help treating her husband with the contempt his profession
evoked in her. No plebeian, however prosperous, seemed to
her to deserve an upper-class wife. For all his wealth he
was incapable of anything but blending wools, setting up a
loom, or arguing over a thread with the girl at the wheel.
His wife decided to dispense with his attentions except
when they were unavoidable. She would look for consolation to somebody nearer her own rank than her homespun
husband. With this intention she transferred to a more suitable man in the prime of life. She fell for him so deeply that
if she didn't see him during the day, she slept very badly on
the ensuing night.

He remained heart-whole and didn't realize the lady's
position. She was much too cautious and far too afraid of
the possible repercussions to reveal herself to him in a letter
or through one of her women friends. But she discovered
the man was intimate with a dull-witted, boorish friar who
was almost universally respected for his piety. The lady decided he would make a perfect go-between for herself and
her lover. Having worked out a plan, she picked her time
and went to his friary. When he was called, she asked if he
would be good enough to hear her confession. He recognized her at a glance, and was only too happy to oblige.
Then she added:

'Father, I have one more thing to confess to, and I must ask your help and advice over it. I think you know, indeed I've just told you, about my husband and relatives. My husband loves me more dearly than life itself, and as he's very rich, he willingly lets me have anything I want. In return he is more precious to me than anything in the world. No woman, however wicked, would so richly deserve damnation as me if I ever dreamed of crossing or dishonouring him in any way. God forbid that I should ever go so far as to commit such a crime. Now there's a man—I don't know his name, but he looks like a gentleman, and I rather think goes about with you a lot. He's tall and good-looking and dresses in respectable dull clothes. Not knowing me or the sort of woman I am, he seems to be practically laying siege to me. I can't appear at a door or a window, or leave the house without him appearing. In fact I'm extremely surprised he's not here at this very moment. This is terribly distressing because when men behave like that, it's respectable women who get blamed—quite unfairly. I've thought of telling my brothers the situation, but I'm always afraid the way men put things is apt to produce just a rude retort. A quarrel ensues. Then some stupid action. I've kept quiet to avoid trouble or scandal. I prefer opening my heart to you, because you're friendly with the gentleman and because it's your job to rebuke both friends and strangers for behaviour like that. For God's sake point his fault out to him and appeal to him to stop it. There must be plenty of other women who'd welcome him open-armed, only too flattered by all this fond attention, but I have no desire to encourage it, and find it excessively irritating.'

With these words, the lady fixed her gaze downwards, as though on the point of tears. The friar had no difficulty in guessing whom she was talking about. He was completely taken in by the story, and congratulated her on being so virtuous. He promised to make sure she would not be bothered again. Remembering her fortune, he didn't fail to stress the value of charity and alms-giving, and touched in passing on his own needs.

'I'm appealing to you, in God's name,' she said, 'and if your friend denies what I've said tell him to his face you had it direct from me, and that I was complaining to you.'

So ended her confession, and when the penance had been given she remembered the friar's hint about charity, and crammed his hand with money, intreating him to say masses for the souls of the dead. Then she got to her feet and went home.

Soon afterwards the gentleman paid the friar one of his regular visits. They talked generally for a little, and then the friar took him on one side and gently rebuked him for giving the lady the glad eye. From what she said, he had gone in for a good deal of this sort of thing. As the gentleman had never given this lady a thought, and practically never passed her house, he was flabbergasted. He was on the point of defending himself, when the friar went on:

'Now don't pretend to be so surprised, and don't waste time in denying it; that'll get you nowhere. It isn't the neighbours that have been complaining; she told me herself, and in great distress. I need hardly mention how ridiculous your behaviour is, but I will say just this: I never saw a woman less inclined to silly flirting than her. So for your own sake and for her peace of mind, leave her alone.'

The gentleman was not so obtuse as the friar and soon tumbled to the lady's clever device. So he pretended to be shame-faced, and promised to leave off. Then he went straight from the friar to the lady's house, where she was permanently posted at a small window, waiting for him to pass. When she saw him approaching, she looked so welcoming and friendly that he couldn't possibly have any further doubt in interpreting the friar's lecture. After that he was only too happy to pass that way every day without fail, which was a source of great delight to the lady. He was always careful to make it look as if he were there for some other reason. It wasn't long before she realized that he was as keen on her as she on him. She was anxious to add fuel to his flame, and convince him of her love, if she got the chance. So she paid another visit to the friar, threw herself at his feet and burst into tears. The friar asked her kindly what was wrong this time.

'Father,' she answered, 'it's still that wretched friend of yours—the one I complained about a day or two ago. His sole function appears to be making my life a misery, and trying to force me into something for which I should never forgive myself, nor dare to ask your pardon.'

'What!' exclaimed the friar. 'Hasn't he stopped pestering you?'

'No he hasn't,' she said. 'Far from it. I suppose he was so riled by my complaining to you that now he deliberately passes my house seven times as often as he did before. And I only wish to God he were satisfied with passing and ogling at me. But he's become so bare-faced in his impudence, that only yesterday he sent a woman to me with wheedling messages and trinkets. He even sent me a purse and belt, as if I hadn't enough already. I've not got over my annoyance yet, and if it hadn't been for my conscience and my respect for you, I'd have gone off the deep end. Needless to say, I controlled myself, determined not to say or do anything until I'd spoken to you. I gave back the purse and girdle to the woman who brought them, and ordered her to get out and return them to where they came from. But then I thought she might keep them and tell him I'd accepted them (I believe that does happen) so I recalled her and got them back, though I disliked having to handle them again. I've brought them for you to hand back to him. I don't need presents like that from him. If he doesn't leave me alone from now on, you must forgive me, father, come what may, I'm going to tell my husband and my brothers. If needs be I'd rather he was shown up than see my reputation ruined by him. That's my last word, father.'

She wept bitterly as she ended her speech, then produced from her dress an exquisite and highly ornate purse and a rich and elegant belt, and threw them into the friar's lap. He believed every word she had said and was most indignant:

'I can't blame you for being angry at his advances, my daughter. But I insist on your following my advice. I told him off several days ago, and he's failed to keep the promise he made me. That and this last exhibition will get him into such hot water with me that he won't give you any more trouble. So for God's sake don't go and tell your relatives in your fury. For he might get more than he deserves. And don't worry about your good name suffering. I shall always be the first to bear witness to your purity before God and the world.'

The lady seemed somewhat consoled by these words. After a moment—pandering to the greed of him and his species, she cried :

'The last few nights, father, the spirits of several relatives have appeared to me in my sleep. They seem tormented and continually crying out for alms. My mother in particular seems to be in dire misery and she's most pathetic. It must be agony for her to see the distress this enemy of God is causing me. So I beg you to recite the forty masses of St Gregory and some of your prayers for their souls, to ensure their liberation from the purgatorial fires.' She slipped a florin into the friar's hand.

He was only too happy to accept it and having bolstered her faith with many instructive words and examples, he gave her his blessing and let her go.

After her departure, the friar, still totally ignorant of the trick being played on him, sent for his friend. The gentleman realized at once from the friar's preoccupied expression that there was news of the lady, so he waited for him to speak. The friar repeated what he had said before, and then on the evidence of the lady's last complaint broke into abuse. The gentleman was still not sure what the friar was getting at, so he hardly bothered to deny the charge of sending a purse and belt. He was unwilling to discredit the lady in the friar's eyes, in case the presents came from her herself. Then the friar exclaimed most heatedly:

'Don't attempt to deny it, you foul-minded man. Why, they're here. She gave them me herself, her eyes streaming. Take a look, and just dare to say you don't recognize them.'

The gentleman pretended to be deeply ashamed, and said:

'Yes, I have seen them before. I admit I sinned, and I swear that now I know what she's like, you'll never hear this affair mentioned again.'

A great deal was said on both sides, before the dunderheaded friar handed his friend the purse and belt. He was treated to a long lecture, and ordered never to behave like this again. Once he had given his word, he was dismissed.

Crowing over this beautiful present and pledge of the lady's love, the gentleman went straight from the friar's to a place where he could show her he had received both the purse and the belt. She was thoroughly satisfied, and delighted that her plan seemed to be going from strength to strength.

The lady only needed her husband to go away, to achieve total success. It wasn't long before he had to go to Genoa for some reason. On the morning he mounted and rode away, she hurried off to the friar. Sobbing with tears, she managed to say:

'Father, I must tell you once and for all, I can't bear it any longer. I promised some days ago that I'd do nothing without letting you know. Now I've come to beg you to release me from that promise. To convince you that I've good cause to complain and be upset, I'll describe how this friend of yours—he's a real fiend in human form—behaved early this morning. As luck would have it, he seems somehow to have discovered that my husband went to Genoa yesterday morning. So this morning he got into our garden early, climbed a tree to the window in my bedroom, which overlooks the garden, and had already opened it and was coming in, when I woke up suddenly. Nothing would have stopped me screaming for help if he hadn't begged me for mercy while he was still outside. He invoked God's name and yours and told me who he was. For your sake I kept quiet, and in my birthday suit ran and slammed the window in his face. I suppose he got away, God rot him, for that's the last I saw of him. I ask you, is that a proper way to behave? I don't intend tolerating it any longer. I've gone through too much already, for your sake.'

The friar was absolutely infuriated by this story, and almost speechless. He could only ask repeatedly if she were quite certain the man wasn't somebody else.

'Good God!' she exclaimed. 'As if I couldn't recognize him by this time! It was him, I tell you! Don't believe a word if he denies it.'

'I can only say that it was the most appalling nerve and a maniacal thing to do. You were quite right to send him packing. Since God has preserved you from shame, I can only entreat you to take my advice, as you've done twice already. Don't complain to any of your relatives. Leave it to me, and I'll try and bring this devil incarnate to book—and he seemed so saintly. If I succeed in breaking him of this utter madness, so much the better. If I fail, then I give you full permission, with my blessing, to deal with him in any way you think fit.'

'Well then,' she answered, 'once again I'll do just as you say. But please see to it that he never annoys me again, for I swear I won't appeal to you about it next time.'

Without another word, and still looking distressed, she departed. She had hardly left the church before the gentleman entered. The friar summoned him, took him on one side, and laid into him with a vengeance, abusing him and calling him disloyal and treacherous. His first two interviews had taught his friend how to deal with the friar's condemnation. He listened carefully and tried to draw him by answering ambiguously:

'What have I done to deserve this fury?' he began. 'Anybody'd think I'd just crucified Our Lord.'

'The fellow's shameless,' cried the friar. 'Just listen to him. He talks as if it all happened a year or more ago, and his lecherous crimes were all ancient history. Have you already forgotten the outrage you committed this morning, a matter of hours ago? Where were you in the early hours of this morning?'

'Where was I?' asked the other. 'I don't know myself. You seem to have got the news quick enough.'

'True enough, I know,' replied the friar. 'I suppose because the husband wasn't there, you were confident she would welcome you open-armed. That was masterly! Every inch the gentleman of honour! You've become a cat burglar, who breaks into gardens and climbs trees. Do you really expect to conquer this lady by sheer insistence, climbing a tree to her window in the middle of the night? She hates you like poison, but you will persist. How well you've taken my warnings to heart, not to mention the ample evidence of her contempt she's given you. But I've one more thing to say: Up to now she's held her tongue about your infamous behaviour, not for any love of you, but because I begged her to. But she won't in future. I've given her a free hand to do what she thinks right, if you annoy her again. What are you going to do if she tells her brothers?'

The friend now knew all he needed to know, and with copious reassuring promises to the friar, went his way. That very night, on the stroke of three o'clock, he entered the garden, scaled the tree, and finding the window open, climbed into the bedroom. He was in the arms of his lady in a moment. She had been waiting anxiously and welcomed him warmly.

'Thanks to the holy father, you knew the way very well.'

They enjoyed a hearty laugh over the naïvety of the fatuous friar, and a good deal of mockery at the expense of the spinning and weaving business. Then they enjoyed each other with great mutual satisfaction. They didn't forget either to organize themselves many other equally pleasurable nights without calling upon the services of the friar as intermediary . . .

MERCENARY

In Milan there used to live a German mercenary called
Gulfardo, who was brave and loyal to his employers (and
that's most untypical of Germans). As he repaid his debts
conscientiously, there were always tradesmen prepared to
give him unlimited credit at low interest. While he was
stationed in Milan, Gulfardo set his cap at a fine woman—
Ambruogia, the wife of a prosperous merchant called Guasparruolo Cagastraccio with whom he had become on very
good terms. He managed the affair so expertly that neither
the husband nor anyone else suspected anything. One day
he sent the lady a message begging her to satisfy his passion.
He swore that for his part he would obey her to the letter
in everything.

Ambruogia made a great deal of song and dance about
it and the upshot was that she'd comply on the following
terms. In the first place no one was ever to know. Secondly
he was to provide the twenty pounds in gold which she
needed for some reason or other. Granted these conditions
she was his to command. Gulfardo was shocked to find someone he had taken for a highly respectable woman was so
sordidly mercenary. His passion became something very
near to hatred, and he meditated ways of double-crossing
her. So he sent her a message that he would be only too
happy to accommodate her in this and in any other way
he could. If she would name the hour, he would bring the
cash with him, and no one would be any the wiser, except
a faithful friend from whom he kept no secrets.

The lady (or should I say the whore?) was overjoyed and
informed him that her husband Guasparruolo would be going to Genoa on business in a few days. When he was away,
she'd contact Gulfardo and fix a time for him to visit her.

Gulfardo then picked his time and went to see Guasparruolo:

'I've come about a business venture of mine,' he said.

'Could you lend me the twenty pounds in gold I need, at
the rate you usually charge me?'

'Willingly,' replied Guasparruolo, counting out the
money on the spot.

A few days later when her husband was in Genoa,
Ambruogia, true to her promise, sent and asked Gulfardo
for the twenty pounds. He and his friend went to her
home where they were expected. He handed her the twenty
pounds on the spot in his friend's presence, and said:

'Keep the money, madam, and give it to your husband
when he gets back.'

She didn't know quite what he meant, but thought he
said this as a cover-up to prevent his friend from guessing
that the money was for services rendered.

'Indeed I will,' she said, 'but first I must check and see
it's right.'

She emptied the gold florins on to the table, checked
there were two hundred and stowed them away with satisfaction. Then she turned to Gulfardo and led him off to her
room. That night and most of the others while her husband
was away, she gave herself to him.

Soon after Guasparruolo got back, Gulfardo paid him a
visit, taking great care that Ambruogia should be there
too. He said in her presence:

'Guasparruolo, I didn't need that twenty pounds you
lent me the other day, after all, because the transaction I
borrowed them for fell through. I returned them straight-
away to your wife, so will you cancel the debt?'

Guasparruolo turned and asked his wife if she'd
been given them. She didn't dare deny it, with the witness
there, so she replied:

'Why yes, and I completely forgot to tell you he had
given them me.'

'Good,' said Guasparruolo, 'then we're quits, Gulfardo.
Don't worry about it. I'll see your account is altered
accordingly.'

Gulfardo then went home, leaving the wife to hand over
her ill-gotten gains. The wily lover thus enjoyed his mer-
. cenary mistress gratis.

Third day: tenth story

THE DEVIL IN HELL

IN the Tunisian city of Capsa there lived a very wealthy man, one of whose children was the prettiest little girl called Alibech. Though she was not a Christian she heard so many of her fellow citizens who were eulogizing their faith and service to the Almighty, that at last she asked one of them the best way of serving God freely. She was told that God's best servants practised entire renunciation of the world and its ways, like those who went to live in the wastes of the Thebaid desert.

Alibech was a naïve fourteen-year-old. Fired by childish enthusiasm rather than a solemn sense of vocation, she received this information in silence, and the very next day set off alone to walk to the Thebaid desert. With great determination she completed the painful journey and a few days later reached the desert. Seeing a small hut in the distance she made for it and met a hermit at the door. He was most surprised to see her and asked what she had come for. She replied that with the guidance of God's spirit she had come to find a teacher who would show her the way to serve the Almighty. The good man saw how young and very beautiful she was, and was afraid that the devil would get him if he allowed her to stay with him. So he congratulated her on her good intentions, entertained her with herb-roots, apples, and dates, washed down with a drop or two of water, and then said:

'Daughter, not far away there is a holy man who is much better equipped to teach you what you want than I am; so go on to him,' and he pointed out the way.

When she got to the man in question, she received the same answer as before. She went on and finally reached the cell of a young and admirably holy hermit called Rustico. She repeated her request and Rustico decided to put his spiritual strength to this most rigorous test; so he did not fob her off like the others. He allowed her to stay in his cell and made her up a bed of palm-leaves that night, and told her to sleep there. Almost at once the powers of the flesh began to undermine his spiritual defences. These soon gave way and Rustico crumpled before the attack, and wisely admitted himself beaten. He abandoned his devotions, prayers, and mortification, and took to considering his visitor's age and beauty and the best line of approach. He must get what he wanted from her without giving her the impression of being lecherous. With a few leading questions he discovered she had never slept with a man, and was every bit as naïve as she seemed. He devised a plan for getting his fun with her on the pretext that she was serving God. He embarked on a long dissertation on the enmity between God and the Devil. He then explained to her that since the Almighty had condemned the Devil to hell, putting him there is the surest way of serving God. Alibech asked how this was done. Rustico answered:

'I'll tell you in a minute, you just have to follow me.'

He then stripped off his skimpy clothing, and dropped stark naked on to his knees as if in prayer. This made the girl follow suit and take a similar position opposite him. In this posture, Rustico's desire increased and the sight of her beauty caused the resurrection of his body. At the sight of this Alibech asked in astonishment:

'Rustico, what's that thing sticking out in front of you there, which I haven't got?'

'Oh, daughter,' he replied, 'that's the devil I mentioned to you. Do you see? He's giving me such terrible anguish now, I can hardly bear it.'

'Thank God,' said the girl, 'I can see I'm better off than you, because I haven't a devil like that.'

'That's true,' agreed Rustico, 'but you've got something else which I haven't got.'

'Oh, what?' she asked.

'You've got hell,' he replied, 'and let me tell you, I think God sent you here to save my soul. This devil gives me such agony that if you would be kind enough to help and allow me to put him in hell, it would be a great relief and a praiseworthy service in God's sight, and that's really what you say you came for.'

In all innocence Alibech answered :

'Father, as I've got hell, make it whenever you like.'

'Blessings on you, daughter. Let's do it now, and get rid of him. Then he'll depart from me.'

With these words, he led the girl over to one of their beds, and showed her what to do so as to trap this scourge of God. The girl had never put any devil in hell before. She felt some pain—it being the first time—and cried out to Rustico :

'Oh, Father, this devil must indeed be horribly evil, a real enemy to God, for even when he's put back in hell, and is no longer on the loose, he hurts.'

'It won't always be like that, daughter.'

And to make certain of this, he put the Devil in six times before getting up off the bed, and for the time being the Devil was so crestfallen that he was quite prepared to relax. But on the next occasion he had to be put back more often, and the girl was always prepared to accommodate him dutifully. Soon she began to enjoy the activity, and this prompted her to say to Rustico :

'Now I realize how right those fellows in Capsa were, for service to God is absolute bliss. I really can't remember finding anything so wonderfully satisfying as putting the Devil in hell. In fact I think anybody who's not interested in serving God is a mere animal.'

That's the reason she so often went to Rustico and said:

'Father, I came here to serve God and not to laze. Let's put the Devil in hell.'

Once when they were performing, she said:

'Rustico, I don't see why he doesn't stay in hell. If he were as happy there as hell is to have him, he'd never be out of it.'

The pace Alibech set with these frequent invitations to Rustico, and their mutual pleasure in serving God, rather took the stuffing out of the poor man. The moment when anybody else would have broken out into a sweat, sent shivers down his spine. So he suggested to the girl that the

E

Devil need not be castigated and replaced in hell, unless he were looking thoroughly uppish.

'By the grace of God we've reduced him to such a state, that he's cringing to be left in peace.'

This argument kept the girl quiet for a time. But when she noticed that Rustico had stopped asking her to put the Devil in hell, she said one day:

'Rustico, your Devil is subdued and not giving you any trouble, but my hell is unbearable. So it would be a good thing if you soothed the anguish in my hell with your Devil, for my hell helped control your Devil when he got uppish.'

On a diet of herb roots and fresh water Rustico did not respond well to this appeal. He told her that it required a good number of Devils to soothe her hell, but that he couldn't do more than he was capable of. These occasions served to give her some satisfaction, but they were so far and few between that it was a drop in the ocean. The girl didn't feel she was doing her duty by God sufficiently, and grumbled about it.

This was the position—a limited supply of Rustico's Devil faced by the excessive demands of Alibech's hell—when a fire broke out in Capsa. Alibech's family home was burnt down. Neither her father, brothers, nor anyone else survived, so Alibech inherited the entire estate. A young man called Neerbale who had frittered away a fortune in generous good living, discovered that Alibech was still alive and set out to find her. He tracked her down just in time to prevent her father's estate being confiscated as an intestacy. He bore her off to Capsa, to her own disgust and Rustico's relief. There he married her and secured a share of the enormous inheritance. But before the couple slept together several ladies questioned Alibech and asked how she had served God in the desert. She told them she had habitually served Him by putting the Devil in hell. The women were so keen to know how to put the Devil in hell, that the girl set their curiosity at rest with a combination of words and gestures. They laughed themselves silly—and in fact they have not stopped yet.

'Don't worry, my girl,' they said consolingly, 'that's done

here as well. Neerbale will know all about performing that service to God with you.'

This story became traditional in that town, and now it's proverbial there that the surest way of serving God properly is putting the Devil in hell. The phrase has travelled and is used to this day.

So, girls, if you want God's blessing, do learn how to put the Devil in hell. It's profoundly pleasing to God, highly satisfying for those involved, and produces astounding results.

Third day: sixth story

THE JEALOUS WIFE

THE ancient city of Naples is probably the most attractive
town in Italy. There lived there a young man called
Ricciardo Minutolo, well known because of his noble birth
and his splendid fortune. He had a very beautiful and
affectionate wife, but this didn't stop him falling in love
with a lady who was generally considered to be far and
away the greatest beauty in Naples. Catella—that was her
name—was married to an equally aristocratic young man
called Filippello Fighinolfi. She idolized him and was
utterly faithful. Ricciardo was so in love with Catella that
he tried every possible device for winning her love, but his
passion seemed absolutely in vain. He became deeply despondent, for he really was infatuated. Life was intolerable,
but death impossible. Seeing him wallowing in misery, some
women relatives begged him to give up this suit since it
was clearly getting him nowhere. Catella wouldn't look at
anyone apart from Filippello, and was so bitterly jealous of
him, that she suspected every bird of the air of having
designs on him.

When Ricciardo realized the extent of Catella's jealousy,
he started thinking how to make use of it. He pretended to
have given her up as a bad job, and transferred his affec-
tions elsewhere. He started enlisting in tournaments and
such-like in honour of this other lady instead of Catella. It
wasn't long before practically everybody in Naples, including Catella, became convinced that he really had forgotten her and was passionately in love with someone else.
He kept up this pose until everybody was so sure that even
Catella's reserve towards him as a potential lover began to
melt. Whenever they met she was as friendly and sociable in
her welcome as everybody else.

In the dog days it was customary for many groups of

Neapolitan ladies and gentlemen to go and picnic at the seaside. Ricciardo happened to know Catella was going there with a party, so he took some friends himself. However, he pretended he wasn't keen to stay and turned down several invitations from ladies of Catella's circle before accepting one. When he joined the ladies, they all, including Catella, started twitting him on his new love. His imaginary burning passion gave them plenty of food for discussion. Finally most of the ladies drifted off somewhere or other, as they tend to on these occasions. Only Catella, Ricciardo and a few others were left. He then casually alluded to one of her husband Filippello's love affairs. Her jealousy was immediately aroused, and she was dying to ask Ricciardo what he was referring to. She controlled herself to begin with, but when she couldn't bear it any longer, she implored Ricciardo in the name of his lady love to explain what he meant about Filippello. He replied:

'Having invoked that lady, you can ask absolutely anything. I will explain myself provided you promise not to mention a word I tell you either to him or anybody else, until it's visibly proved. I can also show you how to get that evidence if you want it.'

Catella accepted his conditions—they seemed added proof that he was speaking the truth—and swore secrecy. They drew a little apart from the others so as not to be overheard, and Ricciardo began:

'Madam, if I still loved you as I used to, I shouldn't dare tell you anything I thought would pain you. Now that's all over, I'm readier to tell you the truth. I don't know whether Filippello resented my love for you, or thought you returned it. If so, he never gave me that impression. Anyway, he seems to have waited until I was more likely to be off guard, and is now trying to treat me the way he thinks I treated him. He wants to sleep with my wife, and I've discovered he's been bombarding her with furtive notes. She's been telling me everything and answering him as I've dictated. But only this morning, just before I came away, I saw her in a huddle with another woman at home. I soon guessed what type she was and why she was there. So I called my wife and asked her what the woman was after.

She admitted: "It's this persecution from Filippello—and it's all your fault for insisting I should encourage him. Now he's saying he's in anguish to know my mind. If I'm prepared to, he'd secretly get me let into a bath-house in town. He's very insistent for me to agree. If only you hadn't made me keep this affair going, I could have settled him once and for all and never had him poking his nose in again."

'Then I saw it had gone too far. I was determined to put a stop to it, and to tell you how he treats that utter loyalty of yours that was so nearly the death of me. In case you regard all this as mere moonshine, you can prove it if you like—see it and touch it. I made my wife tell that woman who was still waiting for her answer, that she would be at the baths tomorrow at about noon, during the siesta. The woman went away thoroughly satisfied. You'll hardly suppose me capable of sending my wife of course, but if I were you, I'd go myself, in place of the one he's expecting. When I had been with him a bit, I'd let on who I was, and he'd be getting no more than he deserved. I'm sure he'd be shown up so badly, that you'd have got your own back for the dirty trick he's done you, and I for what he's been hatching against me.'

As is typical with a jealous person, Catella listened to Ricciardo's story without remembering how double-faced he could be. She believed him at once, and started twisting certain previous events to fit. Then in a burst of indignation, she swore she would go to the baths. It wouldn't be at all difficult and if Filippello came, she'd make him so ashamed he'd never be able to look at a woman again without his ears tingling. Ricciardo was satisfied that his plan would be effective. He added some more details to back up the story, and when Catella was thoroughly convinced, he extracted a solemn promise from her never to tell a soul.

Next morning Ricciardo went off to the superintendent of the bath-house, the woman he'd directed Catella to. He told this woman his scheme and asked her to do her damnedest to help him. She was already in his debt over something else and gladly promised to help. They planned how it was all to be organized. There was a pitch-black windowless room in the bath-house. Under Ricciardo's guidance it was got ready, and as good a bed as possible made up there. As soon as he had eaten Ricciardo got into this bed and waited for Catella to appear.

Catella, still giving Ricciardo's story more credit than it deserved, went home the night before in a bitterly resentful mood. Filippello had returned that evening with something on his mind and wasn't quite as affectionate as usual. She noticed this, and her suspicions increased. She said to herself :

'He's brooding about that woman he expects to enjoy himself with tomorrow, no doubt. But over my dead body.'

So she spent most of the night turning over in her mind what she'd say to him when they met at the baths. Well, to cut a long story short, on the stroke of noon, Catella with just one servant, but otherwise in exact accordance with the original plan, went off to the baths Ricciardo had directed her to. She was met by the manageress and asked her if Filippello had been there that day. The woman had been briefed by Ricciardo, and only asked Catella whether she was the lady who was expected. Catella said she was.

'In you go then,' said the woman.

Catella, still in pursuit of what she was so reluctant to find, was shown into Ricciardo's room. She entered without lifting her veil, and locked the door behind her. Ricciardo was overjoyed to see her. He sprang out of bed, took her in his arms and whispered sweetly :

'Welcome, my love.'

So Catella played up to her part and kissed and petted him—in total silence, for fear her voice would give her away. The room's pitch blackness suited them both, and they weren't there long enough for their eyes to get used to it. Ricciardo led Catella to the bed. Neither said enough words to give themselves away. They made love a long time, a much greater pleasure for Ricciardo than Catella. At last Catella thought the time had come for her to spill her pent-up bile, and she burst out furiously:

'Oh, curse the fate of women ! How often their love for their husband is abused. Poor me ! For eight years my whole life has revolved round my beloved husband. Who do you think you've been sleeping with? The very person you've been double-crossing so long with fake flattery, pretending to love when you lost your head to somebody else. It's me, Catella, not Ricciardo's wife, you crooked devil! See if you recognize my voice—it's me all right. If only it weren't dark. Wait till I see you face to face. I'll show you up as the rotten, dirty swine you are. Oh, curse it! This is the sort of man I've thrown my love away on so long. This two-faced louse, thinking he's got somebody else in bed with him has swamped me with more affection in just a few minutes, than all the rest of the time I've been married to him. You're limp, listless and impotent at home, but you've been passionate enough today, you damned hypocrite. I'm not surprised you kept off me last night. You were reckoning to shed your load elsewhere, and you wanted to be fighting fit. But for all that, the bird came home to roost. Try and talk yourself out of this one, you filthy crook. Why don't you answer? By God, I can hardly keep my hands off you! You thought you'd get away with it, and no one would be any the wiser. Thank God, two can play at that game. You came a cropper. You didn't realize how well I had you covered.'

Ricciardo was secretly crowing over these words, but he didn't say a thing, only held her tighter, kissed her more fiercely than ever, and swamped her with love. But she went on abusing him.

'Oh yes, you think you'll get round me with all this fake affection, you little creep—but you're wrong. I shan't be satisfied until I've shown you up before all your friends, relatives, and neighbours. Aren't I every bit as good as Ricciardo Minutolo's wife, you swine? But what's she got that I haven't? Go on, tell me, skunk! Get away from me, don't touch me! You've done quite enough damage for one day. Now you know who I am, you would only be able to do it with an effort. Well I'm not giving you that satisfaction. I've a good mind to send for Ricciardo. He loved me to distraction, but didn't get so much as a glance out of me. There's nothing to stop me now. If you'd have had your way, you'd have enjoyed his wife, so you could hardly blame me for having him.'

Things had gone far enough. Catella was desperately upset. Ricciardo thought that if he allowed her to go away under her present delusion the consequences might be disastrous. He decided to reveal his identity and settle the misunderstanding. He took her in his arms, held her tight, and whispered:

'Darling, don't be angry. Just loving you didn't get me anywhere, so love taught me a trick. I am Ricciardo.'

Catella recognized the voice, shuddered, and attempted to jump out of bed. As this was impossible she tried to scream, but Ricciardo held his hand over her mouth, and said:

'There's no good crying over spilt milk, my dear. You could scream till kingdom come, but if you broadcast this in any way at all, two things are bound to happen. In the first place—and this should mean a bit to you—your reputation will be ruined. You can swear till you're black in the face that it was me who tricked you into coming here. I'll deny it. My version will be that I bribed you with money and presents into coming, and it's only because you weren't satisfied with what you made out of me that you're kicking up such a rumpus. You know people always prefer the nastiest version, so I'm more likely to be believed. A further result will be a violent quarrel between your husband and me, and I'm as likely to kill him as the other way round. If I did, that would be goodbye to your peace of mind. So, light of my life, don't ruin your good name, and risk losing your husband or me, as well. You aren't the first woman who's been double-crossed, and you won't be the last. Besides I wasn't trying to trick you out of anything. Your humble servant was prompted only by his life-long passion for you. All I am and all I own have been yours for a long time, and from now I want to be yours more than ever before. I know what a sensible woman you are in other respects, and I'm sure you'll be the same over this.'

Catella cried bitterly over Ricciardo's appeal. Despite her anger and her misery, what Ricciardo said was so obviously true, she had to admit to herself that things would probably turn out just that way. So she replied:

'I just can't bear to think about the dirty trick you've played on me, Ricciardo. God help me. Even if I hold my tongue here—and what a jealous fool I was to come—when I get out, never you fear, I shan't be easy until I've got my own back on you somehow. So you can take your hands off me, and let me go. You got what you wanted, and you've taunted me to your heart's content, now for God's sake leave me alone.'

Ricciardo saw how het up she was, however, and hadn't the least intention of letting her go until he was forgiven. He put himself out to soothe her, and with a great deal of coaxing and cringing he finally got her forgiveness. In fact by mutual agreement they stayed on a long time and thoroughly enjoyed each other. Indeed Catella found her lover's charms greatly superior to her husband's, and her severity disappeared. From then on she became most tenderly devoted to Ricciardo. With careful organization they managed to enjoy each other's love often. God give us the same good luck.

Eighth day: sixth story

PIGS HAVE WINGS

I NEED hardly tell you who Calandrino, Bruno, and Buffalmacco were, for they're well enough known to you. I need only mention that Calandrino had a small estate outside Florence which he had acquired as part of his wife's dowry. Each year it yielded a pig among its produce. It was an annual custom for Calandrino and his wife to go out to the farm in December, to superintend the killing and laying down of the pig. One year Tessa wasn't well, so Calandrino went on his own. Bruno and Buffalmacco discovered he was down at the farm alone, and off they went to stay with a priest who was a particular crony of theirs, and a near neighbour to the farm. Calandrino had killed the pig that very morning, and came up to them saying:

'How nice it is to see you. Do come and see what a good farmer I am.'

And he led them home and exhibited the pig. They saw what a good specimen it was, and gleaned the information that Calandrino was intending to salt it for home eating.

'Don't be a fool,' protested Bruno. 'Sell it, man, and let's have a good time on the proceeds. You can tell your wife it was stolen.'

'Not me!' answered Calandrino. 'She'd never believe me and she'd throw me out of the house. There's no good trying to persuade me, I wouldn't dream of such a thing.'

The others hammered at him, but it was no use. Then Calandrino asked them to dinner but so unenthusiastically that they refused the invitation and went home. Later, Bruno said to Buffalmacco:

'Why don't we pinch the pig from him tonight?'

'How can we?' asked Buffalmacco.

'It would be easy enough—I've already thought of a way

117

of doing it, as long as he doesn't move it somewhere else,' said Bruno.

'All right, then,' said Buffalmacco. 'Let's pinch it. Perhaps afterwards our worthy host, the reverend, will help us do justice to a blow-out.'

'Indeed I will,' the priest replied.

'It'll need some planning, though,' warned Bruno—'You know how mean he is, Buffalmacco, and how he'll drink like a fish when it's on somebody else. Well, we'll go and take him to the local. Once there the reverend must pretend to treat us to all the rounds, and not let Calandrino put his hand in his pocket for anything. Calandrino will get tipsy and then we can't go wrong, because he's on his own in the house.'

They did just as Bruno suggested. Calandrino, finding the priest wouldn't let him pay for a thing, drank a great deal more than was good for him, and supper time came and went. It was pretty late before he finally left the inn, and stumbled home. He thought he had locked the door, but in fact he went to bed leaving it open. Buffalmacco and Bruno went back to the priest's for dinner. After the meal they armed themselves with some tools for breaking into Calandrino's house, as Bruno had planned. They approached noiselessly. Finding the door open, in they went, unhooked the pig and bore it off to victory. Having safely stowed it away, they retired to bed. Next morning when Calandrino had at last slept off the wine fumes, he got up and went downstairs—but couldn't see a sign of his pig. Finding the door open he questioned absolutely everybody, but no one had any idea what had happened to it. This upset him dreadfully and he sobbed:

'Oh! Oh! It's just my luck to have a pig pinched.'

Meanwhile, Buffalmacco and Bruno had also got up. They strolled up to hear if he would mention the pig. As soon as he saw them, he called out almost in tears:

'Oh! Oh! Friends, my pig's been pinched.'

Bruno came very close and said under his breath:

'Well, I do believe you're doing the sensible thing for once.'

'But it's absolutely true,' moaned Calandrino.

'That's right, old fellow,' said Bruno. 'Cry it on the roof-tops, so that everyone knows.'

Calandrino raised his voice and shouted:

'God rot me, it's the truth—my pig *has* been stolen.'

'All right,' said Bruno, 'but louder, louder, man. Shout and make yourself heard, and then they'll all believe it.'

'You're enough to drive a man mad,' yelled Calandrino. 'I'm telling you—I'm not joking! I swear to God the pig's been pinched. It's more than flesh and blood can stand.'

'No? But how could that have happened? I saw it yesterday with my own eyes. Do you expect me to believe it's grown wings and flown away?'

'It's gone, all the same.'

'It can't have!'

'Oh yes it has,' answered Calandrino. 'I'm scuppered. I daren't go home. My wife would never believe me. And if she did, she'd make my life hell for I don't know how long.'

'My word, this is a nasty business—if that's what really has happened,' said Bruno. 'But remember it was only yesterday I advised you to pretend this had occurred. I wouldn't like to think you were pulling our legs as well as your wife's.'

'Ah!' screamed Calandrino. 'Do you want to drive me mad, or make me blaspheme against God and all the saints of heaven? I tell you someone took the pig during the night.'

'Well, in that case,' soothed Buffalmacco, 'we must try and find a way of getting it back.'

'Find a way?' asked Calandrino. 'But how?'

'Well, we can rule out someone from India having come to pinch the pig. It must be one of the neighbours. If you could get them all together, I bet I could do my experiment with the bread and cheese and find out in a jiffy who's got your pig.'

'Yes,' Bruno chipped in, 'do your bread and cheese experiment on the local worthies. One of them's bound to be our man! But don't be silly, they'd smell a rat a mile off, and wouldn't come.'

'What's to be done, then?' asked Buffalmacco.

'You'll have to get some strong ginger pills and a good

white wine; and ask them for a drink. They won't suspect a thing—and they'll come. The ginger pills can be blessed just as well as bread and cheese.'

'Of course! You're quite right,' agreed Buffalmacco. 'What do you say to that, Calandrino? Shall we try Bruno's suggestion?'

'For God's sake do try it,' said Calandrino. 'It would certainly give me some consolation just to know who had the pig.'

'All right,' said Bruno. 'I'll volunteer to fetch the ingredients from Florence, if you'll give me the money.'

Calandrino handed over the forty-odd shillings he had on him. Bruno set off to visit a friend of his in Florence who was a chemist. He bought a pound of quality ginger pills, and added a couple of dog-powders blended with sugar-coated liver pills made of fresh aloe. He put a tiny mark on these so they'd be recognizable and not get muddled up with all the rest. Then he bought a flask of good white wine and returned to the farm with his equipment.

'Tomorrow morning,' Bruno announced to Calandrino, 'you're going to ask all the suspects in for a drink. As it's a saint's day they'll come, sure enough. Tonight Buffalmacco and I are going to say the spell over the pills, and I'll bring them you in the morning. I think it would be only friendly on my part to serve it out and say and do the necessary.'

Calandrino took this advice, and next morning there was quite a gathering round the elm in front of the church. It included young Florentines down visiting, the locals, and Bruno and Buffalmacco who arrived with a box of ginger and a wine flask and proceeded to group the company in a circle. Then Bruno addressed them:

'Gentlemen, I ought first to explain why you've been asked, so that if anything nasty happens, you can't say I didn't warn you. The night before last Calandrino here had a fine pig pinched, and he can't find out who stole it. As the thief must be one of us now present, he wants you all to take a pill and drink some of this white wine. I'll tell you here and now that whoever has taken the pig won't be able to swallow his pill. He'll spit it out like poison. So to avoid anyone being made a public exhibition of, it would be far

better if the thief went and confessed to the priest; then
we could wash our hands of the whole business.'

Everybody was quite happy to take the test, so Bruno
arranged them all (including Calandrino) in a row, and
starting at one end, handed a pill to each of them. When
he got to Calandrino he picked one of the throat scorchers
and passed it to him. Calandrino put it in his mouth and
started chewing. The taste of the aloe was so unbearably
bitter that he spat it out. Everybody had his eyes glued to
his neighbour, watching for him to spit his pill out. Bruno
was still dealing them out with pretence of great absorption,
when he heard a voice behind him say :

'Here, what's going on, Calandrino?'

He whipped round and saw that Calandrino had spat
out his pill.

'Wait a minute,' he said, 'perhaps it was something else
which stopped you swallowing it. Have another.'

With that he whisked out the other bitter pill and shoved
it in Calandrino's mouth. Then he went on serving them
out. Calandrino may have found the first one sharp, but
this one tasted ten times fouler. He didn't dare spit it out
though, but went on chewing it, with giant tears rolling
down his cheeks. Finally, he couldn't bear it any longer and
it went the way of the first. Buffalmacco and Bruno were
by now distributing the wine, but they and everyone else
saw Calandrino's reaction. It was now obvious to everyone
that Calandrino had committed the theft himself, and he
came in for a good deal of abuse. When the party had
broken up and Calandrino was left alone with his two
friends, Buffalmacco began:

'I knew you had it all the time, and were trying to kid
us you'd had it pinched, and so avoid having to buy us a
single drink from your proceeds.'

Calandrino swore bitterly (thanks to the taste of aloes)—
that he hadn't got it.

'Now come on, old fellow,' insisted Buffalmacco. 'Tell us
in confidence how much it fetched. Six?'

Calandrino was on the verge of collapse, but Bruno
added:

'Now be reasonable, Calandrino. One of the fellows who

was eating and drinking with us told me you kept a girl down here for a bit of fun, and that you give her whatever you can spare. He reckoned you must have sent her the pig. That's the sort of game you play better than anyone . . . You think if you swear hard enough we'll believe in that so-called stolen pig—which you either sold or gave away. But we know you from experience—you can't fool us that way again. Not to beat about the bush, that spell cost us a good deal of trouble, and if you don't give us a couple of chickens each your Tessa will hear the whole story.'

Calandrino saw he would never be believed. He thought he had quite enough to put up with without adding his wife's fury, so he handed over the four chickens. Back to Florence went Buffalmacco and Bruno with their chickens, and a salted pig, leaving Calandrino out of pocket and down in the mouth.

Tenth day: third tale

THE NOBLEST MAN IN THE WORLD

ACCORDING to the Genoese and others who have travelled in that area, a fabulously wealthy lord called Nathan used to live in Cathay. His estate lay on the road used by travellers between east and west. Nathan was a naturally generous man and liked entertaining. He employed many skilled craftsmen to build and lavishly furnish a huge and most magnificent palace. It was equipped to give the noblest visitors a royal reception. He employed a vast and efficient staff, and all his guests were treated with great courtesy. This paragon of generosity became well known not only in the east but through much of the west as well. It was when Nathan was getting on in life (though that didn't make him any less hospitable) that his reputation reached the ears of Mitridanes. This young man knew he was quite as well off as Nathan, and he envied the other man's celebrity. He made up his mind to destroy or at least weaken Nathan's reputation, by proving himself to be still more generous. He built a palace on the model of Nathan's, and entertained all comers on an unheard of scale. Soon he too was well known.

Mitridanes happened to be alone in his palace court-yard one day. A poor woman came in through one of the gates to beg, and he gave her something. But she wasn't satisfied, returned through a second gate and begged again. Mitridanes gave her something more, and this was repeated twelve times. The thirteenth time Mitridanes said:

'You certainly stick to it,' but he gave her something all the same.

'Ah!' cried the old woman. 'Now *Nathan's* a really generous man. His palace has thirty-two gates and I came through each of them and begged, but he never let on he recognized me and he never refused me. Here I've only come in thirteen times, and I've been recognized and told off already.'

Then away she went and never came back.

Mitridanes regarded the mere mention of Nathan as a personal slight, and the old woman's words infuriated him. He said to himself:

'Oh, how can I ever hope to rival Nathan, let alone improve on him as I'd like to, when I can't even touch him in little things like this? It's obviously no use my trying, unless I can get rid of him. As he shows no signs of dying, I shall have to take action myself.'

Still boiling with indignation, he jumped up, and without telling anyone his intention, set off with a small retinue. Three days later they reached Nathan's palace. Mitridanes told his companions to dissociate themselves from him entirely, to find lodgings wherever they could, and await further instructions. Left to himself, he accidentally came across Nathan near the magnificent palace. Nathan was out on a solitary walk, very inconspicuously dressed, so Mitridanes didn't recognize him and asked if he knew the way to Nathan's house.

'My boy,' said Nathan cheerily, 'none better; if you like I'll take you there myself.'

Mitridanes thanked him, but mentioned his desire not to meet Nathan personally.

'Well if that's what you want,' said Nathan, 'I can arrange that too.'

Mitridanes got off his horse, and he and Nathan walked to the palace, thoroughly enjoying each other's conversation. Once there, Nathan called a servant to relieve Mitridanes of his horse, and told the lad in a whisper to make sure that no one in the house gave him away to the visitor. His incognito was preserved. Mitridanes was given a splendid room in the palace undisturbed by anyone except the servants delegated to look after him. Nathan kept him company and lavished everything on him. Mitridanes came to think of him almost as a father, but he couldn't help wondering who he was.

'I'm just one of Nathan's servants,' was the reply, 'I've

been with him most of my life, but despite my ripe age, he's never promoted me higher than my present position. Even though everyone else speaks highly of him, I've got nothing to thank him for.'

This complaint gave Mitridanes some hope of carrying out his evil scheme more systematically and with less risk. When Nathan asked him politely who *he* was, and why he was there, and offered him whatever help and advice he could give, Mitridanes hesitated a little, but finally decided to take the old man into his confidence. With much beating about the bush and appeals to secrecy, he asked his advice and assistance. Then he revealed his own identity, and his motive in coming. Though Mitridanes' unpleasant revelation shocked Nathan deeply, he soon controlled himself enough to reply calmly:

'Your father was a man of honour, Mitridanes, and you're proving a worthy son in this noble mission of showing hospitality to all comers. I also congratulate you on envying Nathan's goodness. If there were others who felt like you, this miserable world would be a great deal happier. Never fear, I'll keep the secret you have confided to me, but I can't give you much practical help, only good advice. What I suggest is this : about half a mile from here there's a small wood, where Nathan takes his exercise nearly every morning. It'll be only too easy for you to find him there and deal with him as you please. If you kill him, you're far more likely to reach home unmolested if you take not the path you came on, but the one you'll see leading out of the wood on the left. It's rougher, but more direct and less risky for you.'

As soon as Nathan had given this information and left, Mitridanes secretly got in touch with his companions, who were also guests in the palace, and told them where to meet him next day. When the time came Nathan had made up his mind to behave in exactly the way he had described to Mitridanes. He set off for the little wood alone, to meet his death. Meanwhile Mitridanes got up, took his bow and sword (the only weapons he had with him), mounted his horse and rode to the wood. From some distance he could make out the solitary figure of Nathan walking through the trees. Mitridanes wanted to see the face and hear the voice of his victim before attacking him. Seizing the ribbon on his hat, he shouted:

'You're a dead man, grandad.'

Nathan's only reply was:

'Then I must have deserved it.'

Hearing the voice and inspecting the face, Mitridanes at once recognized the old man who had been so welcoming and friendly, and so scrupulous in his advice. His fury evaporated, and he was deeply ashamed. He threw down the sword which had been ready-drawn for the attack, vaulted from his horse and flung himself at Nathan's feet, saying through his tears:

'Dear father, your generosity is unequalled. When I think of the cunning way you engineered my finding you here—and the way you gave yourself up—though you knew for a fact I was determined to kill you, for no reason at all. God, however, knew my duty, when I neglected it myself, and at the crucial moment he opened my eyes which had been blinded by jealousy. Your readiness to give me satisfaction should make me more ashamed than ever of my crime towards you. Take your revenge on me in whatever way I've deserved.'

But Nathan raised Mitridanes to his feet, and threw his arms around him:

'My boy,' he said, 'call your action what you will, good or bad, it certainly doesn't call for any apology from you or pardon from me. You weren't acting with any malice, but in a desire to be more highly thought of than I. Don't be afraid of me. Rest assured no one on earth loves you as whole-heartedly as I do. I know how high-minded you are, not keen on increasing your wealth crookedly, but on distributing what you've got generously. Don't be ashamed of having tried to kill me to increase your own reputation. And don't think I'm surprised. The greatest kings and the most powerful emperors have increased their territory and hence their reputation almost entirely through killing; not just one man, as you were intending, but great numbers through devastating whole countries by fire; and through demolishing cities. So if you wanted to increase your reputation by killing me, there was nothing remarkably odd about that—it's common.'

Mitridanes for his part made no attempt to excuse his vile plot, but only blessed Nathan for providing him with such an apologia. He admitted his astonisment at Nathan's not only letting the plan go so far, but even giving helpful advice. But Nathan answered:

'My giving advice and assent shouldn't suprise you, Mitridanes, for from the moment I was my own master and was pledged to the same mission as you are, I have given anybody who entered my house whatever he desired, to the best of my ability. You came wanting to take my life, and when you asked me for it, I immediately decided to give it you. I didn't want you to be the only guest to leave my house dissatisfied. I therefore gave you the best advice I could for killing me, and surviving yourself. So I ask you once again, I implore you, to kill me if you feel like it. I cannot think of a better way of dying. I have had eighty years' very satisfactory use of my life. As is the way of the world, I shan't have it for much longer of course. So I think it would be a far better idea to give it away, as I've always done with my money, rather than keep it until it's snatched from me willy-nilly. A present of a hundred years would not be very generous, so the six or eight years which is all I've got to offer are a mere nothing. Take it, then, if you want it, do please take it. In my whole career here, I've never found anyone else who wanted it. I don't know where I'll find anyone else interested, if you won't take it. And even if I did find somebody, I'm afraid the longer I keep it the less it's worth. So do take it, I beg you, before it depreciates in value.'

Cut to the quick, Mitridanes answered:

'God forbid that I should think of such a thing now, as I once did; let alone do anything to shorten a life that's precious. Why I would far rather add my own years to yours.'

Nathan answered quickly:

'So you would like to lengthen my life, and by putting me in your debt, you'd prove the exception to my rule of never taking anything from anybody.'

'Indeed I would,' replied Mitridanes.

'Then do as I tell you,' added Nathan. 'You're young—stay in my house and call yourself Nathan. I'll go to your house and call myself Mitridanes.'

'If only I dared take on such a responsibility,' answered Mitridanes, 'I'd have no hesitation in accepting your offer. But I'm perfectly certain that anything I did would damage Nathan's reputation. As I'm not prepared to spoil in somebody else what I can't rise to myself, I shan't accept.'

After they had talked on in this way amicably Nathan invited Mitridanes to the palace. Nathan entertained him royally for several days, and his good advice helped to strengthen Mitridanes' high sense of mission. Afterwards Mitridanes parted from his host and set off for home with his companions, firmly convinced that no one could rival Nathan's generous nature.

Eighth day : second tale

THE PESTLE AND MORTAR

In the village of Varlungo, not far from here, as of course
you all know yourselves, lived a good priest who was a great
ladies' man. He wasn't much of a scholar but he never ran
short of pious tags and lavished them on his flock every
Sunday under an elm tree. When the men were at work, he
visited their wives with the best will in the world, took
fairings, holy water, an odd bit of candle now and again,
and gave them his blessing. Among his attractive
parishioners, the one whose house he particularly enjoyed
visiting was Belcólore's. She was the wife of a labourer
called Bentivegna del Mazzo, and was a buxom and sexy
girl, brown as a berry, plump as a bird, the best possible
grist to the reverend's mill. She had the added accomplish-
ments of being able to play the tambourine, and sing *The
water runs in the ravine* . . . and dance a better round or
reel than any other woman in the district (with a pretty
little handkerchief in her hand). This so bewitched our reverend, that he became delirious and did nothing but wander round the village all day on the off-chance of seeing
her. If he sighted her in church on a Sunday morning, he'd
put everything he'd got into singing the *Kyrie* and *Sanctus*
in the grand manner—the effect was rather like a donkey
braying. If he saw she weren't there, on the other hand, he
hardly bothered at all. Nevertheless he was so secretive
about his love, that neither Bentivegna nor any of the
neighbours guessed a thing.

In the hope of ingratiating himself with Belcolore he
sent her occasional presents—sometimes a bunch of the best
garlic for miles, which came from his own garden, tended
by his own fair hands; perhaps a basket of beans or peas;
a bunch of onions or shallots. He used to pick his moment,
give her the glad eye, and flirt a little. She pretended to be

a country bumpkin and not to understand. Belcolore kept her distance and the reverend got absolutely nowhere.

Now one day the priest happened to be wandering aimlessly round the village at midday when he met Bentivegna with a loaded-up donkey. The reverend greeted him and asked where he was off to.

'Why, I'm off to town, sir, to settle a few bits of business. I'm taking this stuff to old Buonaccorri da Ginestreto, so he'll defend me in some case, because the magistrate sent his proctor to serve me a perempt—a contemporary summons.'

'Good work, my boy,' cried the priest jubilantly. 'Blessings on you. Good luck and come back soon. And listen, if you meet Lapuccio or Naldino, don't forget to remind them about the straps for my thresher.'

Bentivegna promised to do this and jogged off towards Florence. The reverend thought the moment was ripe for a visit to Belcolore, to try his luck. Away he dashed, and when he got there, called out:

'Blessings on this house—who's at home?'

Belcolore called from up in the loft:

'Welcome, Father, what are you doing, wandering about in this heat?'

'God bless me, I've only just come to keep you company a bit, because I met your husband on his way to town.'

Belcolore came to join him, sat down and began sifting the cabbage seed her husband had just threshed. After a little pause the reverend began:

'Belcolore, you'll be the death of me.'

She giggled and asked:

'Why, what have I done?'

'Why nothing at all,' he answered, 'but you won't let me do what I long for and God ordains.'

'Get away with you!' replied Belcolore. 'Do priests do that sort of thing?'

'Indeed we do,' cried he. 'Far and away better than anyone else. We're harder workers, and shall I tell you why? We've got more to offer, because we don't do it so often. In fact I'll make it worth your while to keep quiet and let me get on with it.'

'Worth my while,' she cried. 'How do you make that out? Why, you're all a lot of crooks.'

'Tut! Tut! I wouldn't say that,' he answered. 'You've only got to mention what you'd like. Would you fancy a smart pair of shoes? Or a hair band? Or a gay ribbon, perhaps? What do you say to that?'

'Why, I've got plenty of that stuff,' she answered. 'But if you're so keen, you could do me a favour, then I'd be at your service.'

'Say the word. I'll willingly do it.'

'Well I've got to go to Florence on Saturday to deliver some wool I've spun, and get my spinning wheel put right. If you could lend me five pounds—I'm sure you've got it—I could get my dark purple petticoat and my best Sunday belt (which I've had since I was married) out of pawn. You see without them I can't go to church or anywhere. After that I'll do anything you want, most willingly.'

'Bless my soul,' said the reverend. 'I haven't the money on me, but don't worry, I'll see you have it before Saturday, all right.'

'Oh yes,' scoffed Belcolore. 'You're flush enough with your promises, but you don't ever stick to them. You think you can treat me like Biliuzza, who you dropped like hot cakes. Oh, no you don't. That's what sent her on to the streets. If you haven't got the money on you, you can go straight home and get it.'

'Please don't make me go directly. You see I got here at just the right moment, when the coast was clear. It might not be so convenient another time, and somebody might interrupt us.'

She only answered:

'It's up to you. If you're going, go: if not, you can stay exactly where you are.'

The reverend could see he wasn't going to get what he wanted gratis, and he wouldn't win his case if he didn't go bail for something. So he changed his tack:

'Now look here,' he said. 'You don't trust me to bring the money. To set your mind at rest, I'm going to leave you my cloak as a pledge—you can see what good blue silk it is.'

She looked up and inspected the cloak.

'What's it worth?' she asked.

'Worth!' he gasped. 'Let me tell you it's pure cashmere, if not double cashmere. Some people would say it's quadruple. Why, I bought it less than a fortnight ago from Lotto, the second-hand dealer for a good seven quid. Even then, according to Buglietto, who's an authority as you know, I got it five bob cheap.'

'Oh, you don't say?' cried Belcolore. 'My word, who'd have thought it. Let's have a look at it.'

The priest was quick on the draw. He whipped off the cloak and handed it over. When she had stowed it away safely she said:

'Now, Father, let's go to the barn; no one's likely to disturb us there.'

And off they went. The reverend smothered her in kisses, improved her relationship with the Almighty, and enjoyed himself with her for a considerable time.

Then home he went in nothing but a cassock, as though on his way from taking a wedding ceremony. Back in church, it struck him that a whole year's offerings in candles didn't amount to more than two pounds ten. He felt he had been overcharged at five pounds, kicked himself for pledging his cloak, and racked his brains for some way of getting it back without paying up. He was no fool, and soon hit on a clever way of managing it. The day after was a saint's day and he sent the boy next door round to Belcolore, asking to borrow her stone mortar. He said Binguccio dal Poggio and Nuto Buglietti were lunching with him that day, and he wanted to make them a sauce. Belcolore sent him the mortar, and when lunchtime came and the priest reckoned Bentivegna and Belcolore would be in the middle of their meal, he summoned his clerk:

'Take this mortar back to Belcolore,' he told him. 'Thank her very much from me and ask for the cloak back which the lad left as a deposit this morning.'

The clerk took the mortar back to Belcolore's, and found the couple at their meal. He put down the mortar and delivered the priest's message. Belcolore was about to protest, but Bentivegna threw her a filthy look and said:

'So you are demanding a deposit from the reverend now.

By Christ I've got a good mind to clout you one. Give him it back at once, damn you. And in future, you see he's given whatever he has a fancy to—even our donkey.'

Belcolore got up with a very bad grace and went to the cupboard, took out the cloak and handed it to the clerk.

'Tell your master from me, I hope to God he never grinds sauce in my mortar again, after this bit of dirty work.'

The clerk returned with the cloak and gave his master the message, to the latter's great amusement.

'Tell her when you next see her,' he said, 'that if she won't lend me her mortar, I won't lend her my pestle. It's tit for tat.'

Bentivegna ignored his wife's remark, thinking it was provoked by his scolding. Belcolore, however, was thoroughly annoyed with the priest, and didn't speak a word to him until the grape-harvest. Then, what with her terror of the Devil, who the priest threatened would swallow her whole, and the new wine and roast chestnuts he sent her, she finally relented. They often enjoyed each other after that. Though she never extracted her five pounds, he did recover her tambourine, and fitted a new bell to it—and that was some consolation.

Seventh day : second tale

SCRAPING THE BARREL

NOT many years ago there lived in Naples a poor stone-mason who married an attractive and lively girl called Peronella. She eked out her husband's meagre income at the spinning wheel, so they just managed. One day a city gentleman happened to notice Peronella, found her very striking, and fell in love with her. By various devices he very soon succeeded in making her his mistress. They had arranged the following system for meeting each other. As the husband habitually got up early to go to work or to look for a job, the lover used to watch for him to leave the house. They lived in Avorio Street, which was not very busy, so it was easy for the gentleman to be on the door-step almost the moment he saw the husband leave. This operation was carried out many times. Once, however, the husband had only just gone out and Giannello Sirignario—the lover—joined Peronella, than the fellow returned, whereas he was usually out all day. As the door was fastened, he knocked and said to himself:

'Eternal thanks to God that though I am poor, the Lord has recompensed me with a good, faithful little wife. When I'm away she locks the door so that no one can come and disturb her.'

Peronella recognized her husband's knock and cried:

'Oh dear, I'm done for, Giannello. Here's my husband—damn him. He's come back! I don't know what it means, for he doesn't usually return at this time. Perhaps he caught sight of you coming in. Anyway for God's sake get into the barrel you can see over there. I'll go and open the door and see what's brought him home so early.'

So Giannello jumped into the barrel and Peronella went to the door and dourly let her husband in, saying:

'This is indeed a surprise, having you back so early. By

the look of it you're taking a day's holiday, for I see you've brought your tools. If so, what are we supposed to live on? What are we going to do for bread? Am I expected to pawn my dress and the few oddments I've still got? I work my fingers to the bone spinning day and night, just so as to give us enough oil to keep the lamp alight. I'm the laughing stock of very woman in the neighbourhood, you know. They're amazed at how hard I work and what I go through. And you come home to laze about when you should be at work.'

At this she broke down and moaned:

'What a God-forsaken miserable life. I was doomed from the very day of my birth. I curse the unlucky day I came to live here. For you I turned down a fine young man (and it wasn't through lack of asking)—and you don't care a rap for the woman you married. Other women at least get some fun out of their lovers. Why everyone else enjoys two or three of them at a time. They give them a good time, and their husbands are none the wiser. But poor me! Because I'm faithful and don't go in for love affairs like that, I get a thoroughly raw deal. I sometimes wonder why I don't follow their example and get myself a lover. Just you listen to me, my man. If I had a mind to do the dirty on you, I could get a man just like that. There are plenty of young men who are struck on me, and are very attentive. I could have any amount of money, clothes and jewellery from them for the asking. But I'm too proud to fall for it. I'm just not that sort. And yet you have the face to come home when you ought to be at work.'

'For God's sake don't get so upset, my dear,' protested her husband. 'Give me credit for knowing what you're worth. Only this morning you've given me an example. I admit I did go out intending to work. But you obviously don't realize any more than I did that today's St Galeone's day, and a public holiday. That's why I came home at this hour. But, do you know, I've found a way of feeding us for over a month. This man with me has just offered to buy our barrel—you know, the one that's been cluttering up the place for ages—for ten bob.'

'Well that only makes matters worse,' replied Peronella.

'You, who are supposed to be a man of the world, and should have some business sense, want to sell a barrel like that for ten bob! Why I'm only a woman and hardly ever venture out of the house, but I got so sick of that thing taking up such a lot of room, that I've just sold it to a fellow for fourteen bob. The very moment you got back, he'd climbed in to see if it was sound.'

Her husband was delighted at this news and said to the man he had brought:

'I'm afraid I can only send you on your way, my friend. As you've heard, my wife's got fourteen shillings for the barrel, whereas you only offered me ten.'

'Fair enough,' said the man, and off he went.

'Well since you're here,' said Peronella to her husband, 'you'd better come and clinch it with the man.'

During this scene, Giannello had been all ears, so as to know what to say, and what not to say. At Peronella's last words, he jumped out of the barrel. Pretending not to know the husband was back, he began:

'Where are you, madam?'

'Here I am,' replied the husband as he came up. 'What do you want?'

'Who are you?' said Giannello. 'I was addressing the lady I had made my offer to for this barrel.'

'Don't worry, you can deal with me. I'm her husband.'

'The barrel seems sound enough,' said Giannello, 'but I think you left the dregs. It's coated with something dry I can't scrape off. I'm not keen to take it until it's been scoured.'

'Why, of course,' agreed Peronella. 'Don't let's quibble over that. My husband'll clean it out.'

'That I will,' he said.

He put down his tools, stripped off his coat, asked for a light and a file, and in a brace of shakes he was in the barrel, scraping away. Peronella, as though keen to watch the work, popped her head and her whole arm into the bung-hole, though it was not very large.

'Scrape there,' she instructed, 'and just there. There's another bit you've left.'

So she stood, giving her husband directions. Giannello,

who hadn't fully satisfied his desire that morning before the
mason's return, saw that he wouldn't have another chance,
and decided to make do with what he could get. So while
Peronella kept the bung-hole blocked, he sidled up behind
her. Just like some wild stallion of the plains mounting a
mare, he took the edge off a very healthy appetite. The
performance reached its climax and Giannello beat a hasty
retreat precisely the moment the husband emerged from the
barrel. Peronella withdrew her head from the bung-hole,
turned to Giannello and said:

'Take this candle, my good man, and see if it's properly
scoured.' Her lover then peered into the barrel, reported his
full satisfaction with its cleanness, paid the husband fourteen shillings, and had the poor man carry the barrel home
for him.

Tenth day: seventh tale

LOVE'S REWARD

At the period when the French were being driven from
Sicily there was a Florentine chemist living in Palermo,
called Bernardo Puccini. He was very well off with only a
single and very attractive daughter of an eligible age. When
King Peter of Aragon was installed as ruler of the island he
and his court celebrated lavishly at Palermo. During the
festivities he put on a joust in the Catalan style, and Bernardo's daughter Lisa happened to be watching from a
window with other ladies. She saw him ride by, and was so
attracted that there and then she fell deeply in love with
him. When the celebrations were over and she was back at
home, Lisa was obsessed by her misplaced and hopeless
love. What distressed her most was her sense of inferiority,
and she knew that there was no chance of her winning him.
For all that, she went on loving the King, but didn't dare
tell anyone for fear of the consequences.

The fact that the King was utterly unaware of her, increased Lisa's suffering immeasurably. Her love grew and
her misery with it, until the poor girl gave way under the
strain and fell ill, wasting away daily like snow melting in
the sun. Her stricken parents did everything they could to
cheer her up and of course consulted doctors—but it was no
use. Her love was so hopeless that she had decided to put
an end to her life.

Now her father had promised that she should have what-
ever she wished for, so she set her heart on informing the
King of her love and her decision to die, before the end.
One day, therefore, she asked her father to summon
Minuccio of Arezzo. At that time Minuccio had a vast re-
putation as a singer and musician, and was a favourite with
King Peter. Her father thought Lisa only wanted to hear
Minuccio play and sing, and he passed on the message. The

musician obligingly came at once, tried to cheer the girl up, and then played his viol and sang some songs. In his attempt to comfort her he only succeeded in adding fuel to the flames of her love. Lisa finally said she would like a moment's private conversation with the musician, and everybody else retired.

'I've picked on you, Minuccio,' she confided, 'because I thought I could rely on you never to breathe a word to anyone, but to give me some help. Please help me. I should tell you, my dear Minuccio, that the day our monarch King Peter held his great celebration, I saw him tilting. He stirred my heart so deeply that my passion for him has reduced me to the state of anguish you see me in. I know how presumptuous it is of me to be in love with a king, but I can't control it, let alone eradicate it from my heart. The agony has become so unbearable that I've decided on death as the lesser evil. I have made up my mind to die. But I couldn't bear to put an end to my life without his having any idea of my love. I can think of no one better suited than you to tell him my position. Please don't refuse my request, for if I know the news has reached him, I shall die at least slightly comforted.'

She was silent after this tearful speech.

Minuccio felt very sorry for the girl and admired her dignity and her fierceness of purpose. Suddenly the finest means of helping her came to him.

'Lisa,' he said, 'I give you my word and you can rely on that. I admire the spirit of a girl who can fall in love with so great a king. I am only too happy to help if you will keep up your spirits. I think that within three days I will be able to tell you something cheering. I'll start here and now without wasting any more words.'

Lisa promised she would not despair. She appealed eagerly to him once more and then let him go. Minuccio went off to Mico of Siena, one of the most skilful versifiers of the period, and persuaded him to write a song describing Lisa's sad fate. Minuccio set the words to suitably soft elegiac music. Three days later he went to the Court and found King Peter still at his meal. He was asked to play something with a lute accompaniment and he sang his new

F

song. The words and music were so beautifully harmonized that the attention of all the courtiers was immediately riveted, and they stood enchanted. The King in particular was moved, and when the music had finished he asked where this song originated, for it was new to him.

'Both the words and music date from the last three days, sir,' explained Minuccio.

The King then asked whom the song referred to.

'That I can't tell you except in secret,' answered the minstrel.

King Peter's curiosity was excited and when the table had been cleared, he bore Minuccio off to a private room. There he was told the whole story just as Minuccio had heard it himself. The King praised the girl to the skies, and felt that someone of such spirit had earned their sympathy. He asked Minuccio to go and cheer her and promised to pay her a visit himself that very evening. Minuccio was delighted to be the bearer of some welcome news and hurried off to Lisa. When they were alone together he told her exactly what had happened, and sang the song, accompanying himself on the viol. Lisa was enormously cheered and her health showed immediate signs of improvement. She waited with passionate anticipation for the hour of her lord's visit, but no one in the house knew of it or guessed her secret.

The King remembered the girl and her beauty clearly, and he thought over several times what Minuccio had said. His naturally generous and kindly nature was profoundly moved. At about six, he mounted his horse and rode off as though just for an outing. When he reached the chemist's house he asked to be shown round Bernardo's magnificent garden. As they were walking he inquired after Lisa and asked whether she was married yet.

'Not yet, sir,' replied Bernardo. 'In fact she has been very ill, but since midday she has picked up amazingly.'

The significance of this recovery was not wasted on the King.

'It would be a terrible shame if such a beautiful creature were lost to us so young,' he said. 'Let's go in and visit her.'

And accompanied only by a few lords and Bernardo, he

went straight to Lisa's room. He approached the bed where she was lying propped up, waiting anxiously for him.

'What does this mean, my dear young lady?' he asked, taking her hand. 'A girl like you ought to be a joy to others, and not be wasting away herself. I beg you for my sake to bear up. Then we'll soon have you well again.'

Lisa was a little abashed at being touched by the man dearest to her in the world, but felt in the seventh heaven. She could not reply at once. Eventually she said:

'Your Majesty, it was the attempt of a weak girl to bear an intolerable burden that brought on this illness. Thanks to your kindness, however, I shall be on my feet again very soon.'

Only the King saw the implication of this speech, and he was more and more struck by the girl. Inwardly he cursed the fate that had ordained she should be a chemist's daughter. He stayed a little longer to cheer her up and then said goodbye.

It was generally considered that the King had been most kind in paying such a compliment to the chemist and his daughter. No girl in love can ever have been more delighted than Lisa. With the return of hope came a quick recovery of her health, and she soon looked even lovelier than before. Meanwhile King Peter had discussed with the Queen the best way of rewarding such devoted love. When she was well again he and a sizeable escort of lords rode to the chemist's home. On reaching the garden His Majesty sent for Bernardo and Lisa. The Queen too arrived with a considerable entourage, and Lisa was presented to her and warmly received. It wasn't long before their Majesties called Lisa over and the King said:

'My dear girl, the deep love that you bear me has made me respect you considerably. I hope that for love of me you will consider accepting this honour. What I propose is this: since you are now of an age to marry I should like you to take a husband of my choice. However, I have every intention of continuing to regard myself as your champion, and as a reward I would demand one kiss.'

Lisa blushed crimson to the roots of her hair, and in her pleasure at the King's request, she replied in a low voice:

'Your Majesty, I'm quite certain that if it were known I had fallen in love with you, I should generally be considered a mad fool who was oblivious of her position and your own. But the Almighty who alone thoroughly understands the workings of human beings, knows that when I lost my heart to you, I was fully aware that you were the King and I was Bernardo the chemist's daughter, and I knew how presumptuous my love was. As you know far better than I, however, nobody falls in love on purpose or rationally, but purely on impulse and emotionally. It is that law which, try as I might, I could not resist. The law made me love you, as I do still, and always shall. Indeed from the moment I knew myself abjectly in love with you, I resolved to make your wishes my command. So I am only too ready to accept whoever you are kind enough to choose for my husband. I would literally go through fire and water at a word from you if you required it. It goes without saying that I am honoured to have a king like you for my champion. But I will only grant you the kiss you asked for as your sole tribute, with Her Majesty's permission. I cannot attempt to repay the enormous kindness you and Her Majesty the Queen have shown to me, but may God reward you amply on my behalf, and grant you His blessing and grace.'

With these words she ended.

The Queen was extremely impressed by the girl's reply and agreed that Lisa was as sensible as the King had claimed. His Highness then summoned Lisa's parents, made quite certain that his plan met with their approval, and sent for a poor, but well-born young man called Perdicone. King Peter presented him with a ring and—as Perdicone was far from objecting—married him to Lisa. Afterwards the Queen presented the bride with a great deal of valuable jewellery, and the King gave the bridegroom two flourishing and rich estates—Ceffalù and Calatabellotta.

'They are your wife's dowry,' said the King. 'Later you'll learn our future plans for you.'

Turning to Lisa, he added:

'And now I intend to collect your love's debt.'

With that he held her face between his hands and kissed her on the forehead.

Everyone—Perdicone, Lisa's parents, and Lisa herself—was overjoyed and the wedding was celebrated with gaiety.

All the traditions agree that the King faithfully kept his promise to Lisa. Throughout his life he described himself as her champion, and in all military competitions he wore only the token she had given him.

It is behaviour such as this that wins the hearts of a king's subjects, offers a fine example, and wins eternal fame. Few if any would be capable of such understanding these days, for most rulers have become cruel and tyrannical.

Seventh day: fourth tale

DOWN THE WELL

ONCE upon a time there lived in Arezzo a wealthy man called Tofano whose wife Ghita was a beauty. On no apparent grounds he soon became desperately jealous of her. She resented this bitterly and several times asked him the reason point blank, but she couldn't pin him down. He just generalized lamely. Finally Ghita made up her mind to give him a fatal dose of the poison he so dreaded. She remembered a thoroughly suitable young man who had made advances to her. With considerable adroitness she came to an understanding with him. Their affair reached the stage when words should give way to action, and Ghita racked her brains to find a way of achieving this. She was quite aware that one of her husband's nastier traits was an overfondness for the bottle. All at once she started approving of it, and even gave him a certain amount of surreptitious encouragement. The result was that almost whenever she felt like it she could get him to overdrink, and when she saw he was thoroughly sozzled she would put him to bed. She and her lover could therefore meet frequently without the slightest risk. In fact she so came to rely on Tofano's drunkenness that instead of smuggling her lover into the house she often went so far as to spend most of the night at the young man's home—for he lived nearby.

The love-sick lady had been carrying on like this for a good time before her injured husband tumbled to the fact that she egged him on to drink, but never touched a drop herself. He began to suspect the truth: that his wife made him drunk so that she could have some fun while he was asleep. In order to test his theory he came home after a completely sober day, imitating the speech and walk of someone thoroughly blotto. Ghita was entirely taken in by this display. She decided there was no need to liquor

Tofano up further and she soon had him tucked up in bed. Then, as usual, off she went to her lover's house and stayed there till midnight.

When Tofano saw his wife had bunked he got up and went to lock the door. Then he took up his position at the window—to watch for her return and tell her the game was up. There he sat until his wife got back to find herself locked out. She was absolutely livid and tried to force the door. Tofano let her struggle for a time and then shouted down:

'It's no use, woman, you can't get in. You'd better go back to wherever you've been these last few hours. You're not darkening my doors again, don't you worry—not until I've given you your deserts in front of your relatives and the neighbours.'

Ghita implored him to let her in. She said she hadn't been doing what he thought—only spending the evening with one of her woman friends. The evenings dragged and she couldn't spend all the time asleep or waiting up alone. But her appeals got her nowhere, because her silly husband was set on broadcasting his disgrace throughout Arezzo, rather than keeping it to himself. Seeing the futility of appealing to him, Ghita started to threaten instead:

'I'll make you wish you'd never been born, if you don't open that door.'

'How do you propose to do that?'

Love had accustomed Ghita to thinking quickly and she answered:

'I'd rather throw myself into that well over there than endure the disgrace you're charging me with so unfairly. They'll only have to fish up my corpse for everyone to think you did it when you were stewed. Then you'll have to abandon all your property, run for it and become a freebooter. Or they'll execute you for murdering me, and you'll be the guilty party all right.'

But even this didn't budge Tofano from his fatuous intention. So finally his wife cried:

'It's no good, I can't stand your cruelty any longer. God forgive you. I'm leaving my distaff here—see you put it away carefully.'

And she went to the well. It was such a pitch-dark night that you could hardly see the nose in front of your face. Ghita picked up a huge boulder from beside the well and yelling: 'God have mercy on me!' dropped it in. Tofano heard the terrific splash as the stone struck the water, and didn't stop to question whether his wife had really thrown herself in. He rocketed out of the house to her rescue, armed with a bucket and a rope. Ghita had hidden near the door, and when she saw him dashing to the well, she was indoors in a flash, locking the door behind her. She went to the window and called to him:

'You should mix your wine with water when you're *drinking,* not try diluting it at this hour of the night.'

This taunt brought Tofano back to the door and finding it locked he ordered her to let him in. Ghita dropped the quiet voice she had kept till then and almost shrieked at him:

'By God, you dirty drunken swine, you're not coming into my house tonight. I'm not standing for it any longer. It's time people knew what sort you are, and the time of night you come home.'

It was Tofano's turn to be furious, and he started bellowing insults at her. The neighbours were woken by the noise, and a great number of heads appeared at windows, asking what was wrong. This reduced Ghita to tears and she moaned:

'It's this bastard. He comes home drunk of an evening, or falls to sleep at the pub, and then wanders back at this hour. I've stuck him long enough, but I couldn't stand it any longer, so as a punishment I locked him out, hoping it'd make him behave himself.'

As for Tofano, the silly idiot babbled out what had actually happened, and cursed his wife violently.

'Listen to that,' Ghita appealed to the neighbours. 'That's the sort he is. I can guess what you'd think if it was me who was outside and him indoors. I bet you'd believe every word he said. So you can see the state he's in. I'll bet it's him who's done just what he's saying I did. He thought he could put the wind up me by throwing something down the well. I wish to God he'd really thrown himself in and drowned. The wine he's drunk himself silly with might have got watered down a bit.'

The neighbours all shouted abuse at Tofano, held him responsible for everything, and told him off volubly for slandering his wife. In fact the din could be heard at such a distance that Ghita's people got wind of the story. They hurried to the scene of the crime and were told the whole truth by any number of neighbours. Tofano was seized and beaten black and blue from head to foot. Then his in-laws went into the house, impounded everything that belonged to Ghita, and bore her off home with them, firing a few parting shots at Tofano.

The poor man was left in despair, bitterly regretting the ill-effects of his jealousy, especially as he was really very fond of his wife. He got some friends to patch up relations and eventually persuaded his wife to pardon him and come back to the house. But he had to promise never to be jealous again. He was to allow her perfect freedom to do what she liked so long as she did it tactfully enough for him not to notice her goings-on. So the silly idiot was beaten and had to sue for peace.

Up with love, and down with meanness and the whole rotten crew who practise it.

Seventh day : seventh tale

THE FAVOURITE SERVANT

You probably know the story of the Florentine gentleman who lived in Paris. Poverty had driven him into trade, and he had done so well that he had become a wealthy man. His wife had borne him a single son, Lodovico. The boy had an aristocratic loathing of commerce, so instead of an apprenticeship his father got him a position at the French Court. There he could mix with gentlemen, perfect his manners, and polish himself. When serving the King one day, Lodovico overheard some other young sparks discussing the ladies of France, England, and elsewhere. Some knights just back from the Holy Land, joined in the conversation. One of them claimed that with all his experience he couldn't think of a lady in the whole world to compare with Lady Beatrice, the wife of Egano de'Galluzzi of Bologna. All the others who had come across her in Bologna agreed with him.

Lodovico was still unattached, and this eulogy fired him with an obsession to set eyes on the lady. So he decided to go to Bologna to see her, and to stay if he liked her. He told his father he was keen to visit the Holy Land and got very reluctant paternal permission.

Having renamed himself Anichino, he set off for Bologna. As luck would have it he saw Beatrice at a party the very day after he got there. She was even more beautiful than he'd expected, and he fell head over heels in love with her. He vowed not to leave Bologna till he had won her love. The best way to set about this, he came to the conclusion, was to get himself employed by her husband. This didn't seem too difficult to arrange because Egano had a considerable staff. So Lodovico sold his horses and billeted his servants, ordering them to cut him if ever they chanced to meet.

He was friendly enough with his host to refer to his desire to enter some nobleman's service.

'You would be ideal for a gentleman here called Egano,' said the host. 'He keeps a large household and likes fellows as presentable as you. I'll mention your name to him.'

And so he placed Anichino, for Egano was only too pleased to employ him. Living in Egano's house gave Anichino ample opportunity of seeing the beautiful Beatrice and making himself useful to her husband. Egano soon relied a great deal on his advice and entrusted him with personal as well as all administrative duties.

One day Egano happened to have gone out hawking, leaving Anichino at home with Beatrice. She had as yet no inkling of his love, though she had occasionally noted his good manners with approval. They sat down to a game of chess together, and Anichino adroitly managed to give her the satisfaction of winning. Beatrice's attendants watched the game for a little but then drifted away, leaving the players to themselves. Suddenly Anichino heaved an enormous sigh. She eyed him and said :

'What's the matter with you, Anichino? Do you mind being beaten by me that much?'

'No, Madam,' he replied. 'I was sighing about something far more serious.'

'Then if I am anything to you,' cried the lady, 'you must tell me the reason.'

At hearing such an appeal from the woman he loved more than anything else in the world Anichino sighed even more deeply. She once again begged him to tell her the cause. So he answered:

'Madam, I'm afraid I may only annoy you by opening my heart. Besides you might mention it to someone else.'

'Rest assured,' replied the lady, 'I shan't be annoyed. And I wouldn't breathe a word to another soul without your permission.'

'With that promise,' said Anichino, 'I'll be frank with you.'

And with tears in his eyes he told her who he was, the account of her he had heard, where and how he had fallen in love with her, and why he had entered her husband's service. Then he begged her to have mercy on him and, if she possibly could, to satisfy his secret and consuming desire. If she weren't prepared to offer him this consolation, he only asked permission to keep his position and love her silently.

What an extraordinary make-up the ladies of Bologna have! How well they rise to the occasion! They're allergic to sighs and tears but are susceptible to persuasion and are not immune from desire. It needs far greater eloquence than mine to describe them as they deserve.

The lady's eyes didn't leave Anichino's face during his speech. She believed every word, and in answer to his appeal she accepted his devotion. She was so moved that she caught his habit, and after several sighs, she replied:

'My dear Anichino, cheer up. I've never been won by presents or promises, nor any man's attentions, whatever his rank (and I've been courted by a good many in my time). But already your few words have moved me so much that I am more yours than I am my own. I think you fully deserve my love. My heart is yours and I promise you will enjoy me before the night is out. So come to my room at about midnight. I'll leave the door open. You know which side of the bed I sleep on. Be there, and if I'm asleep, just touch me and I'll wake up and satisfy your long-hidden desire. Just to show you I'm serious, I'll kiss you here and now."

And with this, she threw her arms round his neck and they kissed each other passionately. After this interview, Anichino went off to see to some job. He looked forward to midnight with rapture.

When Egano came home, he had supper and, as he was tired, went straight to bed. His wife went up not long after, but left her bedroom door open as she had promised. Anichino kept his appointment, entered the room soundlessly, closed the door behind him and crept up to the bed. He laid his hand on her breast and found she was awake. As soon as she felt he was there, she grasped his hand. Keeping a firm hold on him, she turned over in bed and woke Egano. Then she said:

'I didn't want to mention it, dear, because I thought you

looked tired. But tell me, Egano, and be absolutely frank :
Which of your servants do you think is the best, the most
loyal, and the most devoted to you?'

'What a question to ask, dear!' answered Egano. 'You
know as well as I do. Anichino is quite the most trustworthy
servant I've ever had. But, why do you ask?'

As soon as Anichino heard that Egano was awake and
they were discussing him, he struggled to free his hand. He
was in mortal fear that the lady was double-crossing him.
But she held on too hard for him to get away, and she went
on chatting to her husband.

'Let me tell you a thing or two about him. I used to think
he was all you say, and really was devoted to you. But the
scales have fallen from my eyes, because yesterday, when you
went out hawking, leaving him behind, he picked this time
and had the effrontery to make the most improper suggestion to me. So as to have all the evidence I needed to prove
his guilt to you, I pretended to give in. I arranged to be in
the garden tonight just after midnight, and meet him under
the pine tree. I've no intention of being there, but if you
want evidence of devoted loyalty you can easily go yourself.
Just slip on one of my gowns, cover yourself with a veil and
go down and wait for him. I'm sure he'll come.'

'It'd be best for me to go and see,' agreed Egano.

He got up, and groping about in the dark managed to
put on his wife's gown and veil. Off he went to the
garden and sat down under the pine tree to wait for Anichino. As soon as Beatrice had seen him well out of the
room, she got up and locked the door. Anichino had never
been so terrified in his life. He'd tugged as hard as he could
to get out of her grip, and had silently sworn blue murder
at his love and his trusting nature. But he was tickled pink
by the last twist Beatrice had given to events.

Beatrice got back into bed and invited him to strip and
lie down beside her. They enjoyed themselves delightfully
for some time. But when Beatrice thought the moment had
come for Anichino to make himself scarce, she made him
get up and put on his clothes.

'Light of my life,' she said, 'take a heavy stick and go to
the garden. Pretend to mistake Egano for me, and then lash

him with your tongue and your stick, just as though your suggestion to me was only a test. The result will be terrific.'

So off Anichino went to the garden, armed with a willow stick. As he approached the pine, Egano saw him and got up as though coming to welcome him. But Anichino cried:

'Oh, you wicked woman. So you came. Did you really expect me to do the dirty on my master like that? God damn you for it!'

And he lifted his stick and struck out. This was quite enough for Egano, and without saying a word he ran for it. Anichino chased him, shouting:

'Off with you, you wicked woman. Don't worry, I'll tell Egano tomorrow.'

A somewhat battered Egano returned to his bedroom as fast as he could. Beatrice asked him if Anichino had come to the garden.

'I wish to God he hadn't!' he replied bitterly. 'Because he took me for you, heaped abuse on me, and knocked me black and blue as if I'd been the worst sort of whore. I thought it very odd that he should have dishonourable intentions towards you. Clearly, seeing how gay and pretty you were, he just wanted to test you.'

'Then thank God you got the practical examination, and I only had the oral,' said Beatrice. 'I'm sure he'd have to admit I took his words better than you did his actions. But he's so devoted to you, you must show our appreciation by making a fuss of him.'

'How right you are!' agreed Egano.

So Egano's faith both in his wife's fidelity and his servant's was fully confirmed. The three of them had very good laughs over the incident. It enabled Anichino and Beatrice to enjoy each other with much less interference than they would have risked otherwise, for as long as Anichino stayed in Bologna.

Seventh day : third tale

IN LOCO PARENTIS

You'll have heard the tale of the aristocratic young fellow
called Rinaldo who used to live in Siena. He was desperately in love with a very beautiful lady, the wife of a
rich local figure. Rinaldo felt that if he could only
manage to get a private interview, he might stand a chance
with her. As this didn't seem possible, and as she was pregnant, he toyed with the idea of becoming the child's godfather. So he made up to the husband, and mentioned the
matter as diplomatically as he could. The suggestion
worked, and Rinaldo acquired a godchild. He now had a
better excuse for speaking to Agnesa, and he plucked up
courage and told her openly of his feelings. She had guessed
as much long before from the expression in his eyes.
Rinaldo didn't get an inch further with her.

Not long afterwards, for some reason or other, Rinaldo
retired to a friary. Whether he found satisfaction in this
vocation or not, he stuck to it. Needless to say when he became a friar he abandoned his love for Agnesa, along with
all other worldly vanities. As time went by, however, he resumed them, though without discarding his friar's habit. He
thoroughly enjoyed looking elegant, handsome, and well
turned out, composing ballads and songs, singing them and
doing things of that sort . . .

So Brother Rinaldo went back to his old loves, and took
to visiting his lady-love regularly. With growing confidence,
he started imploring her, more urgently than before, to give
him satisfaction. Perhaps Rinaldo had become more attractive, because one day his appeals drove Agnesa into that
fatal position which shows the opponent is tempted to throw
in the sponge.

'Oh, but do friars do things like that, Brother Rinaldo?'
she asked.

'Madam,' he answered. 'When I take off this habit, and that's easy enough, you'll see I'm made the same way as other men, and I'm not a friar.'

With a look of mock horror, she replied:

'Oh dear! Oh dear! You're my child's godfather. How could we? No it would be very wrong. I've often been told how wicked it is. But if it wasn't I'd certainly do what you ask.'

'You'd be very silly to let a thing like that stop you,' said the friar. 'I'm not saying it isn't a sin. But God forgives the worst sins, if you repent. Just tell me: Who has the greater claim to be considered your son's father—I who held him at the font, or your husband who propagated him?'

'My husband,' she answered.

'Quite right,' answered Rinaldo. 'And doesn't he sleep with you?'

'Why, yes.'

'Well then, I'm not such a close relation to your son as he is. So I should be able to sleep with you if he does.'

The lady was no logician and didn't need much encouragement. So she either believed he was telling the truth, or she gave a good imitation.

'How cleverly you argue,' she said.

And Agnesa quickly gave in to him and allowed his function as lover to replace that of godfather. They did not limit themselves to a single performance. Thanks to the friar being a spiritual relation, they were freer and immune from suspicion, so they met constantly. On one occasion Brother Rinaldo came to his mistress' house and caught sight of a very neat and pretty little maid who worked there. He sent his companion off to teach her the Lord's Prayer. Meanwhile he and the lady of the house, leading her small son by the hand, went to the bedroom, locked themselves in, and started making love on the divan there. The time flew and before they knew where they were the husband got home, knocked on the bedroom door and called out to his wife.

'I'm done for,' cried Agnesa. 'My husband's back. Now he's bound to guess why we're so friendly.'

'How right you are,' replied Rinaldo, who was undressed,

with his gown and hood off, in just his underclothes. 'If only I had my hood and gown on it would be different. But if you let him in and he finds me like this, we can't possibly get away with it.'

Then Agnesa had a sudden happy brainwave:

'Put them on,' she said, 'and lift your godson in your arms and follow closely what I say, so that your story tallies. Leave the rest to me.'

The husband went on knocking, and Agnes called back: 'Coming, coming!'

She got up, switched on a smile and went to the door. As she opened it, she said :

'My dear, it's as well that Brother Rinaldo, the child's godfather, came. He's been literally a godsend. Otherwise we'd certainly have lost our boy today.'

The poor fool was devastated by this, and asked what had happened.

'Oh, my dear,' she answered, 'he's just had a sudden fainting fit, and I thought he was dead. I was petrified, but his godfather Rinaldo came at the critical moment and picked him up. "Woman," he said, "he's got worms. They are liable to reach the heart, and then they're only too likely to kill him. But don't worry, I'll repeat a charm that will destroy them all. Before I'm out of the house you'll see your boy as well as ever." But you had to be here for some of the prayers. As the girl didn't know where you were, Rinaldo got his colleague to say the prayers upstairs and I came in here. It's vital for only the child's mother to be present at this ceremony, and we locked the door so as not to be disturbed by anyone. Brother Rinaldo's still holding the baby. I expect he's just waiting for the other friar to finish his prayers, and then we'll be done. The boy's fully recovered already.'

The poor simple soul took all this for gospel truth, and was so anxious for his beloved son, he didn't tumble to his wife's deceit. He sighed with relief and said:

'I'll go and find him.'

'No, don't,' she replied. 'You'd ruin the effect of the charm. Wait here. I'll go and see if it's safe, and then I'll call you.'

Rinaldo had heard every word, and was properly dressed and calm again by this time. He was carrying the baby, and having checked that everything was in order, he called out:

'Didn't I hear your husband's voice out there, woman?'

'Indeed you did, sir,' called the silly ass.

'In you come, then,' said the friar.

'Certainly, sir.'

Then Rinaldo said:

'I give you back your son, cured by the grace of God. I didn't think he would live till this evening. It would be a good idea to get a statue of the boy made in wax, at least life-size. In thanksgiving, place it in front of the image of St Ambrose, through whose favour God has granted this.'

The boy saw his father and ran to welcome him as children do. His father clutched him in his arms, crying as though the boy had been rescued from the grave. By turns he kissed him and thanked the godfather who had cured him.

Rinaldo's fellow friar had by now taught the maid her Lord's Prayer, once if not four times over. A white fabric purse, a present from a nun, had made her his life-long admirer. When he heard Rinaldo summon the husband to the bedroom, he crept near enough to hear and see everything that was going on. Seeing how well it had all been arranged, he came down to the room. 'Brother Rinaldo,' he said, 'I've recited all the four prayers you asked for.'

'Well done, Brother,' answered Rinaldo. 'You must have great stamina. For my part I had only said two when the lady came in. But thanks to our joint efforts God in his goodness has thought fit to heal the boy.'

The silly husband ordered some good wine and sweets. He entertained the godfather and his colleague as royally as their efforts deserved. Then he gave them God's blessing and saw them off the premises. Right on the spot he had the wax statue made, and put it with the others before the shrine of St Ambrose—not of course St Ambrose of Milan, but the other in Siena.

Eighth day : third tale

THE MIRACULOUS STONE

OUR city has always been well provided with cranks, and
not so long ago whe had a painter named Calandrino. This
great hob-nailed ass spent most of his time with his two
fellow-painters called Bruno and Buffalmacco. They were
not cruel but they kept up with him largely because they
got a great deal of cynical enjoyment out of their friend's
crackpot behaviour.

There was another Florentine called Maso del Saggio,
who was as smart as new paint, and full of bright ideas. He
had got to hear about Calandrino's naïvety, and decided to
play a trick on him, by making him believe something
utterly preposterous.

One day he chanced to come across Calandrino in the
Church of San Giovanni gazing intently at the paintings
and intaglio work on the newly erected canopy over the
high altar. Maso thought that it was the perfect time and
place to carry out his scheme. He gave one of his companions the outlines of his plan, and the two of them sidled
up to where the solitary Calandrino was sitting. Pretending
not to see him they embarked on a discussion of the rival
merits of various stones. Maso spoke so knowledgeably you'd
have taken him for a crack jeweller. Calandrino overheard
the conversation, and soon seeing there was nothing secret
about it, got up and joined them—to Maso's great satisfaction. He went on with his lecture, and when questioned
by Calandrino about where some of these precious stones
were found, replied glibly:

'Mostly in the Basque country. It's the Bun-fight area,
where vines are bound up with sausages, and geese cost a
penny, with a gosling thrown in. There's one hill made
entirely of Parmesan cheese; on another the sole diet
is macaroni and ravioli, boiled in chicken broth and then

thrown on the ground in a free-for-all. Not far off there's a stream of white wine, first-class, absolutely undiluted.'

'It does sound an attractive place,' said Calandrino. 'But do tell me, what happens to the boiled chickens?'

'They all get eaten by the Basques,' replied Maso.

'Have you ever been there?' inquired Calandrino.

'Have I ever been there, he asks!' scoffed Maso. 'Why, if I've been there once I've been a thousand times.'

'How many miles away is it?' asked Calandrino.

'Oh more miles than you can count sheep in one whole sleepless night.'

'Further than the Abruzzi, then?'

'Well yes, a bit further,' agreed Maso.

Our simple-minded Calandrino was fully convinced that the story was gospel truth, merely on the strength of Maso's straight face.

'I'm afraid it would be too expensive for me,' he said. 'If it was nearer, I'd certainly come on one of your trips, just to see the macaroni tumbling down and eat my fill of it. But would you be good enough to tell me whether any of those very precious stones can be found around there?'

'Yes, there are two varieties to be found there,' said Maso, 'they both have extraordinary properties. First there's Mount Pleasant and Muswell Hill sandstone used for making millstones for grinding flour. They have a proverb that says "Blessings fall from Heaven, millstones from Muswell Hill." As we have more than enough of this sandstone ourselves we don't value it. It's just the same with them and their vast mountains of emeralds—bigger than Brighton Rock—which, I swear, shine at night. And I'll tell you this: If you can cut two flawless millstones and set them in a ring without drilling a hole in them, and take them to the Sultan, he'll give you anything you care to name. The other type of stone is what we jewellers call heliotrope, and it has marvellous properties. Whoever has it on him, for as long as he keeps it, is utterly invisible to everyone else— wherever he doesn't go.'

'That's terrific,' said Calandrino, 'but where do you find this second stone?'

Maso answered that there were usually some to be found in the Mugnone area.

'What about its size and colour?' questioned Calandrino.

'The size varies, some are bigger than others, some smaller; but they're all the same colour, practically black.'

Having made a mental note of all these particulars, Calandrino pretended to have an appointment, and parted from Maso fully intending to go in search of the stone. First, however, he had to tell his cronies, Buffalmacco and Bruno, his plan. So as not to waste valuable time, he put everything else on one side. Eager to start on his mission on the spot, he set out to look for them and spent the whole morning at it. Eventually, when it was already afternoon, he remembered that they'd be working in the convent at Faenza. Even the devastating heat did not deter him, and off he went almost at the double. As soon as he'd found them and attracted their attention, he burst out :

'Friends, if you listen to me, we're in a position to become the richest men in Florence. I have it from a very reliable source that in the Mugnone there's a stone which makes its owner invisible to anyone else in the world. So I think we ought to set off at once and not let anyone else get a start on us. We're bound to find it, because I know what it looks like. When we've got it, all we need do is visit the money-lenders' desks which are always thick with cash, as you know, and help ourselves to whatever we fancy. No one will be able to see us, so before you can say Jack Robinson we'll be rich and won't need to go on leaving our marks on walls all day, like a lot of snails!'

Bruno and Buffalmacco laughed up their sleeves at this, glanced at each other out of the corner of their eyes, and pretended that Calandrino's plan flabbergasted but convinced them. Buffalmacco happened to ask the name of the stone, but his dim-witted informant had already forgotten its name.

'What does the name matter?' he said airily. 'It's what it does that counts. I think we ought to start looking for it without wasting further time.'

'All right, all right,' said Bruno, 'but what about its size and shape?'

'They're all sizes and shapes,' answered Calandrino. 'But they're all the same colour—practically black. So I think we'd better collect all the black stones we see until we strike lucky. Let's be off, and not muck about any longer.'

'Now wait a minute,' said Bruno. Turning to Buffalmacco he added: 'I think Calandrino is on to a good idea, but this doesn't seem a good time to start. The sun's high and it's shining into the Mugnone, drying up all the stones, so that ones which are black in the early morning before the sun's rays strike them will look white. Another thing: to-day's a working day and there'll be plenty of people about in the Mugnone, what with one thing and another. If they see us they're bound to tumble to what we're up to and they'll do the same. So they might find the stone and we should have been pipped at the post. Don't you agree, we ought to start in the morning when it will be much easier to tell the black stones from the white; and on a holiday, so that we shan't be seen?'

As Buffalmacco supported Bruno, Calandrino had to agree. They all three arranged to meet the Sunday morning after and to hunt for the stone. Home went Calandrino, having exhorted his friends to keep the matter completely to themselves, as it had been told him in the strictest confidence. Before going he also told them all about the land of Bun-Fight, and swore to the truth of the story.

His two friends worked out a plan of campaign together, while Calandrino waited on tenterhooks for Sunday morning.

When the day came, Calandrino was up at dawn and called on the others. They set off through the San Gallo Gate, to comb the Mugnone for the stone. Calandrino, naturally enough, led the way, bounding from rock to rock, stooping, picking up and stowing away in the fold of his shirt every black stone he saw. The other two followed, picking up an odd stone here and there. It wasn't long before Calandrino filled his shirt, so he hitched up his generously cut gown, fastened it under his leather belt, and started filling this roomy new pocket. It was soon crammed and he did the same with his cloak.

When Bruno and Buffalmacco saw that Calandrino was

weighed down, and that it was high time for a meal, they put their plan into operation.

'Where's Calandrino?' Bruno asked Buffalmacco.

Though Calandrino was in front of his very nose, Buffalmacco made a complete circle, looking for him high and low.

'I don't know,' he replied, 'but he was in front of us just a minute ago.'

'Just a minute ago!' answered Bruno. 'If you ask me he's at home by now eating his lunch, leaving us in the Mugnone on this wild goose chase after black stones.'

'Well I suppose we were just asking to be taken for a ride and then dropped, when we fell for his cock and bull story,' said Buffalmacco. 'Trust us to be damned fools enough to believe there's a stone as powerful as that to be found in the Mugnone.'

On hearing this conversation Calandrino at once imagined he was holding the stone in his own hands, and that he was invisible to the others, thanks to the stone's power. He was cock-a-hoop at this stroke of luck, and decided not to give himself away but to go straight home. So he turned on his heel.

Buffalmacco noticed and said:

'What are we waiting for? Let's go home as well.'

'All right,' said Bruno, 'but I swear to God I shan't let Calandrino pull one on me like that again. In fact if he were still as near us as he's been all morning, he'd get a stone from me and he wouldn't forget this little jaunt in a hurry.'

Suiting his action to his words, he hurled a stone and hit Calandrino on the leg. Though it hurt, Calandrino leapt in the air, gasped slightly, and walked on without another sound. Then Buffalmacco carefully selected a stone from his collection and cried:

'Look at this splendid stone—if only I could land it on Calandrino's behind, Bruno.'

And he chucked it at the retreating figure with all his strength. In fact on one excuse or another they stoned Calandrino all the way up the Mugnone to the San Gallo Gate. There they threw away what remained of their stones and paused to chat with the guards. These officers were splitting their sides, for they had let Calandrino through the gate unimpeded.

Calandrino walked straight to his house not far from San Lorenzo. As luck would have it, not a soul addressed a word to him all the way along the river and across the town. In fact he met scarcely anybody, for they were all at lunch.

The moment he got home with his stones his wife Tessa popped her head over the banisters and saw him. She was annoyed and told him off for being late.

'Why the devil are you so late? I had to keep the meal hot for you long after everyone had finished.'

When Calandrino heard her he came down to earth with a bang, and was livid at not being invisible.

'Oh damn you woman, it's all your fault,' he bellowed. 'You've ruined me. By God I'll get you for this.'

And he was upstairs in a flash, had dropped his quarry-load of stones in the parlour, and rushed at his wife. He caught hold of her hair, hurled her to the floor, and punched and kicked every inch of her, as hard as he could. Not a single portion of her body escaped him—wringing her hands and begging for mercy got her nowhere.

When Buffalmacco and Bruno had finished laughing over their joke with the guards at the gate, they went on slowly, following Calandrino at a respectable distance. They could hear the row as he thrashed his wife black and blue. Pretending to have just arrived on the scene they called out to him. A very red-faced Calandrino appeared puffing and sweating at the window and invited them up. They switched on a sullen look and came upstairs. There in the middle of the parlour sat the master surrounded by stones. He had undone his buttons and was breathing heavily from over-exertion. In one corner lay his wife, sobbing bitterly, her hair bedraggled, her clothes in tatters, and her battered and bruised face the colour of lead. Buffalmacco and Bruno looked round the room and then said:

'What is going on, Calandrino? Are you aiming to build a wall with this vast number of stones?'

There was no answer so they went on:

'And what's this? However did Madam Tessa get into

this condition? It looks as if you've been beating her up. What has been going on?'

The weight of his load of stones, the frenzied activity of beating his wife, and his depression at the collapse of his scheme made Calandrino too fagged to utter a sound. At that Buffalmacco's voice took on a bullying tone:

'However livid you were about something else, Calandrino, you didn't have to play us a dirty trick like that. Dragging us off with you to look for that precious stone, and then skulking off without a word and leaving us looking like a pair of idiots in the Mugnone. We don't take it too well, and it's the last time you pull one like that on us, don't you worry!'

Calandrino pulled himself together and answered:

'Please don't be angry with me, friends. It didn't happen like that at all. Curse my luck! I found the stone. Listen, I'll prove it to you. When you started saying to each other: "Where's Calandrino?" I was ten yards away. When I realized you were passing without being able to see me, I went on ahead, kept a little in front and got home.'

Then he proceeded to tell them the whole story: everything they had said and done from the start, and he showed them where the stones had bruised him on the leg and behind.

'And what's more,' he added, 'though I was weighed down with all the stones you can see, the guards at the gate didn't say a word when I came in—and you know what a nuisance they can make of themselves—they're so hot on examining everything. On my way too I passed several old friends who always say hullo and offer me a drink, but none of them said a word, not a syllable. They just walked past as though they hadn't seen me. When I eventually got home that blasted woman—damn her—met me. You know how none of that magic can stand up to a woman. The luckiest man in Florence and it had to come to that. I thrashed her till my strength failed. I don't know why I didn't bump her off once and for all. Damn the day I first set eyes on her!'

He had worked himself up into a fury again and was about to start beating Tessa some more. Bruno and Buffalmacco had heard his story out with every appearance of astonishment, nodding from time to time in agreement and hardly able to contain their laughter. Seeing him rearing to start on his wife again, however, they managed to restrain him, by assuring him the good lady was not responsible for what had happened. It was his fault. As he knew that things lost their magic in the presence of women he should have seen that she kept away for the day. God had reminded him of this precaution, perhaps because he was not cut out for luck like that, or because he had tried to double-cross his friends instead of showing them the stone as soon as he found it. With a great deal of strenuous persuasion they finally reconciled him to his long-suffering wife and departed, abandoning him to his miserable brooding in a house full of stones.

Tenth day: tenth tale

THE PATIENT GRISELDA

MANY years ago the head of the house of the Marquises of
Saluzzo was a young man called Walter. He was unmarried
and childless and spent all his time hunting and hawking.
He wasn't remotely interested in marriage or children—
which was very sensible of him. His subjects, however, took
it very badly and kept badgering him to marry. They were
so afraid he would die heirless and leave them without a
ruler, that they volunteered to find him the right sort of
wife, from the right sort of family.

'Friends,' Walter answered, 'you're forcing me into something which I had decided against. It is terribly difficult to
find the right woman and only too easy to pick the wrong
one, and live unhappily ever after. It's quite ridiculous to
claim you can select the right girl, merely on the strength of
her parents. Actually I doubt if you'd be able to gauge the
mothers or fathers very confidently; and what if you could?
The daughter might be quite a different kettle of fish. But
as you're set on loading me down with a wife, I'm prepared
to give in. I intend choosing her for myself, then I can't
blame anybody else if it doesn't work out. Incidentally, let
me say here and now, that whoever I choose must be
treated with proper respect by all of you. Otherwise I'll
show you how I feel about being bullied into marriage.'

The good people said they would be quite happy as long
as he married soon.

For a considerable time Walter had liked the look of a
poor but attractive girl from a farm near his house. He
thought that married life with her might be fairly happy,
so he looked no further and decided on the spot to marry
her. He summoned the girl's father, who was miserably
poor, and negotiated with him for the girl. Then Walter
collected all his friends in the district and announced :

'Friends, you've been telling me all along I ought to marry, and more to satisfy you than because I'm particularly keen myself, I've agreed to it. You'll remember you promised that whoever she was, she'd be treated by you like a lady. I ask you to stand by this promise, just as I am about to keep mine. I've found a girl after my own heart near here, and I've every intention of marrying her and bringing her home in the next few days. So set to and arrange a magnificent wedding reception, and a royal welcome. Then I shall be thoroughly satisfied that you've stuck to your word, and you'll be the same by me.'

They all agreed spontaneously that they were perfectly content and promised that the woman of his choice would be treated like a lady. Then everyone, including Walter, started preparations to celebrate the happy event on a grand scale. He arranged a magnificent reception and invited a good many friends and relatives, local dignitaries and others. He had lots of expensive dresses made, and fitted on a girl who had somewhat the same figure as his future wife. He also bought belts, rings, an exquisite crown, and the rest of a bride's trousseau. At about half-past eight on the day he and his guests mounted their horses. Seeing that all the arrangements were completed, Walter announced:

'Gentlemen, the time has come to fetch the bride.'

Away the whole party rode to Griselda's village. When they reached her house there was the girl hurrying back from the well with a bucket of water, anxious to join the other women and watch Walter's bride pass. As soon as Walter saw her, he called out and asked her where her father was. Griselda answered shyly:

'He's indoors, sir.'

Walter climbed down from his horse, and went into the cottage, telling his companions to wait outside.

'I've come to marry your daughter Griselda,' he said to Giannucolo. 'But first of all there are one or two questions I'd like to put to her while you're here.'

He asked whether, as his wife, she would be obedient, obliging, constantly equable no matter what he did or said . . . and various similar questions. To all of them she

answered yes. Then Walter took her hand, and led her outside. In front of all his guests and the many other people
who had collected, he had her stripped to the skin, produced the other clothes he had had made, dressed her up
and placed a crown on her dishevelled hair. To the amazement of everyone, he announced:

'Gentlemen, this is the girl I intend to marry, if she will
have me.'

She stood there in embarrassed astonishment. Turning
to her, Walter asked:

'Griselda will you take me for your husband?'

'Yes sir,' she replied.

'And I will take you for my wife,' he said, and so the
match was made in front of them all.

Griselda was mounted on a palfrey and led home in state.
The ceremony was dignified and beautiful, and the reception couldn't have been more magnificent if Walter's bride
had been the King of France's daughter. With her new
clothes the bride seemed to have acquired a new dignity,
both physically and mentally. I've already mentioned the
beauty of her face and figure; she had besides charming
manners and social grace, that certainly didn't suggest
Giannucolo's daughter, the shepherdess. She seemed aston-
ishingly well-bred, even to those who knew her background.
Walter found her devoted and obedient, and considered he
couldn't have been luckier. She was so kind and consider-
ate to her husband's subjects that she was universally
adored. Everyone respected her, prayed for her increasing
happiness; instead of saying, as they had to begin with, that
it was very silly of Walter to have married her, people now
considered he had shown enormous strength and good taste,
for if it hadn't been for him Griselda's sterling qualities
would have stayed hidden under shabby working clothes.

In fact her goodness and her fine character were soon
proverbial far beyond the marquis' territory. If people had
been damaging about Walter at the time of the marriage,
now nobody had anything but good to say. Griselda hadn't
been married long before she became pregnant, and when
the time came gave birth to a girl. Walter was delighted,
but not long afterwards he became obsessed with a strange

desire to put Griselda's long-sufferance to a lengthy and arduous test. He started taunting her, and referring sadly to his subjects' dissatisfaction over her low birth. The grumbling had increased enormously, he said, when the baby was a girl. Griselda's expression didn't change as she answered:

'You must deal with me just as your position and happiness demand. I shall be quite happy, for I know only too well how unimportant I am in comparison. I'm unworthy of the honour you were good enough to pay me.'

This answer completely satisfied Walter that his respect and that of others had not given her any big ideas.

Not long afterwards, Walter referred again to his subjects' hatred of the idea of Griselda's daughter. Then he sent a messenger to his wife:

'Madam,' said the servant miserably. 'It's as much as my life's worth—I've got to do what his Lordship orders. He's told me to take away your daughter and . . .'

He stopped, but what he'd said, the expression on his face, and the memory of her husband's words were enough to tell Griselda that his orders were to kill the baby. She snatched the baby up from the cradle, kissed and blessed her and without betraying her inner agony, placed her daughter in the servant's hands.

'Do everything ordered by your master and mine but don't leave her as carrion unless he particularly asked it.'

The servant took the baby girl and went to tell Walter what his wife had said. He was amazed at her resignation and sent the baby to Bologna to be deposited with a relative who was asked to bring his little daughter up and educate her properly, but never to tell her who her parents were.

It wasn't long before Griselda became pregnant once again, and to Walter's delight this time it was a boy. But he still wasn't satisfied, and bullied his poor wife even more. One day he said in great distress:

'My dear, since the boy was born, my subjects have been making life unbearable with their continual reproach that a grandson of Giannucolo should succeed me as their ruler. I'm very much afraid that it may cost me my position if I don't do to this child what I did before, and then divorce you and marry again.'

Griselda listened patiently to him and only replied :

'My Lord, see you do whatever is best for you. Don't worry about me, for I only want whatever suits you.'

A few days later Walter sent for his son, as he had for his daughter, and went through the motions of killing him, but he too was sent to Bologna, to be brought up with his sister. Griselda didn't turn a hair, any more than she had over her daughter, and said nothing about it. Walter was dumbfounded and told himself that no other woman in the world would have behaved like that. If he hadn't seen with his own eyes and to his great satisfaction, just how devoted she was to her children he'd have thought they meant nothing to her; but he knew she was acting thoughtfully, not callously. His subjects believed he had murdered his own children, protested violently against his cruelty, and were full of pity for his wife. Griselda, however, answered the ladies who offered sympathy on the fate of her children by saying that her sole desire was Walter's happiness.

It was a good many years after his daughter's birth that Walter decided the time was ripe to put his wife's long-sufferance to the final test. He announced in public that he could no longer bear being married to Griselda. He admitted he had been immature, wrong-headed in the first place. Now he intended to get a dispensation from the Pope to divorce Griselda and marry again. Many good-hearted people protested but he merely said that it was necessary.

When Griselda was told, she suffered silent agonies. She realized she must expect to return to her old home, perhaps back to her sheep, and see her beloved husband taken up with another woman. But with the resignation she had shown in her earlier disasters, she steeled herself against this last outrage. It wasn't long before Walter had fake letters sent him from Rome to convince his subjects that the Pope had granted him a dispensation to divorce Griselda and marry again. He summoned his wife and said publicly:

'Griselda, with the Pope's permission I am now free to divorce you and re-marry. As my ancestors have always been the local landowners, and yours have always been labourers, I intend you to go home to your father with the dowry you brought with you. Then I shall replace you with someone I've found, who's more suitable for me.' When she heard this announcement it cost Griselda a superhuman effort to control herself and bite back the tears.

'I always knew, sir,' she replied, 'that my birth made me utterly unsuitable for a man of your standing. I owed my position in your house to your generosity and to God. I never regarded it as my right—but always as a loan. When you ask for it back I should be only too pleased—as indeed I am—to return it. So here is the ring you married me with —take it back. You order me to reclaim the dowry I brought. That won't call for any transfer of goods or money, for I remember only too clearly that I was stripped to the skin before you married me. If you think it is decent that a body that has borne you children should be a public show, I will go home naked. But I beg you to allow me just a petticoat to my back, in exchange for the virginity which I came with but have lost. That's all I ask of you, in addition to my dowry.'

Walter was on the point of tears, but his face remained set and expressionless as he replied:

'I'll allow you a petticoat.'

Everybody present implored him to give the woman who had been his wife for more than thirteen years at least a dress, to prevent her from suffering the miserable indignity of leaving his house in nothing but a petticoat. Their appeals were in vain, however. Griselda, dressed only in a petticoat, with nothing on her head or feet, gave them her blessing, left the house, and returned to her father's, amid tearful sympathy from everyone who witnessed it.

Giannucolo had never really believed that Walter would keep Griselda as his wife, and had been expecting this development all along. He brought out Griselda's clothes which he had stored away when she discarded them that morning she became Walter's wife. She put them on again and went back to the dull housework she'd been used to, enduring her cruelly bad luck with stoicism.

As soon as Walter had sent Griselda away he led his people to believe that he was about to marry the daughter

of a Count of Panago. During the elaborate arrangements
for the wedding he sent for Griselda again. When she
arrived, he said:

'I'm bringing my new wife home, and on an occasion like
this she ought to have a proper reception. You know none
of the women staff are capable of preparing the rooms, and
making all the other arrangements for this happy event.
You understand the whole thing much better than anyone
else, so would you do everything necessary, invite all the
ladies who ought to be invited, and welcome them as if you
were the lady of the house. Then after the wedding's over
you can go back to your cottage.'

These words went through Griselda like a knife, for she
had not been able to stop loving Walter when fate turned
against her. Nevertheless she replied :

'I am quite ready to do anything you ask of me, sir.'

And so Griselda in her rough, shabby clothes came back
to the house which she had left such a short time before in
her petticoat. She set to and spring-cleaned the bedrooms,
hung curtains, arranged the seats in the hall, got the kitchen
ready and lent a hand everywhere, like a maid of all work.
She didn't stop till the whole place was as spick and span
as the occasion demanded.

Then, in Walter's name she invited all the local ladies to
the wedding. When the long awaited day came it was she,
still dressed in her rags, but every inch the lady, who welcomed each of the guests and made them feel at home.

As I've said, Walter had had his children carefully
brought up by a relative in Bologna who had married into
the family of the Counts of Panago. His daughter was by
this time an exquisite girl of twelve, and his son about six.
Walter had written to his Bolognese relative's husband in-
viting him to bring the boy and girl to Saluzzo. They were
to come with a large retinue of nobles, and their mission
was supposedly Walter's marriage to the girl, for her real
identity was still a strict secret. Walter's instructions were
obeyed to the letter, and the party reached Saluzzo at
about dinner-time after a few days' journey. The visitors
found crowds of local people and many from further afield
waiting for a glimpse of Walter's new wife. When the girl

G

had been welcomed by all the ladies she entered the hall where the banquet was to take place. Griselda came forward and said warmly:

'Welcome, your ladyship.'

The other ladies had tried uselessly to persuade Walter either to make Griselda keep to her room or at least to let her wear one of her old dresses so that she should not meet the visitors in such a shabby state. Down they all sat and the meal got under way. Everybody stared at the girl and agreed that Walter had made a change for the better. Griselda was as enthusiastic as anybody about her and her younger brother. Walter decided he had tested his poor patient wife enough, for she showed no signs of distress at this last turn of events. Walter was certain it was not just indifference, because he knew how sensitive she was. He considered the time had come to release her from the suffering she was enduring so philosophically. He called her, and with a smile asked her openly:

'What do you think of the bride?'

'I'm most impressed with her, sir,' was the answer. 'If she's as sensible as she's pretty—and I should imagine she is—I'm certain you can be sure of being extremely happy with her. But I do beg of you to spare her the trials you subjected your first wife to. With her youth and delicate upbringing I don't think she could put up with them, whereas the other one had been brought up the hard way from birth.'

Walter saw that though Griselda was sure he would marry the girl, she still had nothing but good to say of her. He sat her down beside him and said:

'Griselda, the time has come to reward you for your long-sufferance. I must convince those who have considered me cruel, unjust, and unfeeling, that I knew exactly what I was doing. I intended to give both you and them a lesson; to teach you how to be a wife, and them how to choose and keep one. I wanted to make quite certain of being completely happy with you for the rest of my life. When I got married I was very afraid I shouldn't achieve this, and I decided to test you and make your life the misery it has been. As you never crossed me in word or deed, I know

now I'm assured of the complete happiness I so wanted. Now I'm going to give you back everything I took from you bit by bit, and make up for all your trials and tribulations by making you blissfully happy. Welcome the girl you thought I was going to marry and her brother, because they are yours and mine. They are the children you and everybody else always thought I'd put to death in cold blood. And I am your husband who loves you better than anything else in the world, and I'm convinced no one else on earth can boast of a better wife.'

He threw his arms round Griselda and kissed her. With tears of happiness running down her cheeks she and Walter went to where their daughter was sitting, dazed by the news. Her parents kissed her and their son fondly, and told the whole story to them and everyone else. The ladies, bursting with pleasure, got up from the table and whisked Griselda off to a bedroom. How auspicious it seemed to them to strip her of her old rags and put on one of her most magnificent dresses. Once more dressed like a lady—she had never *looked* like anything else—they led her back to the hall.

Walter and Griselda were overjoyed to have their children back, and everyone was so gay and enjoyed themselves so much that the festivities lasted several days. People decided that Walter had behaved very sensibly though his trial of Griselda was criticized for its excessive harshness. Griselda herself had by general agreement behaved irreproachably.

A few days later the Count of Panago went home to Bologna. Walter retired Giannucolo from his drudgery for the rest of his life and treated him with the respect due to a father-in-law. As for Walter himself, he married his daughter to a very distinguished husband, and lived happily ever after with the wife to whom he was devoted.

What more need I add except that a saint may be born in a poor man's cottage, just as a king may have the mentality of a swineherd, rather than of a ruler of men. Could anybody but Griselda have borne the incredible severity of Walter's trial, not just with patience, but with positive cheerfulness?

Perhaps, however, it would have done Walter no harm if Griselda had been the type that when once shown the door in her petticoat, would have taken herself off, got round someone else and cadged at least one respectable dress.

THE STORY OF THE BIG TOE

IN Florence there lived a very wealthy business man called Arriguccio Berlinghieri. As is typical of his class even today, he stupidly wished to come up in the world through marrying a lady. He chose a very unsuitable one called Sismonda.

Now when Lady Sismonda saw just how often her husband was away, and how he neglected her, she fell in love with a young man-about-town called Ruberto, who had been chasing her for a long time.

They became very intimate and she was probably careless, for she was infatuated with her lover, or Arriguccio may have tumbled to something. Anyway, he suddenly became horribly jealous, gave up his trips, and totally altered his way of life. He devoted himself entirely to guarding his wife, and didn't allow himself a wink of sleep until he had tucked her up safe in bed. This was terribly irritating for her, and completely prevented her from seeing Ruberto. She racked her brains to find a way of meeting him. Finally with a good deal of prompting from Ruberto, she hit on the following plan. Her room looked on to the road. She'd often noticed that Arriguccio found great difficulty in getting to sleep, but that he slept like a log once he had. She decided to arrange for Ruberto to come to the front door about midnight. Then she would go down and open the door, and spend some time with the lover while the husband was fast asleep. In order that she, but no one else, would know of Ruberto's arrival, she planned to lower a cord from her bedroom window. It reached from almost street level at one end, across the room to her bed, and under the clothes. She rigged it to her big toe, when she got into bed. Having set up this line she instructed Ruberto to tug at the string as soon as he came. If Arriguccio were asleep she would untie it and come and open the door. But if he were awake, she'd keep it taut and wind in, so that Ruberto would know not to expect her. He fell in with this plan, and often came and put it into practice. Sometimes it was possible for them to meet, sometimes not.

They had used this ingenious system some time, when one night while Sismonda was asleep, Arriguccio happened to move further over in bed than usual, and his foot found the cord. He could feel it was tied to his wife's big toe, so he said to himself:

'This looks like a trick.'

When he realized the string led out of the window he was more than ever convinced. So he quietly cut it off her toe, tied it on his own, and patiently awaited developments. It wasn't long before Ruberto arrived and tugged at the cord as usual. Arriguccio hadn't been able to tie the cord on very firmly and as Ruberto gave it a fairly hard pull, it came away. Ruberto understood his instructions and waited. Arriguccio jumped out of bed, snatched his weapons, and hurried to the door, determined to deal with anyone he found there. He had considerable guts and brawn, although he was only in business. When he got there he didn't open the door gingerly like Sismonda, so the watching Ruberto guessed that it was the husband who had come to meet him. He took to his heels with Arriguccio in pursuit. After a long chase Ruberto still couldn't throw off his pursuer, so he turned and faced him, sword in hand. They set to and fought it out.

Meanwhile Sismonda had woken up when her husband unlocked the bedroom door. Seeing the cord had been cut free from her toe, she realized at once the game was up. When she heard Arriguccio chase off after Ruberto, she got up at once. She had a shrewd idea of what would happen, so she called her maid, for she kept nothing from her. With a great deal of persuasion the girl was induced to take her mistress' place in bed. Sismonda begged her not to reveal who she was, but to put up patiently with any punishment Arriguccio might mete out. She would be amply recompensed. Sismonda then left the room in darkness and found herself a convenient hiding place to await developments. The bitter tussle between Arriguccio and Ruberto in the street made so much din it woke the neighbours. They got up and hurled abuse at the pair. Arriguccio was so anxious not to be recognized, that he made his getaway without even finding out who the young man was, let alone actually wounding him. He went home livid with rage, blundered into the bedroom and bellowed:

'Where are you, you whore? You've put the light out, so you won't have to show your head. But don't you fool yourself.'

He strode to the bed and grabbed the maid, under the belief that it was his wife. He punched and kicked her violently till he had almost squashed her face flat. He cursed her viciously throughout this operation, and ended by cutting off her hair. The maid, as is hardly surprising, cried bitterly. Though she couldn't help an occasional cry of 'Oh! For God's sake, stop!' or 'Spare me, spare me!' she was crying so much and Arriguccio's fury made him so deaf that he did not notice it wasn't his wife's voice. After giving her a terrible beating and a haircut, he shouted:

'You foul woman. I'll never touch you again. I'm going to find your brothers and tell them how you've been carrying on. They can come here and deal with you as they think you deserve. Then they can take you away with them, because I'm not having you in my house any longer.'

And he swept out of the house, locking the bedroom door behind him. Sismonda had heard everything that happened, and as soon as her husband was gone, she opened the bedroom door, relit the light, and did her best to console her bruised and tearful maid. She carried her back to her own room, and in secret had her carefully nursed. Sismonda then made it up to the poor girl satisfactorily with liberal supplies of Arriguccio's money.

With the maid tucked away in her room, Sismonda quickly returned to her own, tidied it up and remade the bed so that it looked as though it had not been slept in. She lit the lamp again and dressed, leaving no indication that she had been to bed at all. Armed with a lamp and some needlework she sat at the head of the stairs, to sew and wait for the next move.

Meanwhile Arriguccio had hurried straight to his

brothers-in-law. With a great deal of knocking he made himself heard and was let in. When they realized who the visitor was, his mother-in-law and her three sons got up, asking what on earth had happened, to bring him there at that time of night. Then Arriguccio told them the whole story, from his finding the cord attached to his wife's big toe to the last instalment. To cap it all he handed them the hair, cut, as he imagined, off from his wife's head. It was up to them now, he added, to come and deal with her as honour demanded. He wouldn't tolerate her in his house a moment longer.

Sismonda's brothers believed every word and were furious with her. Picking up torches, they accompanied Arriguccio home, determined to read the riot act to her. Her tearful mother followed, begging each of them in turn not to jump to conclusions, without further evidence. Arriguccio might have lost his temper with the poor girl for some quite other reason. Perhaps he had treated Sismonda badly, and this was a trumped up story to cover himself. She would be very surprised if it were true. She had known the girl better than anyone and from a very early age . . . etc.

When they reached Arriguccio's, and were climbing the stairs, Sismonda heard them and called out:

'Who's there?'

One of her brothers shouted back:

'You'll know soon enough, you whore!'

'Lord love us!' she cried. 'What is going on?'

She got up and went to meet them.

'You're welcome, brothers. But what are all of you doing up at this hour?'

They found her at her sewing with not a scratch on her face, though Arriguccio claimed to have trounced her thoroughly. They were somewhat taken aback, and did not open fire at once. They asked her if Arriguccio's charges were true, and threatened her with dire consequences if she was less than honest.

'I don't know what you expect me to say,' said Sismonda. 'And I've no idea what he's charged me with.'

Arriguccio could only stare at her as though he was out

of his mind, for he remembered the innumerable blows, and the scratches on the face, and the general manhandling he had given her. She bore not a trace of any such treatment.

To cut a long story short, Sismonda's brothers repeated everything that Arriguccio had said—the string, the beating-up and all. When they had finished she turned on her husband and said:

'Oh, now what's all this? Shame on you for making me out a wicked woman, when I'm nothing of the sort. And making yourself out a cruel tyrant when you're nothing of the sort. As if you'd been home at all tonight, let alone anywhere near me! And when is it you're supposed to have beaten me? I can't remember it myself.'

'What did you say, you bitch? Didn't we go to bed together? Didn't I come back from chasing your lover? Didn't I lay into you, and cut your hair off?' began Arriguccio. But his wife interrupted him:

'You certainly haven't slept here tonight. But let that pass, you've only my word for it. What about the beating and the haircut you're supposed to have given me, though? You didn't touch me. I challenge you all—Arriguccio included—to find a sign of a beating on me. But I warn you, don't lay a finger on me, or, by God, I'll do you an injury. Incidentally, I'm not aware that my hair's any shorter. But perhaps you did it without my knowing, so let's see if it's any different.'

And she lifted her veil to reveal a full head of hair. At this her mother and brothers turned to Arriguccio and shouted:

'What does this mean? This doesn't tally with your version. And how are you going to prove the rest?'

Arriguccio was too dazed to have any answer to all this. He saw that all the evidence was against him, so he kept quiet. Sismonda then turned to her brothers and said:

'I see what he's getting at. He won't be satisfied until I've told you what I have always meant to keep from you— what a miserable specimen he is. Now nothing is going to stop me. I'm quite sure that he really did do what he claims. This prize gentleman you married me to—worse luck—calls himself a merchant and is always on about his "good name". He should be better behaved than a monk, purer than a virgin, but he spends all his evenings boozing in pubs, and going with any old street girl. And I have to wait up for him until twelve, or even into the small hours, like tonight. No doubt he got thoroughly soused, went to bed with one of his tarts, and woke up and found this thread tied to her foot. When he'd done what he claims he did, he came back to her, beat her, and cut off her hair. The effects of his drunkenness hadn't worn off, so he thought—and probably still does—he'd beaten me up. If you look at him closely you'll see that he's still only half sober. You can count all he's said about me as the drivel-lings of a tipsy man. Please forgive him—as I do myself.'

Her mother, however, kicked up a terrible fuss about this:

'By God, we're not leaving it at that,' she thundered. 'That a daughter of mine should be married to someone so far beneath her. He's vicious, a dirty dog like that ought to be done away with. It's a pretty kettle of fish. Anybody would think he'd found you in the gutter. Damn it, you've had more than enough trouble from this dabbler in donkey's droppings. Some country crook who escaped to town when the local squire sacked him, looking like a tramp, with baggy trousers. Just because he'd got a bit of money, he set his heart on marrying a real lady, investing in a coat of arms and then saying: "I'm one of the so-and-sos. My ancestors were such-and-such." Oh, if only my boys had taken my advice. Your reputation would have been safe enough with Count Guidi's family, and you could have married there though you hadn't a penny to your name. But they had to give you away to this miserable specimen. There isn't a purer girl than you in all Florence, but that hasn't stopped him shamelessly calling you a whore tonight in front of us; as if we didn't know you better than that. Good God, if I had my way, he'd feel it where it hurts.'

Then she turned to her sons, adding :

'Didn't I tell you boys, you shouldn't have done it in the first place? Now you know what sort of treatment she gets from that precious husband of hers. The tuppenny-ha'penny tradesman. If it were for me to say, rather than you, after what he's said and done to her, nothing would stop me from getting rid of him once and for all. If I were a man—instead of a mere woman—I wouldn't need anyone to settle this business for me. God rot the miserable drunken swine!'

This was enough to make the young men turn on Arriguccio furiously. They gave him the most terrible dressing down, which ended as follows:

'We'll let you off this once, as you're drunk. But if you know what's good for you, you'll see to it we don't hear of anything like this again. If we do we'll make you suffer for both times.'

And thereupon they left. Arriguccio was flabbergasted, uncertain whether it had all happened or was a dream. He didn't say a word and never gave his wife any further trouble. Thanks to her ingenuity she had not only survived the immediate danger, but engineered a way of getting what she wanted in the future, without any interference from her husband.

First day: first tale

THE DEATH OF A SAINT

THERE was once a very wealthy big business man called
Musciatto of France, who became a knight. He was obliged
to accompany Charles Lackland, the King of France's
brother, on a duty visit to Tuscany ordered by Pope Boni-
face. This gentleman, like so many business men, found his
commercial interests were too involved in a variety of areas
to permit of hasty withdrawal. He therefore decided to
commit them to several agents. Everything was tied up except some loans in Burgundy, which he doubted any
agent's ability to recover. He knew the Burgundians were
aggressive, unreliable, and mean. He could think of no one
he could depend on to beat them at their own crooked
game. After a great deal of thought he remembered a certain Ciapperello of Prato, who had visited him in Paris.
Since the man was short and brusque his name could
roughly be translated 'Stumpy', but the French in their
ignorance derived it from their word for a garland
(chapelêt) and called him Ciappelletto. His way of life was
as follows:

A lawyer by profession he prided himself on his speciality
—drawing up false documents. He would draw up any
number to order, and was prepared to do it gratis, where
most of his colleagues would have thought twice about a
commission, even for a fat fee. He hardly ever produced a
document which was not fraudulent, when he did it was
with shame. He also enjoyed committing perjury, whether
it was necessary or not. As oaths were taken seriously in
France in those days, his lack of scruple won him every case
where he was called upon to swear to the truth.

Another pleasurable occupation was fomenting enmity,
dissension, and hatred between friends and relatives. The
greater the damage, the greater his satisfaction. He took on

murder or a similar crime with unhesitating enthusiasm. He willingly killed or wounded people with his bare hands, and he would viciously blaspheme against God and the saints, on the slightest provocation. He was never seen at church, and considered the sacraments as a dirty word. He was a regular visitor, however, of the inn and places of that sort. His attitude to women was that of the dog to the stick, for he was a thorough pervert. He stole as a matter of principle, like a saint offering a sacrifice. He overate and drank grossly, and sometimes did himself an injury as a result. He was a confirmed gambler and was never parted from his loaded dice. What's the point of describing him in greater detail? He was probably the foulest crook ever born.

Ciappelletto had long relied on Musciatto's powerful position to protect him against individuals he had injured and the court he had so constantly outraged. Musciatto had only to remember Ciappelletto, and recall his character, to pick on him as the perfect person to cope with Burgundian cunning. He sent for him and told him the position:

'As you know, Ciappelletto, I'm retiring from here. There are still some crooked Burgundians who owe me money. To my mind you are the perfect person to extract the money for me. As you don't seem to have anything on at the moment, if you'd take the job on, I'll get you backing from the courts, and you'll get a share of the money you recover.'

As Ciappelletto was out of work, out of pocket, and about to lose the support of his patron, he accepted the job without much hesitation. In fact he could ill-afford to refuse. They came to an agreement.

Armed with the power of attorney and letters patent from the King, Ciappelletto set off for the unknown territory of Burgundy. Once there he embarked on the task of collecting the money, but in a manner quite alien to his character. He was mild and friendly as though severity were only a last resort. While on the job, he stayed with two Florentine brothers and money-lenders who treated him respectfully on Musciatto's account. In their house he fell ill. The brothers immediately called in doctors and supplied servants to nurse him back to health. All their efforts were useless, however. The patient was old and (the doctors diagnosed) had led a debauched life, so his disease got worse and appeared fatal. The brothers were distressed, and one day discussed the problem in a room very close to Ciappelletto's.

'What can we do with him?' they both wondered. 'He's put us in a very awkward position. It would be ridiculous to kick him out in *his* state of health, and we'd be bound to get criticized. Everyone will remember the welcome we gave him to start with, the care we've taken of him during his illness, so how can we possibly throw out a mortally sick man, when he's done nothing to offend us. On the other hand he has led such a foul life that he'll never confess himself or take the sacraments. If he dies unconfessed, no church will allow him burial and his body will end up in some ditch—like a dog's. Even if he did confess, his crimes are so staggering, no priest or friar would give him absolution. If he dies unabsolved he'll end up in that same ditch anyway. Then the neighbours, who hate our profession and everything to do with it and would love to get their hands on our property, will raise hell. They'll scream: "Down with the Lombards. The church won't have them, nor will we." They're bound to sack our house, and they may kill us while they're at it. Either way, we stand to lose if he dies.'

Ciappelletto, as I said, was lying within earshot. His ears, like many invalids', were sharpened by his illness and he didn't miss a word of the discussion. He called the brothers in and said :

'Please don't worry about me, nor about what you stand to lose by my death. I overheard what you were saying and agree with your estimate of the situation. But things are going to work out quite differently. I have sinned so consistently against God during my life, that a final fling on my death-bed will make no difference. Please bring me the most saintly friar you can find, and leave me to settle your affairs and mine satisfactorily.'

The brothers were not very optimistic of the results but they went to a friary and asked for a good, saintly friar to hear the confession of the Lombard invalid in their house. They came back with an old friar who was good, learned, religious, and highly respected by everyone in the town. He entered Ciappelletto's sick-room, sat down by his bed and began to give him words of comfort. He asked the invalid when he had last confessed. To this Ciappelletto (who had not been near a confessional all his life) replied:

"Father, I regularly confessed at least once a week— many weeks more than once. But I'm afraid I've been so ill for the last eight days, that I've not been at all.'

The friar answered:

'Well done, my son, carry on the good work. As you've confessed so regularly, I can see we shan't take long with my questions and your answers on this occasion.'

'Oh!' said the invalid, 'don't say that, father. I may have confessed regularly, but I would still dearly love to make a general confession of every sin I can remember from the day of my birth onwards. So please question me in every detail, as though I'd never confessed in my life. Don't make allowances for my ill-health. I'd rather punish the body than endanger the soul, which my Saviour redeemed with His precious blood.'

The holy man was overjoyed with these words. They seemed typical of a soul in a state of grace. He warmly congratulated Ciappelletto on his attitude and first asked him if he had ever sinned carnally with a woman. To which the sick man answered with a sigh:

'Father, I am reluctant to admit the truth about this, through fear of pride.'

'Speak out,' said the friar. 'Telling the truth is never criminal, in the confessional or outside it.'

'Then,' replied Ciappelletto, 'to be frank, I must admit I'm as chaste and virgin as the day I was born.'

'God bless you,' said the friar, 'you have done well. Your achievement is the more remarkable as you had far more temptations and opportunities of weakening than we who are bound by the rule.'

Then he passed to gluttony, and asked whether Ciappelletto had offended in this sin. The invalid had to admit, with a sigh, that he had committed this sin often. He used to fast not only in Lent, like all churchgoers, but at least three days a week besides. He would take nothing bar bread and water, but he swallowed the water with as much gusto, especially when tired out by prayer or pilgrimage, as

the alcoholic took his wine. Sometimes his mouth watered
for those herbal salads country women prepare when they
come up to town. Sometimes too, he felt he was more enthusiastic about food than he should be, considering that he
fasted out of pure devotion.

'My son,' said the friar, 'these are natural and venial sins,
and you must not judge yourself too seriously. No one,
however saintly, can help enjoying food after a long fast, or
drink after heavy work.'

'Oh father,' begged Ciappelletto, 'don't give me false
comfort. We both know only too well that what is done in
God's service, should come from a pure and open heart.
Otherwise the action is wicked.'

The friar answered with great satisfaction:

'I am delighted that you realize this. The purity of your
soul does you credit. But tell me : have you been guilty of
greed, either wanting more than was your due, or with-
holding what rightfully belonged to others?'

To this the penitent answered:

'Father, please do not misunderstand my being in a
money-lenders' house. I have no connexion with them. I
only came to plead with them, point out the error of their
ways, and persuade them to give up this appalling trade. I
think I'd have succeeded, had God spared me. You should
know that I inherited a fortune from my father, but be-
queathed most of it to God. Since then, I have indulged in
a little profit-making trade just to keep myself and relieve
Christ's poor. Such money as I have made, I have halved
with the poor. God's hand has been so with me in this that
my financial position has steadily improved.'

'Congratulations,' said the friar. 'But tell me, do you
frequently lose your temper?'

'Only too often, I'm afraid,' said Ciappelletto, 'but who
can help it when everywhere you look men behave like
criminals, breaking the Commandments and ignoring God?
Several times a day I feel ashamed to be alive, when I see
the frivolity of the younger generation. They commit perjury, they practically live in the pubs, and never go near
a church. In fact they go their own worldly way and not
God's.'

'My son,' answered the friar, 'this is righteous indignation. I do not take you to task for it. But haven't you ever
been angry enough to kill, to insult, or wound anyone in
any way?'

To which came the answer:

'I blush for you, father. How can you, a man of God, say
a thing like that? If I had ever been so much as tempted
to commit one of the sins you've mentioned, how could I
possibly believe that God has been with me? To that type
I say: "Go, and may God help you to see the light." '

'God bless you,' continued the friar, 'but tell me this:
have you ever borne false witness against anybody, or been
malicious, or stolen?'

'Indeed I have,' said Ciappelletto. 'I've certainly spoken
evil of someone. I once had a neighbour who used to beat
his wife regularly without rhyme or reason. I felt so sorry
for her when he started drunkenly thrashing the poor
woman, that on one occasion I spoke up against him to his
wife's relations.'

Next the friar asked:

'Now, you've told me you've been in trade. Have you ever
double-crossed anybody, as merchants tend to do?'

'Yes, indeed,' said Ciappelletto, 'but I never knew *who*.
A fellow brought the money due on some cloth he'd
purchased from me. I put it in a box without counting it.
A month later I discovered there was a penny more
than there should have been. I kept it for a year, so as to
give it back, but I never saw him again, so I gave it to a
charity, for the love of God.'

'That was a trifle,' said the friar, 'and you were right to
do what you did.'

The holy friar asked him many other questions, all of
which he answered in this style. But when he was on the
point of receiving absolution, Ciappelletto added:

'I have another sin to admit to you.'

The friar asked him what it was.

'I remember,' he replied, 'once making my servant sweep
the house on a Saturday afternoon. I'm afraid I haven't
taken Sunday as seriously as I ought to have done,
either.'

'Oh,' said the friar, 'that's fairly slight.'

'No,' said Ciappelletto. 'Do not call it slight. Sunday is all the more important because it's the day of Our Lord's resurrection.'

'Have you done anything else?' asked the friar.

'Yes, father, I once spat in the church of God by mistake.'

The friar answered with a smile :

'That's nothing to worry about. We religious are continually spitting in church.'

'The more shame to you,' replied Ciappelletto. 'Nothing should be kept cleaner than the house where we sacrifice to God.'

He went on like this for some time and then suddenly sighed and piped a few tears (he was quite capable of that).

The friar asked:

'Why are you crying, my son?'

'I'm ashamed to say,' came the answer, 'that there's one sin I've never confessed to. Whenever I'm reminded of it, as I am now, I cry, because I'm sure God won't ever forgive me for it.'

'Come, come,' coaxed the friar. 'What do you mean? Why, if all the sins ever committed in the world, not to mention those which are yet to come, were concentrated in one man, God in His love and mercy would forgive him—if he were penitent as you obviously are, and confessed them. So you can speak out boldly.'

Ciappelletto was still crying bitterly.

'Father,' he replied, 'unfortunately my crime is too serious. Unless you bring your prayers to bear, I fear God will never forgive me.'

The friar repeated :

'Speak out. I promise you my prayers.'

But Ciappelletto went on weeping and despite the friar's promise, seemed incapable of speaking. When he had kept his confessor on tenterhooks for some time, he sighed deeply and said:

'Father, as you have promised to intercede for me I will own up. To be frank, when I was young I cursed my mother.'

With these words he dissolved in tears again.

'Oh, son,' said the friar, 'does this seem to you so unforgivable? Men are continually cursing God, but he pardons them if they're truly repentant. So why shouldn't he pardon this? Don't cry! Why, even if you had crucified Him, He'd certainly forgive someone as penitent as you are now. Do not distress yourself.'

'Oh dear, father!' said Ciappelletto. 'What are you saying? Cursing the dear mother who carried me in her womb day and night for nine months and breast-fed me at least a hundred times—that's a terrible crime. It's much too serious for God to forgive, unless you pray for me.'

When the friar saw that Ciappelletto had nothing more to confess, he absolved him and blessed him. He had believed every word and considered the dying man very saintly. (Who wouldn't have swallowed it, hearing someone talk in this vein on his death-bed?) Finally he said:

'Ciappelletto, if God wills it, you will soon be well again. But if it is God's wish that your soul should return to Him in this state of grace, would you like to be buried in our friary?'

'Most certainly, father,' came the reply. 'I should hate to rest anywhere else, as you have promised to pray for me. Besides, I've always been particularly devoted to your Order. I beg you, on your return to the friary, to have the very Body of Christ which you consecrate on the altar every morning, sent to me. Unworthy though I am, I intend with your permission to take it and afterwards to receive sacred extreme unction. I may have lived a sinner, but I shall die a Christian.'

The holy friar was very impressed with these words and said he would be only too pleased to have the Host sent to him. So it was done.

The two brothers, sceptical of Ciappelletto's ability to hoodwink the friar, had taken up posts behind a wooden partition wall in the invalid's room. They listened and registered everything Ciappelletto told the friar. When they heard his admissions they could hardly keep themselves from laughing, and said to each other:

'What a character he is! He's incorrigible! Nothing

seems to alter his crookedness, or make him turn over a new leaf—not even the fear of God.'

But seeing his confession ensured him church burial, they were not too worried.

Soon after, Ciappelletto took communion, and then as his condition did not improve, he was given extreme unction. Just after vespers on the day of his full confession, he died. The brothers saw to it that he had a proper burial —at his own expense. They asked the friars to keep the customary vigil that night, to take charge of everything and collect the corpse in the morning. On hearing of the death, the holy friar who had heard the dead man's confession, discussed the matter with his prior. A chapter was convened, and the assembled friars were told how saintly Ciappelletto had been. It was obvious from his confession. The friar asked to receive the body with all due reverence and piety. It was quite possible that God might work miracles through it. The prior and the friar's gullible colleagues agreed to this, and the whole body went that evening to where Ciappelletto's corpse lay, and solemnly watched over it all night. In the morning they donned their surplices and copes, armed themselves with books and crucifixes, and formed a procession. A chanting column brought the corpse back to the friary church with enormous pomp and ceremony, followed by nearly all the townspeople. The body was laid down in the church and the confessor himself went into the pulpit and preached enthusiastically about Ciappelletto, detailing his life, fasts, chastity, simplicity, and saintly innocence. Among other things he described what Ciappelletto had tearfully confessed as his greatest sin, and how reluctant he had been to believe that God could forgive him for it. This prompted the preacher to reprove his congregation:

'Whereas you, who are damned, blaspheme against God and His Mother and all the angelic court, on the least excuse.'

He gave a great many further details about the man's faith and purity. In fact he worked the people to such a pitch (for they believed every word of it) that they surged forward at the end of the service and passionately kissed the hands and feet of the corpse. They tore off the grave-clothes, and lucky was the man who managed to keep a scrap. It was arranged that the corpse should be left on show all day. That night it was ceremonially buried in a marble tomb in a side-chapel. The day after, people came singly, lit candles, prayed, made their vows to it, and dedicated wax images. The fame of Ciappelletto's sanctity and of the devotion paid it spread so much, that almost nobody in trouble would have dreamed of appealing to any other saint. He was known, and still is, as Saint Ciappelletto, and all can bear witness to the innumerable miracles God performs through him every day, for all those who devoutly ask his help.

You have heard the life and death of Ciappelletto of Prato, and how he became a saint. Far be it from me to say that he couldn't possibly be among the blessed in God's sight. Although his life was evil he may have repented at the last moment, and God in His mercy may have received him into His Kingdom. But this is outside our knowledge. I'd judge from the evidence that he's keeping company with the devil in hell, and not in the other place . . .

THE POT OF BASIL

IN Messina there lived three brothers—all merchants. They inherited a great deal of money from their father, who had come from San Gimignano. There was one sister, Lisabetta, a beautiful and gifted girl, who for some reason had not yet been found a husband. The three brothers employed a young Pisan called Lorenzo to help them in the shop and act as manager. He was handsome and well-mannered enough to attract Lisabetta's attention, and she soon fell in love with him. When Lorenzo saw how the land lay, he abandoned all his other love affairs and paid court to her. It wasn't long before they expressed their mutual love and became lovers.

The affair progressed very pleasurably for them both, but they didn't take enough trouble in preserving their secrecy. One night Lisabetta's eldest brother saw her going into Lorenzo's room, though she didn't see him. He was very perturbed by his discovery, but was politic enough to keep it to himself, and to spend the night considering various solutions. Next day he told his brothers what he had discovered was going on betwen Lorenzo and Lisabetta. After much debate they agreed to salvage their own reputation and their sister's by saying nothing of what had been seen and heard. They waited patiently for the right moment to end this disgraceful affair neatly. With this at the back of their minds, they were outwardly as gay and friendly with Lorenzo as before. One day they suggested a jaunt and rode into the country, taking him with them. When they reached a very lonely place suitable for their plan, they took Lorenzo completely off his guard, murdered him, and buried him inconspicuously. On their return home they announced that he had been sent away on business. This was quite credible as it had often happened before. When Lorenzo failed to return, Lisabetta questioned her brothers frequently and urgently, for his absence seriously worried her. One day, after a very pressing inquiry, one brother replied:

'What do you mean? Why is he so important to you that you keep asking? One more question, and you'll get the answer you deserve.'

The girl's sinister forebodings only increased. She gave up asking questions, but on many nights she called pathetically for her lover and begged him to come to her. She cried bitterly, longed passionately for his return, yet despaired of it. One night in her misery over Lorenzo's absence, she had cried herself to sleep when he appeared to her in a dream. He was pale and dishevelled, his clothes torn and damp. He seemed to be saying:

'Lisabetta, you do nothing but call me, blame me for my long absence, and accuse me with your tears. You must realize that I can never return, because your brothers murdered me on the day we last saw each other.'

Then he described to her the place where he was buried, and telling her not to call him or expect his return, he disappeared.

When Lisabetta awoke, she believed in the vision and once more dissolved in tears. Next morning she got up, and without risking a word to her brothers, decided to go to the place described in her vision, and test its accuracy. She got permission to make an outing beyond the town. Taking a woman who had lived with the family and was in on all her secrets, she hurried off to the spot. Lisabetta swept aside the scattered leaves and began to dig in what seemed the softest patch of ground. She soon struck against her poor lover's body, for it had not yet begun to decompose. Her vision was proved only too true. The most miserable woman alive, she longed to remove the body and give it a more fitting burial, since she could not mourn it properly there. As this was impracticable, she drew a knife and severed the head from the body as best she could. She wrapped it in a cloth, and passed it to her companion. Then she replaced the earth round the rest of the body and set off home, unseen by anyone.

She shut herself in her room, clutching the head, kissing

it long and tenderly, and bathing it with her tears. Then she placed it in a large decorated pot, the sort used for growing marjoram or basil. She wrapped the head in a fine cloth, covered it with earth, and planted sprigs of the best Salerno basil. The plant was watered only with her tears or rose and orange-water. She used to sit beside the pot, concentrating all her love upon this shrine to Lorenzo. In her long vigils she would cry over it until the plant was moist with her tears.

The basil was so constantly and carefully nurtured, and its soil was so enriched by the decaying head, that it blossomed magnificently and fragrantly. The strangeness of the girl's behaviour attracted comments from the neighbours. When her brothers saw Lisabetta's beauty ruined and her eyes staring from her head, the neighbours drew attention to her obsession, saying:

'We have noticed her at it every day.'

Her brothers caught her too and reproved her several times, but to no avail. So they furtively removed the pot. As soon as she missed it she urgently demanded it back. As they would not return it, Lisabetta broke down and became ill. Throughout her illness she showed no interest in anything except the pot of basil. This amazed the brothers and they decided to examine the pot's contents. They removed the earth and noticed the cloth. There lay the head, and it was not decayed so much that they failed to recognize the curly hair of Lorenzo. They were so frightened by this strange affair and so anxious for it not to get about, that they buried the head as inconspicuously as possible and secretly fled to Naples. Lisabetta wept and asked repeatedly for her pot. Still weeping, she died.

Thus ended Lisabetta's doomed love. As years went by, however, many people got to know the truth. One of those who heard it, wrote the song which is still sung:

> 'Accursed are their ways, and evil,
> Who took from me my pot of basil.'

Eighth day: eighth tale

THE BITER BIT

LET me tell you the story I once heard about two rich middle-class young men from Siena. One was called Spinelloccio Tanena and the other, Zeppa of Mino. They lived next-door in one of the suburbs, did a lot together and seemed as close or closer than brothers. They had both married fine-looking women.

Through being a very frequent visitor to Zeppa's house, whether its master was at home or not, Spinelloccio became so intimate with Zeppa's wife, that he sometimes slept with her. The liaison continued for a good while without anyone finding out. One day, however, Zeppa was in, without his wife's realizing it. Spinelloccio came to see his friend, was told that he'd missed him, but went upstairs in any case. He found the lady of the house alone in her parlour, and they fell into each other's arms. Zeppa saw all this but kept hidden and wondered what was coming next. Soon he saw his wife and Spinelloccio, still entwined, go off to her bedroom and lock themselves in. This enraged him, but he realized that making a violent scene would do more harm than good. He racked his brains for a way to wreak his revenge, without any loss of reputation. A great deal of thought finally produced a workable plan. So he sat tight until Spinelloccio had left his wife.

At once Zeppa entered the room and caught his wife just putting straight the veil her lover's attentions had untidied.

'What are you up to, woman?' he asked.

'Can't you see?' she replied.

'Only too well, and I've just seen something else I wish I'd been spared.'

He cross-questioned her about what had just happened and finally frightened her into coming clean about her

195

affair with Spinelloccio. She begged him tearfully to forgive her.

'Now look here,' he said, 'you've done wrong. If you want to be pardoned you must do exactly what I tell you. Ask Spinelloccio to make some excuse for parting from me at nine o'clock tomorrow morning, and coming to see you. While he's here, I'll come back. When you hear me, get him to hide in this chest, and lock him in. Then I'll instruct you what to do next, but you needn't worry about it, I promise I won't do him any harm.'

His wife dutifully promised to do what was asked, and she was as true as her word.

Next morning at nine o'clock, when the two men were together, Spinelloccio remembered he had promised to visit his mistress.

'I've got to have lunch with a friend,' he explained to Zeppa, 'and I'd better not keep him waiting. So, goodbye!'

'But it isn't lunch-time yet.'

'Never mind. I've got to talk business with him, so I must be there in good time.'

With that, Spinelloccio left his friend and went to Zeppa's house by a slightly roundabout way. He was met by the lady and was taken into her bedroom. They hadn't been together long, before Zeppa returned home. Hearing his footsteps she pretended to be panic-stricken. She bundled Spinelloccio into the chest, as ordered, locked him in and left him there. As Zeppa came upstairs, he called:

'Is it lunch-time, my dear?'

'Yes, it's ready,' she answered.

'Spinelloccio's gone to lunch with a friend,' Zeppa went on, 'leaving his wife on her own. Do go to the window and call her. Ask her to come to lunch with us.'

His wife was so frightened for her skin that she obeyed with alacrity. With much persuasion, Spinelloccio's wife accepted their invitation, though she was told her husband wouldn't be there. When she arrived Zeppa welcomed her very warmly. He took her by the hand, and in an undertone ordered his wife to the kitchen. Then he led his friend's wife into the bedroom and locked the door. On hearing the key turn in the lock, she cried:

'What are you doing, Zeppa? What have you asked me here for? So much for your feeling for Spinelloccio. Is this your loyalty to your best friend?'

By the time she said this, they were near the chest her husband was locked up in. Zeppa didn't loosen his grip on her, but said:

'Please don't blame me until you've heard what I've got to say. I had, and still have, the feelings of a brother for Spinelloccio. I found out yesterday, without him realizing, that he repays my trust in him by sleeping with my wife as well as with you. As I'm fond of him, my only possible revenge is to do the same to him. He's enjoyed my wife, so I'm going to enjoy you. If you're not prepared to give me what I want, I'll take it, don't you worry. I'm not letting him get away with a dirty trick like that. I'm going to get my own back and wipe the grin off both your faces once and for all.'

The lady heard Zeppa out and was finally convinced by his assurances.

'My dear Zeppa,' she said, 'I'm happy to be the victim of your vengeance. As long as what you're doing won't spoil my friendship with your wife. Though she's done me wrong, I want to stay on good terms with her.'

'Don't worry about that,' replied Zeppa. 'I'll look after it, and I'm going to present you with the finest jewel you've ever seen, into the bargain.'

With this, he took her in his arms and started kissing her. Lying down on the chest where Spinelloccio was safely under lock and key, they enjoyed each other to the full.

Spinelloccio in his chest heard everything Zeppa said, all the lady's answers and the succeeding ball game that went on overhead. For a good time he was so livid, he thought he'd burst.

If it hadn't been for his fear of Zeppa, he would have lashed out at his wife, even from his prison. But then he remembered that he'd fired the first shot and that Zeppa was quite justified in what he was doing. He realized he had been treated in a very sporting fashion, and made a resolution that they should be even closer friends, if Zeppa was prepared to. When Zeppa was thoroughly satisfied, he got off the chest. The lady reminded him of the promised jewel. He opened the door and called his wife. She appeared and said with a laugh:

'Well, madam, now we're quits'—that was all.

Then Zeppa asked her to open the chest. She obediently did so, and showed the lady her husband lying in it. It would be difficult to know which was the more ashamed: Spinelloccio facing Zeppa in the knowledge that he'd been shown up, or his wife meeting her husband's eyes in the knowledge of what had gone on over his head.

'Look, this is the jewel I meant,' announced Zeppa, pointing to Spinelloccio, as that gentleman emerged from the chest crying: 'We're quits, Zeppa. So, as you've just been saying to my wife, let's go on being friends. We used to have everything in common except our wives; let's share them in future.'

'Agreed,' said Zeppa.

And they all four sat down to lunch very amicably. From then on, each lady had two husbands, and each man two wives. There was never any disagreement or feud between them under this arrangement.

AN EXERCISE IN EXORCISM

THERE lived in Florence at San Brancazio a wool-worker called Gianni Lotteringhi. He had done well in business, but was ignorant about everything else. He really was a bit simple, so he was often made leader of the Santa Maria Novella choir, and superintended its school. He held various positions of that sort, and was thoroughly smug about them. Actually they were all due to the fortune which enabled him to give liberal donations to the friars. In exchange for the breeches, cloaks, and hoods he subsidized, they taught him practical prayers, or the vernacular version of the Paternoster, or St Alexis' chant, or St Bernard's lament, or the laud of Lady Matilda, or some such rubbish. Gianni set enormous store by them. He preserved them jealously and was convinced they would ensure salvation for his soul.

This naïve wool-worker was married to a very beautiful, alluring, and intelligent wife called Tessa, who was the daughter of Mannuccio of Cuculia. She and a handsome and dashing young man called Federigo di Neri Pegolotti fell in love with one another. Knowing how silly Gianni was, she, with some connivance from her maid, invited Federigo to pay her a visit at a very pleasant holiday cottage her husband owned at Camerata. Tessa usually went there for the summer and Gianni came down occasionally for dinner and the night, returning to business (or psalm-singing) next morning. Federigo was delighted at the invitation and got there punctually on the evening in question. Everything passed off very well, as Gianni did not put in an appearance. Federigo thoroughly enjoyed the hospitality of Tessa's table and bed. She lay in his arms and in one night put him through about six of her husband's psalms.

Neither of them reckoned on this being their one and only meeting. To avoid the maid having to go every time

199

to arrange the liaison, the lovers evolved the following system. Every time Federigo passed the house on the way to or from a place of his own a little further on, he was to take a look at the vineyard beside the house. He'd notice a donkey's head stuck on one of the poles in the vineyard. Whenever the donkey's muzzle was facing towards Florence, it was safe to visit Tessa. If he found the door closed, he was to tap three times and she would open up. But when the donkey's muzzle was turned towards Fiesole, he was to make himself scarce, because Gianni was at home. This system worked satisfactorily on a good many occasions.

But one evening when Federigo was due to share a couple of plump boiled chickens with Tessa, Gianni arrived unexpectedly very late at night. His beloved wife was thoroughly put out. She had boiled a little salt meat separately, and she served this up for their supper. The maid was ordered to take into the garden the two chickens wrapped in a snow-white cloth, with plenty of fresh eggs and a good bottle of wine. The garden was accessible from the road as well as from the house, and she and Federigo often ate their supper there. The maid placed the food under a peach tree on the edge of the lawn.

Tessa was so upset she forgot to order the maid to wait for Federigo, tell him Gianni had come, and ask him to eat his supper in the garden. Tessa, Gianni, and the maid were only just in bed, when Federigo arrived and tapped once on the door. It was so near the bedroom that Gianni heard the tap. So did Tessa, though she pretended to be innocently asleep. Federigo waited a moment and then knocked again. Wondering who on earth it was, Gianni poked his wife and said:

'Tessa, do you hear what I hear? I think someone's at the door.'

She had heard the noise all too clearly, but she pretended to have just woken up.

'Eh? What did you say?' she asked.

'I said, I think someone's knocking at the door.'

'Knocking at it? Why, my poor Gianni, don't you know what it is? It's that spook that's been terrifying me for several nights now. Whenever I hear it, I bury my head in the bedclothes, and don't dare emerge until daylight.'

'Come, come, my dear,' he consoled her. 'If that's what it is, don't worry. Before we went to bed I said the *Te lucis* and the *'ntemerata* and some other very good prayers. I made the sign of the cross at the corners of the bed, in the name of the Father, Son, and Holy Ghost, as well. So there's no danger of it having power to harm us, however potent it is.'

However, Tessa was afraid Federigo would be offended and suspect he had a rival, so she decided to get up and let him know that Gianni was there. She said to her husband:

'Well that's what you say, but I won't feel easy until we've exorcised it. We can, now you're here.'

'Oh, how do we go about exorcising it?'

'I know all about it,' replied his wife, 'because I went to Fiesole for the absolution the other day. One of those hermit ladies—my word, what a holy woman she was, Gianni! —realized how terrified I was about the spook. She taught me a highly reliable and sacred prayer, which she said she had often used herself before she became a hermit—and with a hundred per cent success. God knows, I wouldn't have dared try it on my own, but now you've come, I suggest we go and exorcise it together.'

Gianni fully agreed, so they got up and crept to the door. Outside, the now thoroughly suspicious Federigo was still waiting.

When they had taken up their positions beside the door, Tessa ordered:

'When I give the word, Gianni, spit.'

'Right!'

Thereupon his wife began her prayer:

> *'Spook, spook, traveller by night,*
> *Leave as you came, with tail upright.*
> *A peach tree stands in our garden:*
> *A hundred droppings of chicken*
> *And a lardaceous object lie beneath.*
> *So put the bottle to your mouth.*

Away then like the wild wind flee.
And leave unharmed Gianni and me.'

When this doggerel was over, she added:
'Now, Gianni, spit!'
And Gianni spat.
The listening Federigo heard all this, and his jealousy disappeared. In fact, despite his disappointment, he could hardly hold back his laughter. When Gianni spat, he muttered under his breath:
'Now spit your teeth out!'
When Tessa had exorcised the spook three times in this way, she retired to bed with her husband. Federigo, realizing he had missed the supper he was expecting, interpreted the incantation correctly, and made for the garden. He found the two chickens, the eggs, and the wine under the peach tree, and bore them off home, where he ate them in comfort. He and Tessa had many hearty laughs together over the exorcism; and it might work even today.

Seventh day: sixth tale

SAFETY IN NUMBERS

OUR city is well equipped in every way and used to boast
a young lady of really outstanding beauty. She was married
to a thoroughly worthy and distinguished man, but people
do tend to get tired of a monotonous diet and long for a
little variety, and this lady began to find her husband wasn't
absolutely her cup of tea. She fell instead for a young man
called Leonetto. He didn't come from a very good family,
but he had beautiful manners and great charm. Leonetto
fell quite as deeply in love with her. You know as well as I
do that if two people want the same thing enough, they
usually get it, so it wasn't long before they enjoyed each
other.

Since, as I've said, our heroine was devastatingly attractive, another gentleman, called Lambertuccio, fell madly in
love with her too. She found him unsympathetic and
tedious, and she had no intention of granting him her love.
Lambertuccio got sick of sending useless begging messages to
her. As he was a powerful man, in the end he sent her a
message in a different vein, threatening to ruin her reputation if she didn't give in. She knew her man and was so
terrified, she reconciled herself to giving him satisfaction.

Isabella (for that was the lady's name) happened to have
gone to stay on her delightful country estate, like so many
Florentines in summer. One morning when she was by herself because her husband had gone away for a few days, she
sent for Leonetto to keep her company. He was delighted,
and came on the spot. While they were together, Lambertuccio knocked at the door. He had heard that Isabella's
husband was away, and had set off at once with no escort.
The maid came straight to Isabella, who was cloistered with
Leonetto.

'Madam,' she called out: 'Lambertuccio's downstairs, and he's come alone.'

Her mistress was infuriated, and pretty frightened as well.

'Please,' she begged Leonetto, 'would you mind going behind that curtain, and keeping out of sight until Lambertuccio's gone.'

Leonetto hid himself, because he was just as afraid of Lambertuccio as Isabella was. The maid was sent to let Lambertuccio in. He dismounted, tied his horse to a ring, and came upstairs. At the top he met Isabella, and she welcomed him with a smile and as much friendliness as she could muster. She asked him what she could do for him. He put his arms round her and kissed her.

'I'm told your husband's away, my love,' he said, 'so I've come to keep you company for a bit.'

With this they went into the bedroom, locked themselves in, and Lambertuccio started to enjoy her.

While this was going on, Isabella's husband happened to return home, though she hadn't in the least expected him. The maid saw him approaching the house, and ran straight to her mistress' room.

'Madam,' she called. 'The master will be here in a moment. I should think he's in the courtyard already.'

With two lovers in the house, and one of them with a horse in the courtyard that completely gave him away, Isabella despaired. Then suddenly she realized what to do, and jumped out of bed.

'Sir,' she said to Lambertuccio, 'if my reputation and my life mean anything to you, do as I tell you. Draw your sword, look as fierce and furious as you can, and go downstairs, bellowing: "By God, he won't get away with it!" If my husband stops you or asks any questions, don't say a word. Just get on your horse and go.'

'Just as you say,' said Lambertuccio.

He was still flushed from his recent exercise and furious at the husband's return, so all that was needed was to draw his sword, as ordered. When Isabella's husband dismounted in the courtyard he was somewhat surprised to see a horse there already. He was on the point of going upstairs, when

down strode Lambertuccio, looking and speaking his extraordinary part.

'What *is* going on?' asked the husband.

But his visitor merely swung his foot into the stirrup,
climbed to the saddle, and rode off, having done nothing
but repeat:

'By God, I'll catch him somewhere.'

At the top of the stairs stood Isabella stiff with horror.

'What's wrong?' asked her husband. 'Who's Lambertuccio following with such a murderous expression?'

Isabella backed towards her room so that Leonetto could
overhear.

'I've never been so terrified in my life,' she answered. 'A
young man came running in here—a total stranger—hotly
pursued by Lambertuccio with a drawn sword. The poor
boy must have seen me through the open door of this room,
for he cried out, shaking from head to foot: "Madam, for
God's sake help, or I'll die in your arms." I got up and was
going to ask him who he was and what was going on, when
in dashed Lambertuccio yelling: "Where are you, you
traitor?" I posted myself in the doorway to keep him out.
When he realized I had no intention of letting him in, he
had the good grace to depart—after a good deal of argy-
bargy, as you saw for yourself.'

'You did absolutely right my dear,' her husband congratulated her. 'There would have been a fearful scandal
if anyone had lost his life in our house. It was outrageous
of Lambertuccio to break into it pursuing somebody.'

Then he asked where the young man was.

'I really don't know where he can have hidden, dear,'
replied Isabella.

'Where are you?' shouted the gentleman. 'Don't be afraid
to come out.'

Leonetto emerged from his hiding place very jittery. He
had heard everything and had the fright of his life.

'What did you do to Lambertuccio?' questioned the husband.

'Absolutely nothing,' he answered. 'I honestly think he's
either gone mad, or mixed me up with somebody else. The
moment he saw me in the road near the house, he clapped

his hand to his sword and yelled: "Traitor, you're a dead man." I didn't stop to ask questions, but ran for it, and dashed in here. Thanks be to God and to this lady, I escaped his clutches.'

'Well don't worry any more,' said his host. 'I'll see you home safely, and then it's up to you how you deal with him.'

So after supper, the husband escorted Leonetto to Florence, right to his door. That very evening, on instructions from Isabella, Leonetto had a private discussion with Lambertuccio and settled everything. The incident may have given rise to a good deal of conjecture, but Isabella's husband never knew how he had been hoodwinked.

Third day : eighth tale

THE TRIP TO PURGATORY

THERE was in Tuscany, and is to this day, an abbey, built, like so many, in a lonely place. The monk who was appointed its Abbot was a saintly enough man except when it came to women. Even in this, he organised things so well that no one guessed—let alone discovered—his secret vice, and he kept his reputation for sanctity and justice untarnished.

This Abbot was friendly with a wealthy local farmer called Ferondo. Though he was both stupid and common, the Abbot enjoyed his company occasionally, because his fatuousness was good for a laugh. It came out in conversation that Ferondo had a wife who was a beauty. The Abbot fell so much in love with her, that he could think of nothing else. To his despair, however, he discovered that Ferondo, for all his thickness in other ways, knew how to take very good care of his wife. Our prelate was astute enough to get Ferondo to bring his wife occasionally to the abbey garden and the pair would then be treated to a dissertation on the joys of life eternal, and on the good works performed by saints gone by. This filled the wife with a desire to confess to the Abbot, and her husband gave his permission. She therefore came to make confession and, to the Abbot's delight, sat at his feet and started with these words:

'If only God had blessed me with a different husband, sir, or had spared me from having one at all, I might, with your guidance, be able to follow the path that you describe as having led others to eternal life. Considering what a useless specimen Ferondo is, I might just as well be a widow, but I'm saddled with him and I daren't look at another man while he's still about. He may be an idiot, but he's so fiendishly jealous (and with no justification) that he succeeds in making my life a perpetual misery. So, before I

207

come to my confession proper, please may I have your advice in this matter. You, if anyone, should be able to help me. If I can't find some way out, any amount of confession and good works will be useless.'

The Abbot was delighted by this speech, for he felt that Fate was playing into his hands. So he answered :

'My daughter, a husband who is stupid and, worse still, jealous, must be agony for a woman as beautiful and sensitive as you. As he is both, I can well imagine your predicament. Let me be frank, I can only think of one possible cure : that is to remove Ferondo's jealousy. I do in fact know the right prescription, but it must be kept secret.'

'You needn't worry about that, father,' said the lady. 'I'd rather die than breathe a word if you ordered me not to. What's the medicine to give him?'

'If you want him cured,' replied the Abbot, 'he'll have to go to purgatory.'

'How do you do that,' asked the wife, 'while he's still alive?'

'He must die, then he'll go there. When he's been through enough to cure him of jealousy, we'll employ some of our special prayers for the restoration of life. God will grant it.'

'Must I stay a widow, then?' asked the lady.

'Yes, for a time,' replied the Abbot. 'You will have to be very careful not to be married off to anyone. God would be deeply offended, and besides when Ferondo was resurrected, you'd have to go back to him, and he'd be more jealous than ever.'

'I must take your word for it,' said the lady. 'I shall be only too happy to have him cured of his jealousy, so long as I don't have to spend the rest of my life in prison. Do what you think best.'

'I will; but what will my reward be?'

'Father,' she said, 'anything you like that's within my power. But what can a woman like me do for a man like yourself?'

'Lady,' said the Abbot, 'you can do for me as I'm going to do for you. My scheme will ensure your future happiness and peace; you can save my life.'

'If that's so,' she said, 'I'm only too happy.'

'Well,' he answered, 'you have only to grant me your love and satisfy my burning passion for you.'

The lady was appalled:

'Oh dear, father, what do you mean? I thought you were saintly. Is it right for a religious man to make such suggestions to a woman who comes to him for advice?'

'Don't be surprised, my dear,' replied the Abbot. 'Sanctity does not suffer from this request, because it belongs to the spirit, and I am only referring to a sin of the flesh. Anyway your beauty has so enslaved me that love forces me to this. Let me remind you to be particularly proud of your looks, since they attract saints who are used to the contemplation of heavenly beauty. I need hardly add that, though I am an abbot, I am only human. As you can see I'm still not old. You shouldn't be making difficulties, but welcoming my idea. While Ferondo is in purgatory I'll keep you company every night and give you some fun to make up for what he owes you. Nobody will ever know, for they all think me as holy as you did a minute ago, if not more so. Don't spurn this favour offered you by God. It's yours for the asking and if you're a sensible woman you'll take my advice and get what many women would give their eyes for. Besides, I've got some rare precious stones which could have been meant for you. Now, my love, I do hope you don't grudge me some little reward when I'm only too happy to do you a service.'

The lady hung her head. She didn't want to give in to him, but she didn't know how to say no. The Abbot saw she had registered every word but was hesitating over an answer. He knew the game was already half-won, and he followed up his advantage until he convinced her it was better to throw in her hand. With a great deal of embarrassment she agreed to obey him, but only when her husband was safely in purgatory. He was satisfied with this promise.

'We'll pack him off at once. All you've got to do is make him stay here tomorrow or the next day.'

And with that he slipped a magnificent ring on her finger and sent her off. Pleased with her first present and confident of more, the lady rejoined her servants and went home, talking rhapsodically of the Abbot's holiness.

A few days later Ferondo came to the abbey, and the Abbot decided that he must be sent to purgatory on the spot. He had a drug of great potency, a present from an Eastern prince, who had sworn that this was the powder used by the Old Man of the Mountains for sending people to sleep, and to paradise and back painlessly. According to the size of the dose, it could induce a sleep so heavy that while it was operative its victim would be taken for dead. The Abbot measured out enough to produce three days' sleep and served it in his cell to the unsuspecting Ferondo in the dregs of a glass of wine. He then led Ferondo to the cloisters where he and some of his monks started making fun of their silly guest. The potion began working immediately, and Ferondo was overcome by a violent tiredness, fell asleep on his feet, and dropped to the ground in a coma. The Abbot seemed very distressed, had Ferondo's clothes loosened, sent for cold water to sprinkle on his face, and tried other remedies to revive him. He pretended to think Ferondo had been struck with an ailment of the stomach or some such trouble. Despite the Abbot's attempts and those of his monks, Ferondo did not come to. After feeling his pulse and finding no sign of life, they all had to admit he was dead. His wife and relatives were informed, and hurried to the abbey to mourn. Then, on the Abbot's order, the corpse was laid fully clothed, in a tomb. The widow went home, repeating that nothing would ever part her from the little son Ferondo had left her. She devoted herself entirely to the boy and the estate.

That night the Abbot and a very intimate friend, a monk who had just arrived from Bologna, got up silently, lifted Ferondo from his tomb and carried him to a vault that let in no light and was built as a prison to house delinquent monks. They stripped the clothes from the man, put on a monk's habit, placed him on a pile of straw and waited for him to regain consciousness. The Bolognese was fully briefed by the Abbot and stayed behind for Ferondo's recovery, but no one else knew anything of this plot.

Next day the Abbot and some monks paid the widow a pastoral visit. He found her in deepest mourning. With a few words of consolation he reminded her of her promise.

She felt herself completely free now, unhampered by Ferondo or anyone else, and having noticed another fine ring on the Abbot's finger, promised obedience and arranged for him to come to her that night. So when the time came he put on Ferondo's clothes, and accompanied by the Bolognese went to the house. He had a very enjoyable time in the lady's bed until early next morning, when he returned to the abbey. He repeated the visit frequently—always to good purpose. If he chanced to meet people on this mission, they thought it was Ferondo's ghost haunting the area as a penance. This gave rise to a good deal of comment among the villagers, some of which reached the ears of the widow. She put her own interpretation on the stories.

Meanwhile Ferondo had regained consciousness, but was completely ignorant of his whereabouts. The Bolognese monk entered his tomb with blood-curdling cries, seized him, and gave him a tremendous beating up. Ferondo screamed through his tears of pain:

'Where am I? Where am I?'

'You are in purgatory,' said the monk.

'What!' screamed Ferondo. 'I'm not dead, am I?'

The monk assured him that he was. He then began lamenting his own fate, his wife's, and his son's in a ludicrous fashion. The monk brought him food and drink, and this prompted the question:

'Oh! Do you eat too?'

'Yes,' said the monk. 'This is what your widow sent to the church this morning to pay for the masses said for your soul. God has seen fit to give it to you.'

'God save her,' said Ferondo. 'I loved her tenderly when I was alive. I used to spend all night kissing and hugging her, and went even further—when I felt like it.'

He then fell on the food and drink greedily, but finding the wine bad, he said:

'Well, God damn her! Why didn't she produce the wine in the flask nearest the wall?'

When he had finished his meal, the monk grasped him and gave him another terrible thrashing. Ferondo bellowed with pain and yelled out:

'Oh dear! What have I done to deserve this?'

The monk answered:

'God has ordered this treatment twice a day.'

'Why?' asked Ferondo.

'Because you were jealous,' came the answer, 'even though you were married to the most remarkable woman for miles.'

'Oh dear!' admitted Ferondo. 'You're quite right about her. She couldn't have been sweeter. I didn't know God disapproved of jealousy. Otherwise I never would have been.'

'Well,' said the monk, 'you should have thought of that at the time, and behaved better. If you ever happen to go back, take a tip from me, and avoid jealousy.'

'Oh,' said Ferondo. 'Do the dead sometimes go back to earth?'

'They do,' said the monk, 'if God ordains it.'

'If I ever go back, I'll be the best husband in the world. I'll never tell her off or beat her, except for sending that wine this morning and forgetting to include a candle, so that I had to eat in the dark.'

'Oh, she sent them, but they were burnt at mass.'

'I expect you're right,' said Ferondo, 'and if I ever get back, I'll give her her head. But tell me, what about yourself?'

'I'm dead too. An ex-Sardinian. Since I encouraged my master in his jealousy, God has appointed me to give you food, drink, and your disciplinary thrashing, while he decides what to do next with the pair of us.'

'Are we the only two here, then?' asked Ferondo.

'No, there are thousands of others,' answered the monk, 'but you can't see or hear them, and vice versa.'

'How far are we from home?' inquired Ferondo.

'Oh,' said the monk, 'it's some miles out of shit-range.'

'As far as that,' gasped Ferondo. 'Why, we must be out of this world.'

In this way Ferondo was kept for ten months on a combination of thrashings, food, and tall stories. The Abbot, meanwhile, was thoroughly enjoying himself with frequent visits to the widow, who gave him the time of his life. But all good things will come to an end, and the lady became pregnant. As soon as she knew, she told the Abbot. They both agreed that Ferondo should be recalled from purgatory, and given the glad tidings of his imminent fatherhood. So next night the Abbot went to the prison and called to Ferondo in a disguised voice:

'Ferondo, cheer up! God has decided to restore you to the earth. When you get back, you will have a son by your wife. Call him Benedict, for it is the prayers of your holy Abbot and your wife, and the love of St Benedict that have procured you this privilege.' Ferondo was ecstatic at this news and said:

'I am overjoyed. God bless the Lord God and the Abbot and St Benedict and my darling, my honey of a wife.'

The Abbot mixed in the next ration of wine enough of the drug to put Ferondo to sleep for four hours. He dressed him in his own clothes again and with the other monk's help, replaced him in his original tomb. Early next day, Ferondo came to, saw through a chink in the tomb the light he had done without for the last ten months. So he was alive and started shouting: 'Let me out, let me out!'

He wedged his head against the tomb's lid and heaved. It was not fixed down and started moving. He was just prising himself out when the monks passed on their way to matins, ran up, recognized Ferondo's voice, and witnessed his resurrection from the dead. Everyone was so terrified by this supernatural event that there was a mass deputation to the Abbot. He went through the motions of just rising from prayer and said:

'Do not be afraid, my children. Take the cross and the holy water and follow me. Let us see what the Almighty has revealed.'

He led the way to the tomb, where Ferondo stood, looking deathly pale after his long exile from the light. He no sooner saw the Abbot than he threw himself at his feet:

'Father, it's been revealed to me that thanks to the prayers of St Benedict, my wife, and you, I've been let out of purgatory and restored to life. So I invoke God's blessing on you today and every day, now and for ever.'

The Abbot replied:

'Praise be to the Almighty. Go, my son. God has restored you to this world, so you must go and comfort your poor wife who has cried ceaselessly since your death. May you live from now on in love and service to God.'

'Sir,' answered Ferondo. 'I'll do just that. You leave it to me. I'll kiss my wife just as soon as I see her, I'm that fond of her.'

With these words he went off home. The Abbot, left alone with his flock, pretended to be astonished at what had happened and had the *Miserere* solemnly sung. Ferondo returned to his village, but everyone fled in horror at seeing him. He called them back and testified to having risen from the dead. His wife was at first as terrified as anybody. But all the people were gradually reassured at seeing him alive, and bombarded him with questions. He replied to them all with the wisdom of a man who has gone through a lot, and gave them news of their relatives' souls. Drawing on his imagination, he described purgatory with delightful vividness. He gave a public account of the revelation he had heard from the Mongrel Goobriel (sic) just before his resurrection.

So Ferondo regained his estate, was reunited with his wife, and, as he thought, gave her a child. Since it is a common theory that a child must be in its mother's womb for exactly nine months, it was most convenient that his wife produced a boy exactly that period after Ferondo's return. They called it Benedict.

Ferondo's return from purgatory and his report on it, enormously increased the Abbot's reputation for saintliness. While Ferondo, having had his jealousy beaten out of him, proved the Abbot's theory and never bothered his wife with that sin again. She continued to live with him as before—apparently faithful enough: but she was always ready to accommodate the Abbot when the opportunity offered. After all, he had served her most faithfully in her hour of need.

POSTSCRIPT

Giovanni Boccaccio was born in Paris in the year 1313. He was
the illegitimate son of a visiting Italian business man and a
French girl. Brought back to Florence as a baby, he spent his
early years there and at Certaldo, his father's native town. When
he was still at what we should consider school age, Giovanni was
sent to the royal capital of Naples to be trained in business. It
was there, at the age of twenty-three, that he met Fiammetta,
an illegitimate daughter of King Robert of Naples—we are fairly
sure of both the date and the scene of their first meeting.

Boccaccio's passion for her consumed him for twelve years. She
died in the worst plague that has ever swept Europe, the Black
Death, but her presence suffuses every word her lover wrote up to
1348, and her spirit still haunts him in the opening of the
Decameron, started in that year.

Boccaccio introduces the reader to plague-infested Florence.
Ten citizens meet in this shambles and decide to escape together
to the gardens and palatial villas of Fiesole and of the nearby
hills. To while away the time, and to keep their minds off the
devastation that their city is suffering, the seven ladies and three
gentlemen agree that each one shall tell a story a day over a
period of ten days. This is the setting and frame for the collection of one hundred stories which make up the *Decameron*.
Boccaccio does not, however, as did his admirer Chaucer when
he came to write *The Canterbury Tales*, suit his stories to their
narrators. His framework is unashamedly artificial, it merely
links batches of ten tales together under vague headings. On
each of the days one of the ten evacuees is in command and
chooses a topic for illustration; it may be husbands who have
tricked their wives, or wives who have tricked their husbands.
As the tellers of the stories never emerge as individuals, and the
stories themselves are not in character, this pattern tends to become monotonous. In the present version, setting and order have
been abandoned. The best of the stories are left to stand on their
own, and the reader is spared much repetition.

It is easy to forget, at a distance of six hundred years, how
revolutionary the *Decameron* was, both for Boccaccio and for
Italian literature. It is often said that with the Black Death the

Middle Ages came to an end. Significantly, the new age was issued in, for Italy, with the first prose work to be written in the vernacular: the tight grip of Latin was loosened.

The *Decameron* represents a break with Boccaccio's own earlier work. He had always written variations on the theme of his all-consuming love for Fiammetta. In his collection of short stories, we may feel, there is more talk of lust than love. Yet the psychological acuteness that had characterized his early poems is evident on every page. The writing is caustic, satirical, unsentimental in its observation of human foibles, and richly humorous in its comment on kings and beggars, prostitutes and princesses, big business men and sharp fr ars. The scope of the *Decameron* is enormous: it is no less than Italy in the fourteenth century. Even stories derived from elsewhere, from Arabic or Persian, are imbued with the spirit of their author and the world he knew so well. Just as it is impossible to think of Shakespeare's Bottom as an ancient Athenian, it is difficult to consider Boccaccio's characters as anything but Italian. But the stories are by no means dated. It is their freshness and modernity that delight the reader and urge him on. What commercial traveller will not feel a little uncomfortable at the thought of Brother Onion, what husband or wife will dare to say that Boccaccio understands nothing of marriage? For all their six hundred years, the stories are as contemporary and as eternal as the human nobility and ignobility they describe.

The *Decameron* was a turning point for Boccaccio in another sense. By the time he had finished writing it he was a changed man. Under the influence of his friend Petrarch he turned away from the vernacular, from the earth-bound world of the *Decameron*, to Latin, to the academic and the religious life. Here again he exemplified much that we would now call Renaissance. He compiled dictionaries and encyclopaedias of information. Through him Europe rediscovered Homer. Petrarch was the guiding spirit of this second epoch of Boccaccio's adult life, as Fiammetta had been of his first.

Boccaccio died a year later than his friend Petrarch, in 1375, but the *Decameron* had only just started to live. It has remained popular in many languages and in every generation. Boccaccio influenced Chaucer very strongly, in both *Troilus and Criseyde* and *The Canterbury Tales*, while Shakespeare found in the *Decameron* much of the plots for *All's Well That Ends Well* and *Cymbeline*. These are only two of the countless writers who have profited from acquaintance with Boccaccio. In fact, it is almost impossible to tell or hear any story without feeling that one has heard it before—or something like it—in the *Decameron*.

In my version I have freely used not only English weights, measures, and coins instead of the Italian terms belonging to Boccaccio's period, but also colloquialisms of our own times. The style of the *Decameron* is elaborate. English translators who attempt to match it find themselves halfway between William Morris and the Hollywood epic. But surely the spirit of the work should be preserved rather than stylistic and historic accuracy. The stories must pulse with something of the fierce life Boccaccio gave them. It is better to have them alive and somewhat anachronistic than historically accurate and dead.

M. C.